THE RUNNER

TWIN FLAMES (BOOK 3)

RACHEL HENKE

RED BALLOON PRESS

DEDICATION

This one is for Rusty

TWIN FLAMES TIMELINE GUIDE

Present day: Continuous throughout the series - York and London

Georgiana: The historical timeline for this novel. (Book 3) Set mainly at Willow Manor, York. During the reign of King George II (1729)

Caroline is Cara's name in her past life in Georgiana so the names are used interchangeably when she time travels back

Tudorville: The main historical timeline in Books 1 and 2. Set at the Tudor court in London during the reign of Henry VIII, and in York (1536)

Victoriana: The other historical timeline in Books 1 and 2. London, York and Seville. During the reign of Queen Victoria (1840)

TWIN FLAMES SERIES

Book 1: Twin Flames

Book 2: The Uprising

Book 3: The Runner

Book 4: The Covenant

TWIN FLAME QUOTE

"Love at first sight is a rare experience of instantly recognising someone on a soul level. It's a feeling of deja-vu —like coming home."

Twin Flames (Book 1)

CHAPTER 1

Willow Manor, York - Present day

The estate was bathed in a soft, golden morning glow, characteristic of a quintessential English summer's day. Cara and George strolled hand in hand through the lush green gardens of Willow Manor, on their way to check out the latest developments in the old barn which was steadily being transformed into the new Tudor Heritage Centre.

Cara loved seeing the progress being made each day, and a giddy joy filled her heart as she turned to look at her husband.

'It's coming along nicely after the initial problems of getting started,' said George. 'I thought we might need to delay the opening, but it looks as though we'll make it, after all.'

It had been a hectic and exciting year so far, overseeing the renovations of Willow Manor, the ancestral home which had been in the Cavendish family for centuries. The newly married couple invested heavily in refurbishing the main house and renovating one of the massive old barns into what they hoped would become the premier Tudor Heritage Centre in the world. With George's considerable historical manuscript experience from his former career, the Cavendish link to the royal house of Henry VIII, combined with Cara's Tudor historian's PhD and expertise, they made a formidable team.

Cara raised George's hand to her lips and kissed his fingers. 'You've been brilliant at handling the project while I finished my book. We would never have got this far so quickly without you overseeing everything with such dedication.'

'Well, I do recall saying last year that I wanted a new challenge to occupy me, didn't I? I certainly got what I asked for... and much more when we bought this rambling old place,' said George.

'Sometimes I can't quite believe this is all ours and we're really free to build our dream life.'

George brushed a lock of chestnut hair aside to reveal her eyes, which shimmered with emotion like pools of fine grey mist. 'It's okay to be happy,' he said, pulling her close and hugging her tightly to him. 'The struggle is behind us now, my darling. Let's allow ourselves to relax and enjoy having Willow Manor back in the Cavendish family, just as it should be.' He held her shoulders and tilted her backwards slightly as he said, 'Although we can't relax completely. There is far too much to do... but you know what I mean.'

And then he gathered her back into his arms, and the fragrance of his sandalwood aftershave on his warm skin caressed her senses. Cara was secure in his love, but after all they had been through to get to this place, sometimes she was overcome by the depth of their connection and worried something might snatch their happiness away again.

They swayed together gently, standing on the manicured lawn in front of the grand Tudor manor house, which was now their forever home, breathing each other in and enjoying the quiet moments before they entered the bustle of the barn building site.

'Ready?' asked George.

Cara nodded, disentangled her arms, and straightened her now crumpled white shirt, which had escaped from the waist of her fitted black jeans. She followed George through the barn door, and they greeted the builders, who were a cheery lot and were pleased to stop for a cup of tea to give them the latest updates. They spent an action packed few hours watching the Tudor Heritage Centre slowly come to life.

At midday when the chatty crew took their break and wandered off for lunch, George organised a picnic while Cara found a blanket in one of the almost bottomless kitchen cupboards which she discovered were an eclectic treasure trove of useful household items. They gathered their picnic and crossed the grass, weaving through a woody mass of willow trees until they came to the clear bubbling stream that cut through the estate. Cara arranged the blanket, and they settled down in the pale sunshine to munch on their egg and mayonnaise sandwiches and to drink coffee. Between mouthfuls, they fine-tuned the details of the grand opening of their dream business and new life. They buzzed with excitement and the thought that she had never been happier flashed through Cara's mind.

Let's stay like this forever.

The next morning Cara rose and dressed, and entered the basement kitchen, which still had a whisper of the night's chill in the air. She poured herself a cup of steaming coffee from the pot that George had left on the machine. He was an early riser and made the most gorgeous coffee and was in the habit of leaving her some. She added a dash of milk, took a sip, and then carried her cup cautiously up the stairs, taking care not to spill any as she walked slowly through the maze of corridors towards the library. She planned to tackle some boxes of old books she'd been meaning to organise for ages. Cara had been so busy completing her book to submit in time to meet the publisher's deadline, and getting involved in the renovation plans, that she hadn't even made a start.

The library was her favourite room. It was the place where she always felt most at home in the grand house. There was a magical energy to it—and she recalled passing many pleasurable hours there in her Tudor time travelling days.

She pulled back the heavy chintz curtains and a wave of contentment washed over her as glints of morning sun cast golden rays into the room, lighting up the antique oak furniture and opulent wall panel hangings, making the room sparkle. The previous owners had clearly taken great care to retain much of the library's authentic style, which attractively combined Tudor, and a smattering of more modern touches added over the years, presumably for comfort. Cara thought the effect timelessly elegant. She took another sip of coffee as her eyes scanned the room once more, and then she rested her cup carefully on a Tower of London coaster on the wooden table, before she turned to tackle her first task with solid determination and withdrew one of the faded bound tomes from a storage box.

Cara took a step back to survey the floor-to-ceiling oak shelves laden with the Cavendish book collection, some of which must be as much as five-hundred-years old. She didn't know the details, but somehow the book collection had remained intact as a valuable feature of the library even after the house was converted into a hotel.

I bet these shelves can tell a tale or two. Never mind the books...

Cara blew the dust from the sleeve of a book titled *The Tudor Queens*, which made her sneeze violently, and then she gently wiped the cover and manoeuvred the book into a space on the shelf. The book was heavy and there wasn't enough room where she wished to slot it in, so it wasn't as easy as it looked. Her weight pressed against the wooden frame, and she heard a sudden creak. She abruptly stepped back, not wanting to risk breaking the shelf.

Cara lost herself in a daze of dusting the book covers and then, after some time, decided to try to fit them into the spaces on the shelves. She leaned forward again, her weight pressing against the wood, and she heard the same creak. Before she could move backwards and decide what to do, the bookshelf shifted noisily and swung open as if it had come away from the wall. Cara almost fell with it, but steadied herself by clutching another portion of the shelves and moving swiftly to one side.

Her breath snagged in her chest as she stared at the dark gap in the wall, revealed by the shifting bookshelf which stood ajar at a precarious angle. A vision of one of her favourite childhood books, *The Lion, the Witch and the Wardrobe*, entered her mind. Her fertile imagination kicked into overdrive. Had she discovered a hidden door to a secret world? She was unnerved and took a succession of quick steps backwards and as her calves hit the firm surface of the sofa base, she collapsed onto the brown leather chesterfield.

On the right of the sofa lay a pile of dusty books waiting to be organised on the library shelves. Cara's heart revved like a formula one engine, and she sat there for a few minutes, staring at the dark gap in the wall, wondering what it meant. It looked like a hidden passageway.

Where the heck does it lead?

Gradually, her heartbeat slowed and returned to normal as she reminded herself that it was okay—she was just scaring herself as she sometimes did with her tendency to overthink. Ever since she'd begun time travelling, she was prone to occasional bouts of panic and anxiety about what might happen unexpectedly if the vortex came for her or George.

After a few seconds, she rose in one smooth motion and walked towards the gap in the wall. It was likely just an undiscovered priest hole, which, although exciting, was nothing to fear. She told herself not to make a mountain out of a priest hole and chuckled at her own silly humour. Priest holes were routinely discovered in Tudor homes, dating back to the Dissolution of the Monasteries when Catholic and Jesuit priests were hunted down and persecuted in England.

Cara's first present day time travel experience had occurred in her favourite York bookshop, so it was no surprise she should be a little nervous. The shifting bookshelves had brought back memories of what had heralded the start of the most traumatic period in her life.

What is it with me and bookshelves?

Cara was too intrigued to ignore the mysterious hole and reached out to push the shelf, even though she hadn't consciously decided she would. It was cumbersome and took all her might to shift. As she pressed her weight against it and leaned into it, the gap gradually widened until there was enough space for her to enter. Her historian's curiosity made it impossible for her to resist, even though she was fearful of dark, confined spaces and her pulse raced at the thought of what awaited her behind the old musty wall. She drew a deep breath, and took one tentative step through the gap and placed her right foot forward until it hit solid ground. She sighed with relief, but her heart still raced.

Cara and George had bold plans and the last thing she wanted was to have to deal with the drama of time travelling to Tudorville again. She worried she might be swallowed up and instantly swept away by the vortex. But no—there had been no sign of swirling, freezing cold air enveloping her and no feeling of being unable to control her movements. Everything seemed perfectly normal, apart from the black hole taunting her to step inside and explore its hidden depths.

She hesitated, one leg in the ominous gap in the wall, and for a second, she considered whether she should call George to join her, rather than entering alone. But then she remembered he would still be busy on an early morning conference call. Not renowned for her patience, she swung her other leg into the vacuum and planted her left foot firmly next to the right. She looked about to try to make out her surroundings, but the dark was too dense to see anything. Her nose crinkled at the smell pervading her nostrils, and the air was cold. Not vortex cold—just old house cold and what one would expect in an unheated portion of a hundreds-of-years old building. She took a few shallow breaths to calm her racing heart without inhaling more of the stale, dank air, and then she stood there wondering how she could continue on in such dense blackness.

After a moment, she stepped back into the safety of the library. She couldn't explore the passageway without a torch, and she reminded herself that she didn't have to go in at all. Everything wasn't paranormal just because she could time travel. There was nothing strange about finding an old passageway or a secret tunnel in a house as ancient as Willow Manor.

Was there?

As she crossed the room, she chided herself for being fanciful, and then quickly rallied her spirits and got down to practicalities, guided by her historian's sharp instincts. She rummaged through the drawers in the ornate writing desk, one by one, until her fingers touched and then grasped a small torch in the bottom, dustiest drawer.

Memories of Tudorville filled her mind once again, and she saw a version of herself sitting at the elegant writing desk which overlooked the gardens, writing her correspondence almost five hundred years ago. She clearly remembered the events of 1536 when Anne Boleyn was beheaded, and later that year she became Queen Jane Seymour's lady-in-waiting, and her and George were embroiled in the Pilgrimage of Grace, which was the most dangerous of the Tudor uprisings.

Cara was happier than she'd ever been. After a tumultuous start to their present-day romance, everything had worked out perfectly between them. More than perfectly—she never imagined she could be so in tune with her partner, but they were aligned in every way and more content than she had ever dared hope.

The Twin Flames were not only blissfully married but had even managed, through a series of fantastical time travel events, to bring the Cavendish ancestral estate, Willow Manor, back into the family.

Sylvia, the psychic and Cara's trusted advisor, had explained that their Twin Flame mission was triggered because thousands of years ago, their souls had created a spiritual contract to attain unconditional love. Only when they succeeded would they reach what the mystics called "Ascension". And their souls wouldn't rest until they did. Twin Flames were typically put through a series of heart-wrenching and seemingly impossible to overcome challenges until they learned the lessons their souls were on earth to learn. Cara and George's mission was even more complex because they were multi-generational Twin Flames, which is why their ability to time travel had been activated and they were conscious of their past lives.

Cara stood, straightened her stiff back, and stretched her arms above her head, trying to get some energy running through her body for the task ahead. She was getting distracted, and the sooner she checked out what was in the hidey-hole, the sooner she could get on with organising the books as she had intended when she entered the library. There was a mountain of work to do before the grand opening, and the library was one of the key rooms they planned to open to the public, so she couldn't afford to spend any more time on fanciful fools' errands.

Cara squared her shoulders, took another deep breath, and resolutely entered the black opening in the wall until her whole body was tucked neatly behind the open bookshelf and in the space. She moved forward, one cautious step at a time, following the narrow beam of the torch, trying to make out what was in front of her. There was a wall on either side and a narrow passage lay in front of her for as far as she could see the tip of the light.

Nothing extraordinary, so far other than the space seemed larger than a traditional priest hole. The parts of the walls she glimpsed were coated in thick cobwebs and illuminated the old stone to give the walls a shiny hue, which cast an eerie glow throughout the passage as she moved. Cara pulled her cardigan tightly around her, but it did nothing to stop the tremor reverberating through her body. She was cold, and she second-guessed her decision to explore alone.

The floor was hard and freezing beneath the soles of her sandals, and the chilly air clawed at her skin as she continued to edge forward cautiously, shuffling like an elderly person on an ice rink. She sneezed abruptly, and the torch shook and created a prism of light effect. The torch illuminated an enormous spider, which scooted across the wall, and Cara let out a high-pitched scream.

Her heartbeat raced ever faster. She regretted not waiting for George to join her. It would be so much more fun with him alongside. He wouldn't like that she'd rushed in without him, and she imagined him telling her off in his good-natured fashion, when she told him what she'd done. The thought of being back with him; telling him what had happened, calmed her down and distracted her.

He said she was too hasty for her own good. Despite her reaction to the spider, her mind soon churned with positive possibilities as she moved forward through the narrow space. Her desire to uncover something new from the past spurred her on through her veil of fearful thoughts.

If it was a priest hole, they could open it up for visitors and she was certain it would be a wonderful attraction for the Tudor Heritage Centre. They could get a spread in *The York Press* and be featured in some specialist history magazines, which would be brilliant for the opening. Her mind continued to whirr with ideas as she inched forward through the dark tunnel.

How big is this priest hole?

After several more steps, she approached what looked like a wall ahead of her and she assumed she must be reaching the end of the priest hidey-hole. Cara shone the torch sideways and upwards, but there wasn't anything to see other than the wall and the stone ceiling. She reached out to touch the wall with her left hand and clutched the torch with the other. Both her hands shook slightly, and adrenaline shot through her as another wave of fear clutched at her and her skin tingled. Her hand fumbled about, looking for a firm surface, but to her surprise, her fingers touched nothing solid like she expected. She aimed the torch at the wall, and there it was illuminated reassuringly once more. She reached out to pat it, but her hand met no resistance, so she tilted her upper body further forward in case she wasn't quite close enough. But there was only more air and space. As she continued to lean forward, fumbling about and trying to reach the wall, the torch slipped from her hand and bounced and ricocheted along the hard floor; the noise echoing through the empty space as it disappeared from view.

Oh shoot.

She was about to turn and flee from the dark passageway back to the warmth of the welcoming library because the thought of staying in there without the torchlight freaked her out. But when she heard the noise, her whole body stiffened. The familiar whooshing sound filled the passageway. A cloud of freezing cold air enveloped her and seeped over her skin. She lost her footing and screamed as she tumbled forwards into the vortex. And then she was gone.

CHAPTER 2

Willow Manor, York - Georgiana (1729)

Caroline clasped her hands together in her lap as she sat in the plush velvet armchair in the library of the grand old house. This was her first time inside Willow Manor; she'd only ever seen the magnificent Tudor house from the grounds when she and some of the other village children occasionally ventured near the edge of the sprawling estate.

Caroline discreetly cast her eyes about the room as Lady Margaret Cavendish consulted her diary and gave her details of what would be required of her if she accepted the post as governess and companion to her daughter, Olivia.

'Does the position sound satisfactory to you?' asked the countess, whose demeanour was business like, but whose brown eyes twinkled as though she were secretly amused by life and was not quite as serious as she seemed.

Caroline thought that despite her formal appearance, the countess's eyes revealed a measure of kindness that she hadn't expected to find in the higher classes. Her father had spoken well of the countess and encouraged her to accept the post, so Caroline's intentions were already set as she hurried across the fields and down the footpath, which was a well-known shortcut from the village to Willow Manor. Her father said the lady of the house had a reputation for being formidable, yet fair, and she was well respected by the villagers. He knew the countess when he was a young man earning his teaching stripes at the new local school, which was the unusual initiative of the Cavendish family. Mistress Margaret—who hadn't yet become a countess—had frequently accompanied her mother on charitable duties to the school and in the village. The Cavendish family were popular in the community and, as the only big house in the region, many of the villagers worked on the Cavendish estate and lived on the land.

'Caroline? A penny for your thoughts, dear. Is being governess to my daughter, Olivia, acceptable to you?'

Caroline, deep in thought, imagined her father and the formidable countess meeting as youngsters, and had forgotten she was supposed to be listening and hadn't heard one word her potential mistress said. She snapped herself back to the library and smoothed her shabby skirts with one hand before raising her eyes respectfully. 'I gratefully accept your offer of the position and thank you, my lady.'

The countess released an audible sigh and smiled at Caroline as their eyes met once more. 'That's settled then. I too am very pleased to have you with us; Miss Olivia needs sensible company and a firm hand. She's a good-hearted child but easily distracted with girlish nonsense, so I shall rely on you to guide her to attend more readily to her studies and set a good example of an educated young woman. Your father stated in our correspondence that you surpass most educated men in your learning, which is a credit to you both.

I have no wish to raise my girl unschooled, which is unfortunately how it is for most young ladies.'

Caroline nodded and a thrill of excitement rippled through her as she thought about the wonderful and unexpected opportunity that had come her way. This was a lifeline for her to escape a long and dull life in Willow Wick where the most she could aspire to was to become someone's wife, unless she was to continue to be a burden on her father or be alone and penniless. Ralph Knight wanted her for his wife, but she had no desire to marry him. Caroline didn't know how long she would be able to hold him at arm's length as her childhood sweetheart's ardour grew more feverish each time they met.

No, she must get away from the village, even if it was only by a few miles. By going into service, her father assured her she would be safe and enjoy the protection of the Cavendish household. He vehemently warned her not to marry Ralph, who he pronounced *a bad lot.*

It mattered not how bright she was or that she could hold her own among men with fine academic minds, she would be cast aside to do the laundry because she was of low-class birth. Caroline would miss living with her father and seeing him every day in the tiny cottage they shared, but she was ready for this moment, and she knew this was her chance to set herself free even if going into service didn't seem like an obvious route to freedom. She would earn her own money and when she had saved enough, she planned to leave Willow Wick and ultimately be mistress of her own destiny. The countess's progressive attitude to women appealed to her and made her all the keener to be in her employ.

Caroline was young, but she was ahead of her time, which she attributed to her father's fine tutorage.

The countess raised her opulently jewelled hand to ring the bell on the table beside her. 'Talking of Olivia, she's having a piano lesson, but you shall meet her once you have settled in. The sooner you commence, the better.'

The countess bid a servant girl who appeared as if out of the shadows to bring them tea.

Caroline sat quietly doing her best to stay composed as she waited.

What if her young charge proved a dreadful handful, and she couldn't manage her like Ralph had implied?

Ralph's face loomed in her mind, and she consciously pushed the vision of his handsome, strong features and piercing blue eyes away. Her childhood companion—he always thought he was right and that as a man, he could tell her what to do and she should listen and do his bidding. Well, he was in for a shock because all of that was about to change. She would gradually loosen her ties to him; gently but firmly, and he would meet a girl who would be far better suited to his domineering nature.

Caroline's thoughts turned to Olivia. She herself had only just turned nineteen, so she wouldn't be much older than the daughter of the house. She heard footsteps in the corridor and the door swung open.

'This must be our tea,' said the countess, a second before a tall, fine-looking man wearing an elegant and richly embroidered sky blue waistcoat and breeches, launched himself into the room.

'Ah, my dear boy, we are awaiting our tea, but I'm most pleased to be blessed with your arrival instead. Let me introduce you to Mistress Caroline Radcliff, who has just accepted the position of Olivia's governess and companion.'

George bowed in Caroline's direction, and said, 'Good day, Mistress Radcliff. Welcome to Willow Manor. I am confident dear Olivia will not disappoint you in her studies. She is an accomplished young woman, although I of course confess to being most biased.'

Caroline reciprocated his smile in what she thought must be a rather forward manner, but she couldn't stop herself.

His presence seemed almost too overpowering for the room, and Caroline's heart beat rapidly. A light blush stained her warm cheeks as she studied him. His stare unnerved and thrilled her at the same time. His dark eyes bore into her and, uncharacteristically for Caroline, she found herself unable to hold his admiring gaze and she looked away quickly. Her heart pounded harder—she hadn't been this nervous since her first day at school when she had to prove herself worthy of a place and not just because she was the schoolmaster's daughter.

'This is my son, Lord George Cavendish, who is officially the head of Willow Manor and the new earl, now his dear father is no longer with us,' said the countess, seemingly oblivious to the instant attraction between her son and the newly appointed governess.

George continued to look at Caroline and said, 'I'm still not accustomed to being an earl if the truth be known.'

He stooped to drop a kiss on his mother's heavily powdered white cheek, and Caroline noticed her face light up even more.

'I see I am intruding on your ladies' conversation so I will make myself scarce at once and apologise for the interruption. I will return later to find the book I seek,' said George.

He nodded, bowed once more, and then turned and left the library. Caroline had seen the young master occasionally during her childhood as he passed through the village in the Cavendish crested carriage, but she'd never been personally introduced or exchanged words with him. He was much more charming in person than she would have thought. She'd imagined he would be distant and snobbish, but he had appeared open and friendly, treating her as an equal, which she suspected must be rare for men of his class.

A long-hidden whisper of a memory stirred deep within Caroline's restless soul, but she couldn't put a name to it. She'd never experienced such an intense and immediate reaction to a man and didn't recognise the feeling of a powerful attraction. As a sunflower leans towards the sun, she basked in the rays of the earl's attention. After he exited the room, she had the unexpected urge to call after him not to leave, to ask him to come back and talk to her again, but her grey eyes met the countess's brown ones, and she composed her features into a serious expression. It wouldn't do for her employer to think she was smitten with her beloved son.

Whatever is the matter with me?

She was behaving in an erratic manner most unlike her usual steady self.

'He's a dear boy—well, a man, now...' said the countess, glowing as she talked of her son. 'Always so patient and polite with everyone. The servants positively idolise him, and his former nanny still lives in a cottage on the estate, at his bequest, since he left to study at Eton.'

Of course, he's attentive to everyone. I only imagined he was interested in me—how naïve I am.

The countess turned her attention to the tea tray, which had just arrived. She poured a splash of milk, followed by the steaming tea, into two white, gold-rimmed china cups and carefully passed a cup to Caroline. After taking a sip and replacing the cup on its saucer, she continued, 'Olivia and George adore one another, you know.'

She was a mother who was contented with her lot.

Caroline said, 'Indeed, my lady, he is most attentive, and I am grateful to be joining your household. Olivia is fortunate to have such a caring brother to watch over her.'

The countess took another sip of tea, and her pale green silk mantua gown shimmered in the light. 'That's settled then. You shall live in, of course, but never fear—you may visit your father on Sundays, should you wish. He is well, I hope? I exchanged only a brief correspondence with him concerning the position and haven't had the pleasure of seeing him in person for many a year.'

'He is well, thank you, my lady, and he spoke highly of you. It was he who encouraged me to accept the post.'

'He is an honourable man with an astute mind, which is why I sensed you would be a perfect match for Olivia. We could do with more like him in the village.' She rang the bell once more, and the maid reappeared in the room, as if by magic. 'Ah, Harriet, please prepare the green room for Caroline. She is joining us with immediate effect as governess to Mistress Olivia.'

Caroline rose as the countess indicated their meeting was over. 'Welcome to Willow Manor, my dear. I trust you'll be happy here and I want you to feel at home with us. It's important that Olivia has the company of a woman close to her own age, whom she trusts and may study with. It is difficult for young women of noble birth to find their place in the world without firm guidance and friendship.'

Caroline thanked her once more and curtsied before following the maid out of the library and into the maze of dimly lit corridors which led to the kitchens in the basement.

Harriet, a young, cheerful girl who looked at ease in their surroundings, which bode well for Caroline, beckoned her to follow. 'Come and meet Cook while I prepare your room. She's a good sort and will look after you. You won't go hungry while you're at Willow Manor, that's for sure,' she said with a cheeky grin.

Cook, who was a short, rotund woman with a homely face, greeted Caroline with a hearty smile and settled her in a chair by the large kitchen table where she was preparing batches of generous sized scones ready for the blazing beehive oven. She placed the last scone onto the tray and wiped her pink floury hands on her crisp white apron and said in a strong Yorkshire lilt, 'Would you like a brew, lass?' Her eyes glowed playfully, and Caroline already felt at home in the huge, warm kitchen. She was keen to show her gratitude for Cook's hospitality and wished to find out more about the workings of the grand house, so she nodded enthusiastically to another cup of tea, and said, 'Aye. That'd be grand.'

And so began Caroline's life as governess at Willow Manor.

CHAPTER 3

Willow Wick, York - Georgiana

CAROLINE HUNCHED over the smoky hearth in the tiny cottage, which was nestled in a row of identical buildings on the edge of the village green. She stirred the stew one last time and then scooped a modest portion into each chipped dish.

'Stew is served. Come and eat, Father. I have to leave soon to get back to Willow Manor before it grows dark,' she called.

Her father snapped the book in his hands shut, rose from his armchair, and placed the volume on the chair, ready to resume his reading that evening. He stooped to kiss his daughter's cheek as he passed the hearth and then sat down at the small table where they had shared so many meals over the years.

'I'm going to miss you more than you know, my love, but you're doing the right thing. Marrying Ralph would be a disaster. He's not the man for you and the sooner you distance yourself from him and the rest of the Knight family, the better off we'll be.'

Caroline pulled out a chair and joined him at the table. She touched his arm and said, 'Eat up before it gets cold. You don't have to worry about that anymore. I told you, it's all arranged with the countess.'

'She is a fine woman,' he said, a fond smile lighting up his features. 'I knew her when she was a young woman, you know.'

'Yes, you said. You met her before Mother, and by the sounds of it you were smitten.'

He blew on a spoonful of stew and raised it to his lips.

'We took to one another well enough, but it wasn't meant to be.'

'Do you have regrets, Father?'

'Not at all. I loved your mother dearly. But it took me a while to get over my youthful ardour. She was a slip of a girl, and a fine beauty with a fiery nature, but with a kind and good heart. She wasn't like the others.'

'The others?'

'You know, the children of the aristocracy, they didn't have the time of day for us village bairns.'

Caroline nodded. 'I don't think I mentioned earlier, but I met her son, the earl, today.'

Her father raised one eyebrow and looked at her as he ate.

'He was polite and courteous,' continued Caroline.

'I would expect no less of the countess's son.'

'Are you sure you're not still holding a candle for her, Father? Her husband died, and she's free now. As are you…'

'Don't be daft, lass.' He raised his eyes and shook his head before taking his last mouthful of stew and laying down his spoon. 'I've never forgotten her, but it would be quite out of the question.'

'Why? You're an educated man with fine manners, and you know the ways of the rich. You've drilled them into me since I was a child. Wealth surely isn't still more important than true love, is it?'

'You have always been a dreamer, my dear, and I love that about you, but unfortunately, the world doesn't work this way. People like us do not wed people like them, no matter how finely educated.'

The words hung in the air between them, and then Caroline cleared up after their meal and went to collect a handful of her dearest possessions that she wished to take with her. Her father would continue to live at the cottage, at least while he still taught at the village school, so she didn't need to take everything; not that she owned much.

Once she was ready to leave, her father offered to walk her to Willow Manor.

'Thank you, but you stay here. It's still daylight and it'll be good to have a quiet walk to clear my head. You have lessons to prepare.' She gave him a tight hug and stepped into the small yard, and exited the front gate. 'I'll visit on Sunday, all being well.' She looked back again and saw him standing on the doorstep, watching her. She waved and blew him a kiss, before turning to wipe the tears from her eyes so he wouldn't see her crying. What a fuss she was making.

There was something emotional about leaving home for the first time, even if she wasn't going far, and planned to return soon. Caroline carried a basket on her arm and weaved her way through the narrow lanes, towards the outskirts of the village. She passed by the line of Willow trees along the riverbank—the lime green leaves skirted the sparkling water, and Caroline fell into deep thought as she walked, imagining what it would be like to live in a house as grand as Willow Manor.

When she was a child, she often played at being the lady of the manor. Her father indulged her make-believe games but teased her he didn't know where she had got such ideas.

Butterflies flitted around her stomach as she approached the footpath that led out of the village and towards the Willow Manor estate which lay on the outskirts, but as she was about to step onto the footpath, she heard a familiar voice call her name.

Her spirits sank as she realised she wouldn't be able to avoid him after all. Caroline had hoped to settle into her new position before meeting Ralph again to explain to him why she had left against his wishes and without his blessing.

'Caroline, where are you going?' he said, catching up with her.

'I can't tarry. I didn't have a chance to tell you, but I accepted the position at Willow Manor, and I have to get over there now.' She straightened her bag on her arm, and her cheeks flushed pink.

'So, you were going to leave without telling me, like a thief in the night?'

Caroline's patience for Ralph was already in short supply after their previous conversations concerning whether she should accept the post. She sighed, 'Please don't be so dramatic. I'm no thief, and it isn't yet night, but I wish to get there before night falls, which is why I had to leave without stopping to see you.'

Ralph's blue eyes darkened as they appraised her. 'I wish you would listen to me and not take that position. If it's security you crave, let us be wed now, and not wait any longer.'

She looked at him, her heart pounding, fearing he might be about to drop down on one knee and ask for her hand in marriage.

Please God, no. Let him see sense and realise we are not right for each other.

Caroline had tried to let him down gently, but he seemed ever more determined to keep pushing, even though she'd given no indication she wished to marry him. He was the kind of man who didn't take no for an answer, and he wasn't getting any easier to handle with age.

'I'm sorry, Ralph. I can't stay to talk now as Mistress Olivia is waiting for me at the big house, but we can talk again upon my next visit.'

Ralph stood in front of her, and his large muscular frame blocked her way. 'Mistress Olivia,' he sneered. 'Why would you want to be a servant to a young girl when you could be mistress of your own farm?'

She sighed. She knew how to handle him, but she was growing weary of having to. His persistence was tiresome. He always had a wicked temper, which she had learned to snap him out of, but he wasn't usually nasty to her.

'Ralph, would you please move aside and allow me to pass?' Caroline tilted her head to one side, hoping to charm him and quickly extract herself from the unsettling situation and be on her way.

'You promise we'll talk soon, and you'll think about us getting married?'

'I promise we'll talk soon, but I already explained I have no wish to marry,' she said, checking her lace cap was still in place. 'It's not you or your farm. I don't wish to be anyone's wife. You know that. Please don't keep bringing it up. We will remain friends, Ralph, just as we have always been.'

He glowered at her, anger flashing in his eyes, and for a second she feared his temper might get the better of him and he would strike her as she'd seen him do to others, but then he seemed to contain himself and swiftly moved aside and beckoned for her to pass with a mock, deferential bow, 'My lady, please be on your way to the grand house.'

Caroline rolled her eyes. 'Don't be daft, Ralph. I'm just a servant who needs to make an honest living.'

Once he let her pass, she waved him a quick goodbye and hurried down the footpath, eager to get away from him before he changed his mind and came after her again.

She'd always stood up for him when he got into trouble, but the truth was she knew he was a bully and it was getting harder to ignore, and more difficult to excuse his behaviour now he was a grown man. He was becoming more demanding, and she breathed a sigh of relief as she rushed along the footpath, trying to make up the time she had lost so she wouldn't disturb anyone by arriving late. Perhaps it wasn't such a good idea for her to return to the village on Sunday, after all. Caroline had a soft heart but a strong rebellious streak when people tried to tell her what to do. She decided it would be better all-round if she stayed out of Ralph's way for a while; at least until he got used to the idea of her working at Willow Manor. She shuddered at the thought of being his wife. He was a handsome, well-built man, but the thought of him touching her filled her with dread.

No, she must not let that happen.

Willow Manor, York - Present day

Cara lay crumpled and disorientated in the dark space.

What on earth just happened?

She picked herself up slowly and stretched her limbs cautiously. Nothing broken. She crouched back down and fumbled on the ground for the torch and crawled about in the narrow space until her hand touched a smooth, firm object.

Bingo.

Cara clicked the rubber coated button on the base of the torch and the light blazed into full beam. She breathed a sigh of relief and looked around. Nothing obvious had changed since she'd entered, but she remembered the chilled air and the whooshing sound coming for her. After that, she had no memory of anything until just now. She sighed. A version of her must be back in Tudorville, but she had no way of knowing exactly what was going on until her memory updated. She knew from experience she would have to wait and be patient. It was only a matter of time; she'd hoped her time travelling days were over, but it looked as though that was not to be.

She hurried back along the passageway, taking bold steps, anxious to get back into the house and exit the creepy dark hole. A part of her was scared she wouldn't be able to return to her normal life, but there it was. The wonky bookshelf stood open, showing a crack of light, and she hurried towards it and jumped down into the safety of the warm library.

Her cup of coffee stood on the table. There was a thin layer of congealed milk on the surface.

What time is it?

She checked her watch. Only about an hour had passed since she'd entered the library first thing. That would explain the cold coffee, but how long had she been out for? It can't have been long as she'd been faffing about for quite a while before she entered the passageway, and then she'd taken her time to find her way through it.

She sat down once again on the sofa next to the box of books and rested her head against the cool leather and closed her eyes. She needed a moment. Her head was spinning, and the sudden turn of events overwhelmed her.

Think, Cara, think.

The time travel seemed somehow different this time—her intuition told her something had changed. But what? Like in the past, after the vortex took her, she was aware she had time travelled, but couldn't remember the details—not right away, anyway. And sometimes not at all. Who knew how much she didn't remember?

She shook her head, stared mournfully at the piles of untouched books, then stood up and headed towards the door. The books would have to wait. She needed some fresh air.

THAT EVENING, over dinner on the terrace, Cara told George about her strange experience that morning.

George paused mid-fork and said, 'Why didn't you tell me earlier? I've been waffling on about the renovations all afternoon and you had all that on your mind.'

'I thought I'd wait until my thoughts settled and I was calmer. Anyway, you have so much going on with the builders, I didn't want to distract you at such a critical time.'

George stopped eating and rested his fork on his plate. 'It doesn't matter how busy I am—I always have time for you—you know that.'

'Of course I do, darling. Sorry, I should have told you sooner.'

He reached for her hand and continued, 'It sounds as though you're time travelling to Tudorville again. Do you remember any of the details?'

Cara shook her head. 'I don't know where I went.'

She knew he must be seriously worried when he stopped

eating in the middle of his meal. He had one of the most voracious appetites of anyone she knew.

'Eat up, or it'll get cold,' she said.

He picked up his fork and continued eating. 'I was really beginning to believe it was all over.'

Cara swallowed a mouthful of risotto and said, 'Me too. Even Sylvia thought we might have completed our Twin Flame mission and would be left in peace now.'

Sylvia was their psychic advisor who had become Cara's trusted confidante soon after she began time travelling.

'Well, I suppose there's no point worrying about it. There's nothing much we can do, anyway. We're at the mercy of the vortex once more,' said George.

'True. Although it could be just a one-off,' she said, her expression hopeful as she looked at George across the trestle table on the terrace and sipped at her glass of white wine.

He nodded, but neither of them really believed it. They both knew from experience that when it began, it was full on and soon enough they would find out what they were up against.

'On the bright side, at least I'll see the children again. I have such vivid dreams about them, and I never know whether they're real insights into what's happening or whether they're just dreams,' she said.

'They are never far from my thoughts either,' said George.

They both fell quiet as they thought of Thomas and May.

'I just tell myself to trust in what's already happened and that we are both doing our best for them there,' George continued.

'That's a lovely way of seeing it. I shall adopt that way of thinking too.' Cara smiled and felt a rush of love for him. Being a time travelling Twin Flame was never simple.

'Let's go and explore the passageway together tomorrow. It would be terrific if it turned out to be an original priest hole. You said there's a wall at the end and it doesn't connect to another spot in the house, so it's not a true passageway, is it?' George said.

'The wall was there again when I came around, but I swear it disappeared before. I think that's why I fell—I reached out to touch what looked like a wall, but it was just thin air. Then I heard the vortex, and I remember nothing until later. Maybe I just imagined there was no wall.'

CHAPTER 4

Willow Manor, York - Georgiana

CAROLINE CROSSED into the grounds of Willow Manor as dusk descended over York like a dark cape. It had been a warm, sunny day, but the evening chill permeated the air and Caroline shivered as the cold seeped through the layers of the much-repaired skirts of her gown. She looked back once more to check Ralph hadn't followed her. He had a habit of tailing her like a lost puppy. When she asked him about it, he said he only ever wanted to make sure she was safe. When they were younger, she'd found his adoration and attention endearing, but lately it only irritated her, and for some time she'd been doing her best to shake him off without hurting his feelings. She knew she had failed today.

There was no one in sight, and she paused to take a couple of deep breaths of the crisp evening air before she neared the servants' entrance. The stars shimmered like precious stones in the swiftly darkening sky. As she approached the house, she heard the comforting hum of low voices and the sound of pots and pans. The busy household was winding down for the day, and soon the servants would retire to bed, ready for another long day in service. Caroline knocked lightly on the heavy door.

'There you are, lass. I was just saying that you should be back by now. It doesn't do to be wandering about on your own at night,' said Cook, clucking over Caroline as she shooed her inside the warm kitchen. Just as Harriet had predicted, the kind-hearted cook had taken Caroline under her wing.

'I beg your pardon for being late. I got held up in the village,' said Caroline. She wasn't accustomed to having anyone fuss over her. Her father loved her dearly, but she looked after him, not the other way around.

'Would you like a cup of tea, my dear, before we close up and retire?'

Caroline nodded eagerly.

Cook waved her away with her hand as if it was nothing, before beckoning for Caroline to sit down, and turning to pour some tea from the pot on the stove. Caroline waited at the table, pleased to rest her weary legs and warm herself after the long trudge through the fields in her thin shoes. Each sharp stone and twig had made her wince. She gazed dreamily around the comfortable, well-equipped kitchen, the grandness of which she'd not believed possible until that morning. Caroline didn't understand why, but she already felt at peace in the house—her love affair with Willow Manor had begun.

Willow Manor, York - Present day

Cara tossed from side to side in the king size bed she shared with George in their newly refurbished bedroom in the old manor house. She whimpered as she dreamt, and her lips moved.

George sat up and switched his bedside lamp on and then reached out to touch Cara's restless body. 'Cara,' he whispered. She flipped over again and continued whimpering, obviously distressed. He touched her arm firmly this time. 'Darling, wake up,' he said, his voice louder.

Cara heard him and her eyes flipped open. 'I was dreaming about Willow Manor in another time,' she said, still groggy from sleep.

George stroked her damp hair and helped her sit up and drink a few sips of water.

'That was weird,' she said. 'I was here, but not here. I don't even know how to explain it.' She shook her head.

George, now wide awake even though it was only three in the morning, said, 'What was going on, then? You sounded distressed.'

'I remember little. I saw myself—or at least, a version of myself, in a small cottage and I was eating a meal with my father.' She shook her head again. 'But he wasn't my father. He looked different, and we were different. Like we were from another time.'

'I see,' said George, not understanding what she was talking about, but wanting to give his troubled wife a chance to settle down.

'But he wasn't unlike my father. Gosh, I'm making no sense,' she said.

'It's okay, you've just had a nightmare. Dreams don't all have to mean something deep, you know.'

Cara studied the face she loved so much, and as she looked at him, she saw a vision of a different George.

'You're going to think I've lost it, but there was another George too.'

Cara's heart raced as she considered the implications of her dream.

George tried to make light of it. 'You'd think three of me would be quite enough, what with a version of me in the other timelines.'

Cara stared at him, trying to make sense of the moving parts from her dream. 'I'm losing sight of the images already. I can't remember what else happened, but it seems like more than just a dream; it seems significant somehow.'

They stayed like that for a while with Cara resting her head on George's shoulder, his arm around her and him supported by a large, white fluffy pillow, until Cara's eyes drooped.

'Come on—try to get some sleep. You look exhausted.'

She nodded and George pulled the light quilt over their chests and up to their chins and Cara drifted off into a peaceful sleep, cocooned in George's comforting arms.

The next morning after breakfast and some more discussions about the builders, Cara said, 'Do you have time for me to show you the secret passage, or whatever it is, in the library now?'

George took a final slug of his coffee and stood up. 'Absolutely, let's do it now before I get involved with the centre.'

'Goodie. I'll feel better if you see it too,' she said.

They walked slowly up the wide, imposing staircase which led from the basement to the upper floors, and then Cara took George's hand as they zig-zagged through the maze of corridors and arrived outside the library.

'I'm nervous,' she said. 'I don't think I mentioned last night, but the passageway was also in my weird dream.'

'I can't wait to see it—what an exciting discovery,' he said, kissing her and trying to distract her from her sombre mood.

She turned the handle, and the door swung open with a loud whine. 'We'd better oil that door before we open to the public or it will be a nightmare,' he said, touching her gently on the waist to encourage her to enter.

This morning, Cara didn't notice the elegance of the library. Her eyes darted straight to the bookshelf, which hung open at an odd angle.

It's still there as I left it.

She had tried to push it closed but was so agitated she only gave it a brief attempt and then rushed out of the room in a panic. Cara didn't know what she'd expected, but she was relieved.

She opened the heavy chintz curtains, just like the previous morning, and George reached the bookshelf with a couple of strides. She saw him peer into the hole behind the shelves and then he glanced over at her and said, 'This looks interesting. It shows all the signs of a priest hole, don't you think?'

'Yes, I suppose so, although I think it's larger than usual.'

'I'm going in to see,' he said.

'Be careful,' she said, and she felt the fierce flip and thud of her heart.

He gave her an impish grin. 'Don't look so terrified, darling. It's only a hole in the wall. We've faced a lot worse.'

She nodded as though trying to convince herself. 'Sorry, I'm being silly. I don't know why I'm so jumpy. Must be lack of sleep and that weird dream.'

George shoved the bookshelf further in and the entire section of the wall moved with it to reveal the full expanse of the entrance. 'How they disguised it is extremely clever. Do you still have the torch to hand?'

Cara tried to remember where she'd put it after she fled

from the passage. She scanned the furniture surfaces, and then she spotted it nestled against the brown shiny leather of the chesterfield. She picked it up and handed it to George. 'Here you go.'

'Aren't you coming?' he said.

Cara looked at him, tension constricting her chest into a tight ball until she struggled for air. 'There's something I didn't tell you last night...'

Willow Manor, York - Georgiana

Caroline settled into life at the big house as if she'd always lived there. As governess and companion to Olivia, she enjoyed a higher social status than the other servants, and as such, she was designated a private room. For the first time in her life, she had a bedroom of her own, rather than a small space to sleep in, which she must clear each morning. The first evening when Harriet had shown her to her quarters; she could barely speak to thank her, so great was her surprise at being given the beautiful room. She hadn't given it any thought until her arrival, and had assumed she would sleep with the maids in the attic. The green room, Harriet told Caroline, was where Nanny lived throughout Olivia's childhood. Nanny, who was still quite young, had recently vacated the room as she had taken a position in a new household, rather than retire on the estate like George's nanny.

When Harriet bid her goodnight and left, Caroline flew onto the bed and rolled about like a mad thing, hardly able to contain her yelps of glee. The room was strangely familiar, almost as if she had been there before. She'd noticed a similar feeling when she was in the library with the countess. Caroline had no explanation for it, other than that perhaps it was a positive sign she had made the right decision to leave the village.

She barely slept that first night, such was her excitement at being in a proper bed in palatial surroundings. Thoughts of her father alone in the tiny cold cottage whirled around her mind as she tried to fall asleep, and doubt clouded her newfound happiness. She hoped he had eaten well and hadn't forgotten to bank the fire before he retired. Caroline had been mistress of the little cottage for as long as she could remember, and her father wasn't used to doing household chores. A dutiful daughter, she worried she had deserted him and perhaps it had been selfish of her to take the position. Guilt consumed her as she moved from one side to the other in the cavernous bed. Finally, she drifted off to sleep, unable to resist slumber a second longer, seduced by the crisp sheets and comfort of the soft mattress. Her last thought was that she must have died and gone to heaven.

The next few days were busy as Caroline settled into the rhythm of Willow Manor and grew acquainted with her charge, Olivia Cavendish.

'What would you like to do today, Mistress Olivia?'

'I would like you to stop calling me Mistress Olivia,' the girl replied, a mischievous gleam in her eyes.

Caroline noticed she had the same bewitching dark eyes as her brother and had to snap herself back to the moment. 'And what do you think your dear mother would make of such a request? I don't think she would approve, so I fear we must continue with me addressing you formally, at least for the time being.'

'I wish to take a walk into Willow Wick, if we may,' said Olivia, bouncing about on her chair, her youthful energy spilling out of her into the room.

'Whatever for?' asked Caroline, immediately wondering

how she would avoid bumping into Ralph if she were to accompany Olivia into the village.

'It's fine weather today; let us not be cooped up in here on such a beautiful day.' Olivia's golden hair, dark eyes and pale skin made for a striking combination. She was barely more than a child, but was already breathtaking. Caroline guessed it wouldn't be long before the suitors lined up at the door to ask for her hand in marriage. She must help Olivia make the most of her freedom for as long as she was fortunate enough to enjoy it. Caroline shuddered at the thought of the beautiful young maiden being wedded off to some wealthy man old enough to be her father, as was so often the way of society.

'Very well. Get your cloak, in case of sudden rain, and we shall take a stroll to the village, or shall we ride in the carriage?' Caroline asked, realising that could be the way to avoid Ralph.

'Carriages are so very dull,' said Olivia. 'I never get to see anything when I'm hidden away in the carriage under Mother's watchful eye.'

'I hope you don't mistake me for some kind of flighty fool who will let you do anything that takes your fancy, young lady. I have undertaken the responsibility to take good care of you,' said Caroline, smiling to take the sting out of her reprimand.

Olivia tilted her golden hair to one side and smiled alluringly. 'I'm so very grateful that you have come, dear Caroline. I fear I may have died of boredom without you. It's been quite dreadful since Nanny left. Now, let us hurry to the village while the sun still shines.'

They left the grounds of Willow Manor, walking at quite a speed. Olivia chatted happily like a little bird released from her cage, while Caroline tried not to think of Ralph and what would happen if they were to meet him on the way.

CHAPTER 5

Willow Manor, York - Present day

CARA TWIDDLED with the silver pendant necklace George gave her as a birthday gift. Now she regretted not telling him more details about the previous night when he woke her from the disturbing dream.

George paused near the open bookshelf, torch in hand, and turned to her. 'That sounds ominous. What… what didn't you tell me?'

Cara cleared her throat as she struggled to choose the right words. She didn't want to make a big deal of it, but it was only fair to tell him. And she wanted him to know because they didn't keep things from each other. The dark, secretive days when they first met and lived double lives were over, which made it even more precious that they didn't need to hide anything from each other anymore.

It was such a relief for Cara to share her innermost fears with George, and she sensed it was the same for him. Cara had learned they were like mirrors, triggering their wounds and insecurities for each other to heal. When Twin Flames achieve union, it's said they shine so brightly as their true loving selves, they naturally raise the consciousness of the planet with their soul vibration. Cara never felt so fully herself until she met George.

They both experienced deep healing since those turbulent early days. George realised he wasn't responsible for others' happiness, and it was safe to be honest about his own needs and desires. Cara confronted her deepest fear of not being enough, which had followed her like a dark cloud ever since she was abandoned as a child. She had no memory of her parents, but the feeling of being deserted had stayed with her, even after she was adopted by a wonderful man who she thought of as her true father.

Only through the emotional rollercoaster of their intense love affair had she finally experienced unconditional love for herself and for George.

'Darling? What is it?' said George, interrupting Cara's thoughts.

'Oh sorry, I was miles away. Um… it was Ralph Knight in my dream, you know… the karmic warrior. The guy who hypnotised me in Tudorville, remember?' Cara swallowed hard, her pulse tip-tapping in her neck.

'Of course, I remember. The rotten impudence of the man. I thought we'd seen the back of him.' George crossed to where Cara stood, the torch immediately forgotten. He guided her towards the sofa. 'Let's sit down for a minute. The priest hole or whatever it is can wait. What more did you see in the dream?'

Cara sank down onto the sofa, grateful for his calm and compassionate nature. 'I don't know how much I can remember or explain clearly—you know what dreams are like. It's all a bit hazy.'

'Take it slowly, my darling. It's all okay,' he said, reaching for her hand.

'Well, you know I told you I thought I'd seen another version of us?'

George nodded and listened intently as Cara explained the dream was about the young woman, Caroline, who she first saw when Ralph Knight hypnotised her in Tudorville in 1536.

'I have a foreboding that I'm being drawn into that timeline when I was Caroline. What if I actually time travelled to 1729 through the passageway but my memory hasn't updated yet, and the dream was a warning?' She looked at the hole in the wall. 'I wish I'd never found it now,' she said, lowering her head into her hands.

'Let's not jump to any conclusions. It may have just been a dream, and that might just be a priest hole.' He tried to diffuse her worry with his most charming smile. 'Shall we check it out together?'

'I hope you're right,' she said. 'Okay, let's get it over with.'

Holding hands, they moved towards the opening. George picked up the torch, squeezed Cara's hand for a second, and then released it and stepped into the dark space. He shone the torch ahead and then turned back to help Cara join him in the narrow space. They stood there looking about the partially lit passageway.

'Ready?' said George.

'Yes, let's see if there really is a wall,' she said, her voice almost a whisper.

They took cautious steps. George went ahead and Cara was right behind him.

'What do you see? We must be reaching the end by now,' Cara said.

Cara watched George stretch his hand out in front of

him, illuminated by the soft glow of the torchlight. She held her breath.

He said, 'Look, it is a wall. It's solid. I think we have ourselves a priest hole, as you thought. I'll research it when I have a chance and see if there's any mention of a priest hiding out here during the reformation.'

'That's exciting. I wouldn't be surprised if we offered refuge to a priest in Tudorville. I wonder whether he survived, poor thing.'

'Here—touch the wall—it's firm, considering how old it must be. I can't feel any crumbling.' George guided Cara's hand towards the wall and placed her fingers on the rough surface.

The second her fingers touched the wall, she knew. 'It's going to happen again, George.'

'What?'

'The vortex is coming.'

Suddenly he felt it too. The freezing cold air swirled around them and the familiar whooshing sound filled their ears. George gripped onto the torch tightly, but the light fizzled out and he lost sight of Cara.

'I'm going,' she called.

He heard the panic in her voice.

George stood helpless as the vortex surrounded them, powerless to stop it. He'd only witnessed the vortex when it transported him to the Victoriana timeline, but this time, it hadn't come for him. He put his arms out to stop her from going, but they only flailed about in the freezing nothingness and his cold fingers scraped the wall. It was hopeless. He could do nothing to stop it.

She had gone.

Willow Manor, York - Georgiana

The rain drummed relentlessly on the walls of the old Tudor manor and droplets of water slid down the library windowpanes. Olivia and Caroline sat at the table, side by side. They had clicked into an enjoyable rhythm of reading and studying together in the mornings after breakfast, and then taking some form of exercise in the afternoons. Sometimes they would discuss what they had learned, and at other times, Caroline would encourage Olivia to forget her studies and enjoy the day.

Caroline was grateful to have a post where she could continue learning with Olivia, rather than pretending to be an experienced governess who already knew everything she must teach. Caroline shared what occurred to her, and they also explored new themes together as they read, which proved absorbing for the two young women.

'I don't suppose we'll be able to walk into the village today, after all,' said Olivia, glancing up from her book to assess the ferocious rainstorm which had come out of nowhere after a sunny start to the day.

Caroline's eyes followed Olivia's, and she rested her open book on the table. 'We won't even get a turn around the gardens if this downpour doesn't let up, never mind a walk to the village.'

Olivia frowned, and her mouth turned downwards. 'How tiresome. I was so looking forward to it.'

'Is there a particular reason you wish to walk to the village again so soon after our last visit?' asked Caroline. She suspected she knew what attracted the young woman to Willow Wick, and unfortunately, it wasn't only the fresh air.

Olivia shook her head, her expression one of pure innocence. 'No, I just enjoy the long walk. It's pleasing to have an interesting destination rather than wandering around the grounds as I used to with Nanny or Mother. I have grown weary of the same old childhood walks.'

Caroline studied the dazzling young woman, who looked particularly lovely today, dressed in a vibrant blue gown which complemented her golden hair and intelligent dark eyes.

Caroline dreaded the walks to Willow Wick and intended to use every excuse she could to avoid them. They had already been twice in the short time she'd been in service at Willow Manor, and twice was too much as far as she was concerned. Caroline had been on edge all the way during the first walk, worrying they would run into Ralph. She was a bag of nerves by the time they reached the line of willow trees. There was no sign of Ralph, but Caroline didn't find the walk pleasurable, which was a great shame, because Olivia was a pleasant companion with a keen interest in the world around her and a stimulating conversationalist. Caroline was on edge and expected Ralph to jump out at them at any moment. The second time Olivia beseeched her to walk into the village, she was about to use her governess status to divert her, when her brother George overheard the request and chimed in to say he thought it a splendid idea.

When she professed her reluctance, he said, 'But Mistress Caroline, you would not deny my dear sister and your good self the prospect of a wonderful outing on such a fine afternoon as this?'

Caroline's face grew hot, and her cheeks stung as they flushed bright pink. She couldn't think of a good reason to refuse. In fact, she couldn't think at all when he was staring at her like that. He had a way of disarming her with just one look that reduced her to a speechless wreck. He must think her a terribly dull companion for his beloved sister.

'If I wasn't so preoccupied with estate business today, I

would accompany you myself. Perhaps next time, ladies,' he said, bestowing a wicked smile in Caroline's direction, which turned her legs to water.

She suspected he was well aware of the dramatic effect he had on her just by being in the same room, and he seemed to enjoy it. He was a sophisticated young man who had spent much time at court. It was obvious he was already skilled in the art of flirting with the opposite sex and was quite as chivalrous as any knight in the books she read.

She wished she could compose herself when she was around him, but he only had to say two words to her, and she became bashful and quite unlike herself. Caroline struggled to find her usual witty retorts in his all-consuming presence and left the room whenever possible so he wouldn't notice her state of embarrassment.

And so, thanks to George, the two of them had set off on their second walk, wearing warm capes and bonnets, walking arm in arm across the fields and then along the footpath which led to the village. Caroline resolved to do her best to forget about Ralph and make the most of the outing. She chastised herself for allowing thoughts of Ralph to ruin her exciting new life. How could she enjoy the freedom she craved if she lived in fear of what he might do if he saw her with Olivia?

Caroline shook her head and brought herself back to the present.

'This afternoon, I would like to hear you play your latest piece, and later we shall do some needlework to entertain ourselves. This is most definitely not a day for venturing out to the village. Let us hope tomorrow will be dry and we may explore an alternative route I wish to show you.'

Olivia's pretty face clouded over. She looked at Caroline, unable to hide her disappointment, and said, 'I would have thought you'd love to go into Willow Wick, seeing as it's your home. Do you not care to visit your father? I could accompany you and we could take the carriage.'

Olivia had a good point. Caroline hadn't been to see her father yet. She hoped to go the following Sunday when the girl would be otherwise engaged with the family. She must not leave it much longer to visit her poor dear father, who would be waiting to see her, even at the risk of running into Ralph. At least she could go alone and there was no chance of him shaming her and making a fool of her in Olivia's presence. She could just about handle him on her own, but not in front of the Cavendish family.

Willow Manor, York - Present day

George switched the torch off and on again, and it bounced back to life. He shone the flashlight around the small space and saw Cara slumped on the floor by the wall.

'Cara, darling.' He touched her face gently, and she moaned and opened her eyes.

'Where am I?' she said, scrambling to her feet.

George steadied her as she swayed near the wall.

'I feel woozy. What happened?'

'I'm not surprised. Take my hand and let's get out of here.'

They edged slowly along the passageway, following the beam of the torch. George pushed the bookshelf which stood ajar and had almost clicked shut. Bright daylight flooded into their eyes, making them squint.

He jumped out and helped Cara down. 'Are you okay?'

'I think so. It happened when I touched the wall, didn't it? I'm definitely time travelling again,' she said.

'The weirdest thing was how the vortex took you, but not

me. I was in it with you, but nothing happened to me,' he said.

'Are you certain you didn't go too?'

He nodded. 'I know when I travel even if I don't remember the details.'

'I need to get outside,' said Cara.

They headed out and walked around the estate, admiring the gardens. Cara tried to forget about the ominous signs of another phase of time travelling.

'Swifty's doing an amazing job,' she said. And as she mentioned his name, Swifty, who was now their head gardener, but in other lives was an integral part of their time travel team, came dashing around the corner, Cornelius the greyhound at his heels. Cornelius bounded over, and Cara knelt on the grass and stroked his silky coat as he licked her face with great enthusiasm. 'There, there, good boy,' she said.

They chatted to Swifty for a few minutes. He was working hard in the new courtyard garden, planting rows of flowers and fledgling trees ready for the grand opening.

'Isn't it weird how he seems to have no memory at all of our past lives?' said Cara, as they continued their walk. 'He must be a genuine sleeper traveller.'

'It's weird for us, but it's a blessing for him. He's living a lovely uncomplicated life, and he seems content.'

'It's fascinating how we are drawn together again, even though he remembers nothing,' said Cara.

George nodded. 'Yes, we're like a cast in a play that just keeps on running.'

'What did you make of the passageway?' asked Cara.

'Well, it definitely has the markings of a priest hole, but it seems to also serve as some kind of time travelling gateway, for you.'

'It's not the same as when the vortex took me in the past.

Even though this version of me remained here as usual, I was knocked out. How long was I out for, would you say?'

'I'm not sure you were out, as such, but you were on the floor and visibly shaken.'

'I think I must have been out for a minute as I blanked,' she said. 'I'm really confused about what's going on. The mode of time travel is different this time. It's not just the gateway, but I can't put my finger on it.'

They looked at each other and said simultaneously, 'Let's call Eddie.'

Eddie was a quantum physics professor and dear friend to them both. In Tudorville, he was their children's tutor and their time travelling partner. He had helped save them both from the hangman and certain death, and they trusted him with their lives. Literally.

They walked to the rose garden and sat on a bench in one of their favourite spots near the lovers' fountain. George took his phone out of his pocket and clicked Eddie's number.

'Perfect timing, as always. I was just wondering how you two were doing,' said Eddie, his distinctive voice ringing out through the speaker. 'Hold on, let's do video. It's been too long since I saw your faces.'

Eddie wanted to know the latest on the centre developments, so they filled him in on the details. Then Cara, unable to wait any longer, said, 'Something weird has happened, Eddie. We want your take on it.'

'That's good news. I was thinking it was a little dull now we're all living such normal lives.'

'Be careful what you wish for,' said Cara. 'You know it's never dull for long.'

She told him about her discovery of the priest hole and how she suspected she was time travelling again.

'Well, I imagine I'll be seeing you in Tudorville any minute, Lady Cara,' he laughed, looking thrilled.

'It always astounds me how you just take it in your stride,' she replied, shaking her head.

'The truth is, it's a dream scenario for a quantum physics professor. I get to see quantum physics play out in real time. Pardon the pun.'

'Well, I have a feeling this is going to excite you even more,' said George. 'Cara thinks she's travelling to a new timeline.'

'Which timeline?' Eddie's eyes widened.

'I believe I'm travelling back to 1729, to the timeline where my name was Caroline. If you recall, Ralph Knight kidnapped and hypnotised me to rewrite the Georgiana timeline so I would marry him, not George.'

'I remember!' said Eddie. 'That would have wiped out your future lives. And we nearly lost Willow Manor...'

'That's right. But that's not all. I think we may have found a way to time travel on demand,' Cara said.

George looked at her as the significance of her words dawned on him.

'Is there any chance of you coming to York?' Cara continued. 'We could do with your professional opinion.'

'Try and stop me!' Eddie said, his eyes gleaming. 'I'll be on the first train.'

CHAPTER 6

Willow Manor, York - Georgiana

Caroline tried on the new gown that Olivia insisted she accept as a gift. They passed several afternoons, talking and giggling as they altered the garment to fit Caroline. Although they were of a similar build, Caroline was taller than Olivia and the elaborate mantua gown would show her ankles, which wouldn't do. Caroline had hesitated to accept the gift, but Olivia had been so determined that she eventually gave in. She could certainly do with a new gown, even if she was a little overwhelmed by the extravagant style.

Caroline was discovering that Olivia had a very persuasive nature. 'Caroline, I have so many gowns and this particular one doesn't complement my colouring half as well as it would yours.'

Olivia held the pastel lemon brocade against Caroline's cheek to emphasise her point. 'I insist you have it. And besides, we will make the necessary alterations together, and you know Mother wishes me to become more accomplished in my needlework.'

'You are too good to me, Mistress Olivia,' replied Caroline. The girl touched her heart with her generous nature and kind spirit, and not for the first time, she thanked God for her good fortune in having such a wonderful position.

'Really, I do wish you wouldn't address me so formally. We are like sisters, and as such you must call me Olivia.'

A few days after the gown incident, and several weeks after she moved into the grand house, the countess requested she come to her in the drawing room. Caroline was nervous, and as she climbed the staircase, she thought her heartbeat must be as loud as the ticking grandfather clock in the hallway. Was this all too good to be true? Perhaps the countess wasn't satisfied with her performance as governess. As she walked behind Harriet, who led the way as usual, her heart thumped ever harder, and she grew unpleasantly hot and flustered.

Harriet ushered her into the room and then left with a quick reassuring wink at Caroline, for which she was grateful.

'Sit, my dear,' said the countess, beckoning to a chair opposite her own. 'You look well, if somewhat alarmed. Let me assure you there is no need to be.'

Caroline said, 'Thank you, my lady. I do hope I have succeeded in meeting your expectations.'

'You have more than exceeded my expectations. Olivia is positively blooming under your tutorage. I am overjoyed at her progress in your company.'

A wave of relief flooded through Caroline, and she allowed herself to relax in the stiff-backed chair. She wasn't to be banished home to the village, as she had feared when she heard the summons. At nineteen years of age, although confident, she lacked experience in the ways of the world and was easily knocked off balance. She hadn't yet learned to trust her instincts fully and although she thought the position was working out well, for a moment she wondered if she had overstepped her boundaries by becoming too friendly with Olivia and accepting the formal gown which was such a lavish and expensive display of the girl's affection.

'Olivia has requested I invite you to join us for dinner today, which I am more than happy to do. George is keen to hear more about Olivia's studies and your plans, as am I. He also thought it an especially splendid idea that we get to know you better as you're almost one of the family now.'

Caroline cleared her throat—the brief relaxing respite was over. The thought of dinner with George sent her into an immediate spin. What would they talk about? What plans was she supposed to have to discuss with them? She would surely make a fool of herself in such prestigious company.

Caroline was accustomed to eating meals in the cosy village cottage with her father and occasionally they might have a friend join them for dinner, but she had experienced nothing so grand as dining at a house such as Willow Manor. Since she'd arrived, she'd been enjoying meals with the servants in the kitchen. It was wonderful to be part of a team with a common purpose and, following Cook's lead, the members of the household had welcomed her like she was one of their own. The servants were one big family and Caroline loved the camaraderie, which was an unexpected benefit she hadn't even considered would be part of a life in service. The cheerful banter in the kitchen was soothing, and she was not inclined to dine upstairs. Her heart fluttered at the thought of eating with the family.

Caroline brought herself back to the present. She couldn't refuse without seeming rude and so she forced herself to smile. 'Thank you, my lady. I'd be honoured, indeed.'

She slipped out of the drawing room after she was

excused and went to find Olivia in the stables. Anxious thoughts spiralled around her mind and gnawed at her as she wondered how she would get through dinner with George that afternoon.

York - Present day

Eddie called that afternoon to say he couldn't come the same day, after all. Something had come up at the university, so he would take the train the following morning.

That night, Cara had another dream. This time it was more vivid—and she knew for sure it wasn't merely a dream.

It was an update from another timeline.

She saw herself as the nineteen-year-old girl, Caroline—the former version of herself in the early eighteenth century.

Cara woke in a panic, knowing without a doubt that the Twin Flame mission was back on in full force.

Well, that lovely peaceful period is over.

She thought she should be used to it by now, but she had once again dared to believe her time travelling might be over for good, and then was shocked when it resumed. This time was particularly jarring, as it was a new timeline and made her stomach gurgle with nerves.

Cara told George, and he comforted her in his usual stoic manner. 'It'll be okay, darling. We'll figure it out like we always do.'

She knew she was fortunate to be loved by a man who was so grounded and strong. He always knew what to say to calm her fears and make her feel safe.

After breakfast in the kitchen and a quick catch up with the builders, they drove to pick up Eddie from the station.

'It's this very kitchen I saw in my dream,' said Cara. 'The

layout is almost the same. I take my meals in here with the servants and there's this wonderful cook who has taken me under her wing and I think must be trying to fatten me up!'

George covered her hand with his while he drove. 'What year is it there? Do you know yet?'

'Yes, it's 1729, which confirmed my fears.'

'What's significant about that?'

'It's when I… well, Caroline left Willow Wick and went to work as governess to Olivia, your sister. The earl's sister, that is. Gosh, this is even more confusing than usual, with you having a sister in both timelines and me having a different name back then. Anyway, it's the exact period that Ralph wanted to rewrite to keep us from falling in love.'

'Ah,' said George.

When they arrived at the station, there was nowhere to park, so George waited in the car while Cara dashed in to look for Eddie. When she saw his dear beloved face, her eyes welled up, and she had to get a grip on her emotions.

Eddie hugged her tightly. 'Hello dear Lady Cara. I have missed you. But why the sad face?'

'Sorry, I'm so pleased to see you—just a bit overwhelmed, that's all. And why do you insist on calling me by that ridiculous name?' Cara rolled her eyes at the fancy title.

'To me you will always be Lady or Countess Cavendish, talking of which I can't wait to see you and the earl living at Willow Manor again. I've been dying to come ever since you moved in.'

'I wish you had come sooner. We certainly have enough room and can do with another pair of hands.'

They left the platform and jumped into the car. Eddie's long legs curled against the back seat. As they purred through the traffic, he regaled them with stories of his quirky students and told them about his quantum physics experiments at the university. He hadn't had any significant breakthroughs since they last met.

George guided the car steadily through the thick mid-morning traffic around the city, and then darted onto the quiet country road which led to Willow Wick and away from the magnificent city walls.

As they drove through the gates and up the willow tree-lined driveway towards the majestic manor house, Cara spotted Eddie staring out of the car window like an excited child.

'It's amazing to be back, isn't it?' she said.

George parked the car round the back of the house and grabbed Eddie's bag. They headed inside through the kitchen door and Eddie stood looking around, shaking his head, bemused. 'I can barely believe we're here,' he said.

They ate dinner at the table on the pale stone patio, which was decorated with vibrant coloured pots stuffed with a riot of swaying summer blooms. Several hours passed in a flash as they chatted about old times, or old timelines, to be more accurate, and demolished a couple of bottles of Cabernet Sauvignon—the connection between them tangible in the warm evening air.

When an evening chill descended, they cleared away the dinner plates and settled in the snug that Cara and George had refurbished with cosy evenings just like this in mind.

Eddie said, 'Okay, come on, guys. Spill the beans about the time travel on demand. I can't wait any longer to hear your news. I could barely sleep last night, for thinking about it.'

'I wondered how long it would take you to ask for the details,' said Cara, laughing.

'Why do you love to torment the good professor, so?' said George, retrieving his wine glass from the table and taking a large swig as he settled back into the armchair.

'All right, all right,' said Cara. 'Well, seriously, though I don't know for sure that it's time travel on demand, but it seems like it may be. I'm not sure what happened the first time, but the second time George was with me, and we both felt the vortex.'

Eddie rubbed his hands together and proceeded to quiz Cara on the specifics. His fascination and enthusiasm were palpable, and he kept firing questions at them.

Cara held up her hand after ten minutes of intense questioning. 'You are relentless. This must be what it was like in the inquisition,' she said, and took a sip of wine, rolling her eyes.

'Talking of the inquisition, I'm pretty certain we have a genuine priest hole on our hands which is going to be absolutely brilliant for the centre,' said George.

'A priest hole time portal by the sounds of it! Probably best we don't mention that to your visitors,' said Eddie. He rested his head on his hands on the table.

They sat in silence for a while as Eddie processed what they had told him. George reached for Cara's hand and squeezed it as they waited to hear his thoughts.

'Do you think there's a specific reason you're travelling to this new timeline—Georgiana?'

Cara nodded. 'Yes, although I've had several dreams about it, but can't remember a thing in the normal way. I'm not getting any memory updates like I used to about Tudorville.'

'I wonder if the reporting system works differently when it's time travel on demand,' said Eddie, running his fingers through his hair so it stuck up chaotically, and he looked like an archetypal mad professor. 'It could be a positive sign we're getting closer to what we've been trying to do.'

'I don't know, but my gut tells me it's to do with Ralph, the karmic warrior. It doesn't feel positive. It feels scary,' Cara said.

'But we handled him, didn't we? Sylvia undid the hypnotic suggestion, and we had proof it worked because Willow Manor was restored,' said Eddie, swinging his wine glass slowly from side to side, so the wine swirled around the bottom of the balloon glass. 'I wonder why you would be called back to that specific time.'

'What if I've been called back to make sure the timeline stays as we intended?' said Cara. 'It's a critical period. If the undoing of the hypnotism doesn't stick, it could disrupt the timelines again, and we will be in trouble.'

'There's only one way to find out,' said Eddie.

'I don't know what you're going to say, but I'm pretty sure I won't like it,' interjected George, curiously sober despite their copious wine drinking.

Eddie looked at George and then back at Cara.

'We need to run some quantum tests with you in the portal and see what happens,' said Eddie.

'I was afraid you'd come up with something like that!' Cara said.

Willow Manor, York - Georgiana

The stays squeezed Caroline's stomach and chest so tightly that she struggled to breathe. For the tenth time that day, she wished she could join the servants for supper as usual, in the warm, welcoming kitchen. Olivia had asked her to tap on her door a few minutes before dinner so they could walk down together.

'You look beautiful,' said Olivia when she opened her door and slipped out into the hallway. She grabbed Caroline's clammy hand and skipped about like a carefree lamb. Caroline wished she could be as joyful.

'Come. It's only mother, George, you and I. There's no need to look so terrified. I promise they won't eat you.'

This statement, which was obviously designed to allay Caroline's fears, had the opposite effect, and only made her more anxious. The vision of an intimate family dinner with George observing her every move filled her with dread and she shook inwardly. He would see her for the simple village girl she was, and she was certain she would make a fool of herself.

'May I compliment you on your gown? You look as well as the ladies at court, and the colour suits you,' said George. They were shown to their places at the long table in the great hall, and much to Caroline's consternation, she was seated directly opposite George. His dark eyes drilled into hers, and she shifted uncomfortably in her seat, simultaneously electrified by his presence, and wishing she were somewhere else. She blushed and tried to find the right words to acknowledge the compliment.

'I told Caroline it would suit her. It was one of my gowns and we altered it together. She looks beautiful, doesn't she?' said Olivia, oblivious to Caroline's mortified expression.

'You have done well, girls,' said the countess. 'The gown suits you perfectly.' She nodded towards Caroline.

'Indeed,' said George, the admiration in his eyes clear.

Caroline lowered her head and focused on the table to avoid his intense stare. She wondered what it was like to be lord of the manor and a frequent visitor at the famous court of King George and Queen Caroline. She wished she could flee from the room and away from his prying eyes, but dinner with the Cavendish family was no speedy, simple affair, so she tried to steady herself and appear calm. She had no doubt she would be able to hold her own at the dinner if it weren't for his unsettling presence. There was something about him that undid her poise and made her feel naked and exposed.

The sumptuous meal was served. Caroline was relieved there was something to keep her occupied, and as she ate, she paid special attention to how the family ate and she tried to model them. Her father did his best to teach her how to dine in society, but she never had the opportunity until now. She found their table manners weren't all that different to her father's, because he wasn't your average villager. The quality and quantity of the meal differed vastly from the fayre they ate at the cottage, with a rich array of meats from which to choose. There was more food than she and her father ate in a week. There was venison and partridge and beef, and Caroline wished she could relax and enjoy the feast, but she was on edge under George's watchful eyes.

Why did he study her so closely?

Morsels of the succulent dishes stuck in her dry throat as she chewed and tried to swallow. She could barely digest the food and wished only for the meal to end. Olivia chattered on about her riding lessons and asked that Caroline join her the next day.

'Are you an accomplished rider, Mistress Caroline?' asked George in between mouthfuls.

'No, I'm afraid my riding skills are minimal,' she replied, feeling inept and out of her social depth.

She had assisted Ralph occasionally by riding one of his wagon horses on the farm, so she knew the basics, but she certainly wasn't up to Olivia's standard of riding for pleasure.

'You must join Olivia and make the most of the horses. You'll be up to speed in no time,' he said.

'How kind of you,' Caroline replied. 'I shall consider it.'

Olivia said, 'I won't hear of it. We shall ride tomorrow after lessons. Perhaps we may ride into Willow Wick.'

Caroline shook her head. 'I'm definitely not ready for a long- distance ride.'

She would not risk running into Ralph. He was angry enough without taunting him with the sight of her behaving like a lady of the manor on horseback.

'I'm going to need a lot of practice before we get that far,' she said, trying to make light of the suggestion and brush it off.

'Perhaps the three of us could ride out together,' said George, raising one eyebrow as he contemplated her discomfort.

She noticed a wicked smile briefly cross his lips, and she had the uncomfortable realisation that he was toying with her.

Caroline sat up straight in her chair and raised her chin. 'What a wonderful idea,' she said, her grey eyes sparring with his challenging dark ones.

She wasn't going to let him treat her like a foolish girl, earl, or no earl.

CHAPTER 7

Willow Manor, York - Present day

THE NEXT MORNING, George took Eddie on a partial tour of the rambling old house. 'We plan to refurbish it over time and are focusing on launching the Tudor Heritage Centre. The main house needs a lot of updating—it still looks somewhat like a hotel,' said George, pointing to the oak counter near the entrance which had served as a reception area.

'And over there used to be part of the great hall, if I'm not mistaken,' said Eddie, pointing and shaking his head in wonder. 'Thomas, May and I would frequently join you there for meals.'

'I don't recall much unfortunately, but the house has felt very much like home for both of us since the moment we moved in.'

George led the way as they wandered in and out of the downstairs rooms.

'It's incredible you got this place back into the family. I

keep getting flashbacks from Tudorville—it looks so different and yet remarkably similar. It's hard to explain,' said Eddie.

George nodded. 'Cara says that too. It must be the layout and the Tudor furniture because there have been a lot of changes over the centuries.'

Eddie ran his hand over the back of a smooth wooden chair, marvelling at the condition of the fine period piece. 'I almost wish I could be back in Tudorville again. I would pay more attention.'

'Well, if you happen to find yourself back there, that would be incredibly helpful for the refurbishing and restoration work. We only have Cara's memory to go by. Much of what we're planning is based on guesswork and her knowledge of how houses were typically laid out and furnished at that time.'

Eddie studied the impressive rows of paintings lining the walls. 'Is there one of you?'

'I'm not sure. I understand there are some old portraits of the family stored away for safekeeping, but we haven't had a chance to look properly yet. There is so much stuff everywhere and we're trying to get the centre ready to open.'

Cara appeared in the doorway with a circular tray holding three freshly brewed cups of tea, her chestnut hair gleaming in the sunlight like a halo. 'What are you up to? I thought you might fancy a cuppa.'

'Marvellous idea,' said Eddie, beaming at the sight of his through-the-centuries time travelling companion and the mistress of Willow Manor. 'George was just telling me about your plans for the house.'

'Did he mention we are thinking of reopening a wing of the house as a boutique hotel for the centre visitors?'

Eddie reached for one of the cups, raised it to his lips and blew on the tea. 'No, we didn't get that far. I was just remarking how recognisable the place is to me even though I haven't seen much of it since Tudorville.'

Cara passed a cup to George and perched on the edge of a wooden bench as she drank hers. 'It's peculiar, isn't it? George remembers nothing, but I keep getting these flashes of things that used to be in the house and thereabouts.'

'It would be splendid if we could restore it closely to how it was in 1536 when we lived here,' said Eddie.

'Yes, although there's a strong imprint of the Georgian era on the house too, so it's a blend. I think it's a wonderful example of how house styles develop through the years,' said Cara.

They sipped their tea in quiet contemplation as rays of sun seeped in through the stained-glass windows, casting coloured spindles of light onto the flagstones.

'I miss the children, you know. It might be five hundred years in linear time, but in quantum time, it doesn't seem long since we were in the schoolroom working on their lessons,' said Eddie.

'I know what you mean. I miss them dreadfully,' said Cara. 'I try to console myself by thinking that at least we didn't mess up the timeline and they are safe and living their lives.'

Eddie tapped Cara's shoulder, like you might console a small child.

George pushed his floppy hair off his forehead, as though he were swatting away a fly. 'What else would you like to see, Eddie?'

'I bet I can guess,' said Cara, her tone playful, belying the tension in her knotted stomach. 'I imagine you are itching to see the priest hole.'

'You know me too well,' said Eddie.

'Pass your cups and I'll pick up the tray on the way back. Although, our new housekeeper whizzes about the place as silently and fast as a genie, so it probably won't be here when we come out of the library. Did I mention she's Swifty's mother?'

'Swifty? As in our Swifty? I had no idea he was here, never mind his mother too,' he replied, pulling a comical face.

'Oh yes, he's the head gardener. I bumped into him when I visited the hotel to look for the Bank of England vault key George hid in the lovers' fountain. Didn't I tell you?'

'Oh, yes, that's right, you did, but I didn't realise Swifty still worked here.'

'I'll introduce you if we see him, but don't be disappointed if he doesn't recognise you,' said Cara.

Eddie nodded. 'Another sleeper traveller like Carlos…' He followed them up the ornate winding stairs and wondered what surprises they had in store for him in this great old house.

Willow Manor, York - Georgiana

Caroline had turned out to be a proficient rider and looked forward to their outings since she began riding every day with Olivia.

'You're a natural,' observed Olivia. 'It's almost as though you've been riding all your life.'

Caroline hadn't disliked riding—she wasn't given the opportunity to do much of it in Willow Wick and had imagined it would be more difficult, so she hadn't been on a horse for years.

She had no recollection of her past life as Lady Cavendish, mistress of Willow Manor, and the wife of Lord Cavendish, the earl. In 1536, she had been a much-admired horse woman, and as lady-in-waiting to Anne Boleyn and later to Jane Seymour, she rode alongside them regularly. Caroline had no memory of galloping through the grounds of Willow Manor with her husband, cantering around Hampton Court Palace or riding from London to York when they fled from Henry VIII's army with a price on their heads.

She put her sudden ability to ride down to a fortunate twist of fate and then promptly dismissed it.

One early afternoon after lessons, when the weather was perfect for riding; sunny but not too oppressive for their formal riding habits, Caroline and Olivia went racing across the estate at the back of the great house, thundering towards the post they had marked as the end of their race. Olivia was a daredevil and adored riding fast. Caroline liked to win. Her hair tumbled from beneath her hat and flew behind her like a gleaming flag as they galloped, riding neck and neck towards the finish line. Olivia won the race by a hair's breadth and punched her arm in the air.

'I'll beat you next time,' said Caroline.

They didn't notice George riding towards them, and he appeared suddenly and towered over them on his magnificent black horse.

'Good afternoon,' he said, bowing his head formally.

Caroline couldn't say why exactly, but she always worried he was amused by her awkwardness around him, and as usual, when he was near, she grew flustered. Fortunately, her face was warm and her cheeks already a rosy pink from the exertion of riding, as she sat side saddle recovering her breath, feeling like a rabbit snagged in a trap with no way out.

'Did you see the race, dear brother? We've been having a splendid time now that Caroline has discovered she's a much more accomplished rider than she realised. I still won, though!' declared Olivia.

'Yes, I spotted you riding like the wind, although it was

close. I must say, it's thoroughly ungracious of you, dear Livvy, to be quite so smug about your victory.' George punched his sister playfully on the arm. 'My little sister always did like winning,' he said, turning to Caroline. 'I'm afraid you have your hands full with this one.'

'I shall have to practice more,' said Caroline, wanting to say something witty, but not knowing what would be considered an appropriate response. She hoped he didn't think her too presumptuous, riding his horses at her leisure.

Caroline wished she were more used to witty society like Olivia—she was so gauche around him it was crippling.

George held Caroline's eyes for longer than necessary and then he snapped his gaze away as though it were an effort.

'I'm off to meet with John Thornton,' he said, patting his horse's head. 'He's our estate manager,' he clarified for Caroline as an afterthought. 'I recall that you two promised we would ride together. You're clearly an accomplished rider, so I wonder whether you may consider accompanying me today? I think the weather will remain dry and we should make the most of it.'

'Oh yes, please!' Olivia exclaimed before Caroline had a chance to think of a reasonable excuse to decline his alluring offer.

Caroline coughed and cleared her throat. 'Where does your estate manager live?' She knew John and knew which was his cottage, but the question would buy her some time to think about what to do.

'In the village,' interrupted Olivia, who glowed at the prospect of a trip to Willow Wick and jogged about in anticipation on her saddle.

Caroline diverted her with rides around the vast estate, so they had avoided making another trip together. One Sunday, Caroline had nipped into the village alone, taking a shortcut to her home and entering around the back so she wouldn't risk being spotted near the busy green. She spent a lovely hour with her father and then flitted out of the village under-cover of dusk.

Her pledge to Ralph that she would go and see him played on her mind daily, but she was so content at Willow Manor, she couldn't face another showdown with him. She would not allow him to take this newfound joy away from her. Each time his face loomed in her mind, she heard his voice like an ominous whisper, and something deep inside her warned her not to seek him out. Not yet, anyway. And so, she postponed the visit. She told herself she would go and see Ralph soon, when the time was right.

There was no dampening Olivia's enthusiasm, and she snapped Caroline, who was panicking and trying not to show it, back to the present.

What if Ralph saw her riding with the lord of the manor and his sister? He would be livid. He despised the nobility and had made his revulsion about her working for them clear; never mind what he would make of her riding to the village with them purely for fun.

'Oh, please say we may go, and we'll visit Talbot's on the square. I have been simply dying to buy new ribbons for weeks now, dear Caroline.'

The enticing thought of browsing for ribbons in the local store was too much for Olivia to resist.

Caroline found it difficult to ignore Olivia's pleading face. She didn't want to disappoint the sweet girl.

No. She mustn't let herself live like a prisoner just because she was fearful of Ralph's reaction to her new life. It wouldn't do. Not for her or for her charge. She decided she would just have to hope Ralph wasn't around. Perhaps he would be occupied on his farm and wouldn't even know she'd been anywhere near the village. The thoughts jostled around her mind, as she persuaded herself it would be all right.

After several minutes of casual chatter between the siblings, George turned to Caroline and said, 'Well, I must be on my way. Will you ladies join me?'

He studied Caroline's face, and she squirmed beneath his gaze. He could see she was in the grip of some inner turmoil and was intrigued why a ride into the village required such deep consideration. As he found her most agreeable to the eye, he continued to study her.

Caroline nodded. 'Thank you. Let us not disappoint Mistress Olivia. We would love to accompany you.'

She hoped he didn't know just how flustered he made her and thought she was rosy cheeked from the race.

As the words left her lips, Caroline knew she was in trouble. She had grown extremely fond of Olivia in such a short time, but the leap of joy in her heart was for George, and there was nothing she could do about it.

'Very good.' He manoeuvred his horse expertly about, so he faced the same way as the girls. As he did, his hard thigh brushed against Caroline's leg beneath her riding skirt and her senses crackled at his touch.

He looked across at her, calm and steady. 'Shall we race to the footpath?'

And off they shot, George leading, Olivia close behind, and Caroline trying to catch her breath and wondering what the devil she was getting herself into.

CHAPTER 8

Willow Manor, York - Present day

THE CURTAINS WERE open when Cara, George, and Eddie reached the library. The room exuded its usual calming, serene air, and sparks of sunlight bounced off the surfaces of the wooden furniture, giving the room an enchanting aura.

'Ah, lovely. I can see Mrs Lightfoot has already been in this morning and waved her magic wand around in here. I don't know how she does it, but she manages to keep the entire house looking tiptop.'

'This room is exactly as I remember it,' said Eddie. 'The chesterfields are later additions, of course, but the layout and bookshelves are the same. It's remarkable.'

A smile spread across Cara's face. She was proud of this room.

'I'm happy you like it. We've barely had a chance to get started, but it's stunning, isn't it? There's a special energy in here and it's been my favourite room as far back as I remember.'

'Talking of special energy, where is this wormhole?' He scanned the room from side to side, appraising the floor-to-ceiling shelving stacked with layers of old books. It was a special edition collector's dream.

'Wormhole?' said Cara.

'It may well be a priest hole in structural terms, but in quantum terms, it sounds to me like it's got all the attributes of a wormhole,' said Eddie, rubbing his fingers back and forth across the light stubble on his chin. 'Of course, there are various names for these points in the universe. You may have heard people refer to them as wormholes, portals, gateways or even tunnels,' he continued, looking from Cara to George. 'There are all kinds of names made popular by sci-fi books and movies.'

George, who had just discovered a volume of the Cavendish family history and was absorbed in flicking through it, raised his head. 'Aren't wormholes considered possible in Einstein's theory of relativity? I seem to remember something about that from my otherwise deathly dull physics classes.'

'Yes, that's correct.' Eddie's head bobbed up and down as he nodded enthusiastically. And that's all it took to set him off on the complex workings of quantum physics. 'It's known as an Einstein-Rosen Bridge or Einstein-Rosen Wormhole. In simple terms, it's like a tunnel with two ends at separate points, which may be in different locations or times… or even universes. That's when we get into the possibilities of the multiverse where we'd be talking about multiple universes, not just timelines.'

'I suppose we should be grateful we've not been catapulted to other universes then!' said Cara. 'It's mind blowing…'

'It is,' said Eddie. 'It was reading Einstein's Theory of Relativity that got me into this field in the first place. But don't let the science overwhelm you. This is a really exciting development. It's what you've been wishing for ever since you started time travelling.'

'Is it?' said Cara, pulling a face. 'How so, exactly, Professor?'

Eddie sank down on the chesterfield next to the still unsorted boxes of books. 'As you suspected, this could well be the missing piece for being able to time travel on demand. Although, we don't know whether it will work for me or George. Think about it... let's say it is a bona fide wormhole —you stumbled into it by chance, but it sounds as though you were transported to the same timeline on both occasions.'

'Yes, but I would have expected to find myself back in Tudorville, but in Georgiana everything's different... I even have a different name this time.'

Eddie scratched his stubble again and was silent as he considered the ramifications of an alternate timeline.

'Using the wormhole theory as a starting point, it makes perfect sense the tunnel would transport you to one other location only. That's what makes it possible to be explained by science, otherwise it would be too random.' He waved his hands around as he spoke. 'Think of it as a fixed entry point to the vortex.'

'Triggered by that specific location, you mean?' said George, looking bemused.

'Yes but, we'll only know for certain when Cara's been through it again in a controlled experiment.'

Cara squeezed into the narrow space to sit down next to the professor. 'I thought it wouldn't be long before we were back to experiments. I really don't like the sound of "controlled". What on earth would you have me do this time?'

'You have an amazing ability to revisit your past lives, Cara. We can't just ignore it. That would be a great shame, and a loss to the scientific community. If this is as we suspect; the opportunity you have to travel to a specific timeline on demand is one in several billion.'

'How did you work that out?' she said, her grey eyes widening in awe at his instant mathematical calculation.

'Let's just say it's an educated guess,' said Eddie, with the hint of a smile.

George raised one eyebrow and looked at Cara knowingly. They had both experienced the outcome of Eddie's educated guesses and George was reluctant to risk their hard-won happiness for the sake of proving a complex scientific theory.

George laid the book he was reading on the writing desk and came over to join them. 'What do you have in mind?'

'Show me the priest hole and if all is as I suspect, I'd like to send Cara through again and observe what happens,' said Eddie.

George reached for Cara's hand. 'What do you think?'

She shook her head. 'I don't know what to think. I've been having more dreams about Georgiana, so it does seem to be calling me. But I'm reluctant to rush in and risk messing things up again. It's 1729, and everything points to us reaching the exact spot when we were in danger of losing our past and our future after the karmic warrior hypnotised me to force us apart.'

'You didn't say you've been having more dreams,' said George, thin lines creasing his forehead and his dark eyes clouding over.

'I didn't want to worry you, darling, and I didn't know what to make of it. I mean, they could just be dreams, as you said, couldn't they? I remember nothing after going into the priest hole, so we've no way of knowing if I did time travel to Georgiana… the dreams and the vortex showing up at the same time could be a coincidence. The vortex took me for sure, but it could have been to Tudorville as usual,' Cara said. She stood abruptly and crossed the room to gaze out of the window. Cara watched Cornelius dart in and out of the hydrangeas, his thin tail curled near his long, graceful legs, while Swifty, lost in a world of his own and oblivious to her observing him, mowed the lawn which he had explained was a never-ending task. As soon as he completed the lawns on one side of the estate, he returned to the other and began all over again. Watching Swifty and Cornelius, who was a present-day version of the sweet puppy George had gifted her upon their betrothal in Tudorville, soothed her weary soul and not for the first time, she wished she'd never stumbled on the blasted wormhole. Her thoughts wandered again to their children, Thomas and May, and she imagined them in this very house in another time, taking their lessons with Tutor Edward, running about the grounds with the greyhound. She could see their joyful faces as they dashed about with Swifty and Cornelius.

George's parents would be in residence at the estate, and the sixteenth-century version of her and George would likely be in London at the court of Henry VIII. If she hadn't experienced this other life for herself, she would think it impossible. The thought of the children comforted her momentarily, but also reminded her of the magnitude of what was at stake. If she went back in time and changed even one tiny thing, it had the potential to adjust her family's life for every generation.

Eddie said, 'What do you say? Are you up for trying to go through the wormhole again?'

She turned back from the window to face Eddie and cast her eyes from him to George and back again. She sighed. 'I know I kept wishing we could time travel on demand, but now the prospect of it is real, it's terrifying!'

'It's understandable you would feel that way,' said George. 'When we were time travelling at the whim of the vortex and we didn't know what would happen next, the idea of being able to choose when we travelled was a luxury. Now we've stopped travelling and are settled here, it's not remotely tempting...'

'True. I wish it would all just stop,' said Cara. 'It's like we're on an endless mission, and each time we think we're done, it just starts up all over again to test us.'

Eddie's blue eyes shone with empathy. 'Take some time to think about it. I'm not rushing off and will stay on for a few days and help you out around here, if that's okay?'

They assured him it was more than okay. They'd love to have him. Then Cara walked over to the portion of the shelves to reveal the spot where she'd fallen through time. She pushed on the edge of one shelf and heard the familiar creak. The section shifted and swung open to reveal the dark hole. 'Do you want to go in and have a poke about?' She looked at Eddie and smiled, much like one might humour an enthusiastic child.

Eddie jumped up and was at her side in seconds. Cara reached over to the nearby console table and placed the torch in his hand. 'Here you go—you'll need this. It's pitch black in there. It goes on for a while, so take it slowly and then you should come to a wall. My theory is my touching the wall triggered the vortex, but I won't come in and take the chance, in case it occurs some other way. Nothing happened when George touched it, but that's not to say the vortex won't take you.'

'I'm in the other timelines with you. Makes sense I could be in Georgiana, too,' said Eddie, pursing his lips, torch in hand as he considered the possibilities.

'I'll come in with you if you like,' said George. 'I am immune to the wormhole.'

Cara stared at him, alarmed, her heart thumping. 'Really? You've only been in there once. How can you possibly know you're immune?'

'It'll be okay,' he said, kissing her, taking the torch from Eddie, and preparing to step into the gap. He looked back at them both. 'This way, if the vortex comes for Eddie, at least we'll know for sure.'

'Good shout,' said Eddie.

'Be careful,' said Cara. She thought it was an awful shout but knew better than to try and get in George's way once he'd decided. She should have seen this coming and steered him away from it in advance. It was too late now.

George switched on the torch and stepped into the dark space, ready to follow the narrow beam of light. Eddie jumped in after him. It was a high ceiling, so they didn't have to crouch.

'We'll be back soon,' called George, and a faint echo of his voice streamed back into the library.

'Wish us luck,' said Eddie, looking back at Cara before following George.

Cara watched as they disappeared, and the light grew faint.

'You'll need more than luck,' she said aloud, knowing they wouldn't hear her words. Her senses raced into overdrive as she contemplated all the things that could go wrong. A dark veil of gloom descended over her, and she felt her chest tighten as it always did when George was in danger. She wished she had agreed to the experiment because he would now be safe in the library, and she wouldn't be waiting powerless, while her husband led the way into a wormhole, which Eddie said held the power to transport him to another universe, never mind another timeline.

Bloody hell. Why did I get us back into this?

Cara cursed herself for sharing her discovery with them. If they came back safely, she vowed to put an end to this and shut down the whole idea. The present-day timeline was perfect as it was, and she wasn't going to meddle with it, no matter how enticing it was to develop their time travel system. She would not endanger them all again, even for a wormhole.

Willow Manor, York - Georgiana

It was three in the morning, and Willow Manor sat silently in the deepest depths of night. Even the birds still slept and there was not yet a faint whisper of dawn. This hour is known by those who understand such things as *the witching hour*. Folklore has it that between three and four in the morning, supernatural events are most likely to occur.

Caroline writhed from side to side on the mattress, alone in her room, her nightgown damp with perspiration, the sheets twisted around her feverish limbs.

Unbeknownst to her, she had slept in this room many times before.

The layout of the sleeping quarters in the house had changed somewhat in a refurbishment undertaken by George's parents, but this very room had been her and George's bedchamber in Tudorville. She stirred in her sleep and gradually awakened. Or was she still dreaming? She couldn't be certain.

Violent feelings of loss washed over her, and the vision of George kissing her passionately and touching her in a way she had never been touched before consumed her. She could still feel his kisses on her skin. It seemed so real. She shivered, echoes of desire rippled through her body, and she longed for him.

Caroline sat up in the bed abruptly, with only streams of moonlight casting eerie shadows around the room. Her heartbeat quickened, and she had an overwhelming sense of having been in that bedchamber before, perhaps even in that bed, in another time.

She pulled the sheet up to her chin to cover her rapidly cooling body and contemplated her dream. George had been different. He was significantly older, and there had been flecks of grey in his thick hair. Caroline sat unmoving for a long time, thoughts of another George tumbling around her mind.

What was the meaning of the strange dream? Was it some kind of glimpse into the future? She shivered again, having been warned by the local priest at church about the dangers of falling prey to the supernatural.

She sat and pondered the whispers of her vision as the early morning mists slid across the York landscape, coating the field beneath her window until the sun pierced the misty veil and triumphed in revealing a bright new day. It was only when the first shards of light streamed into the room and the witching hour had safely passed that Caroline surrendered to her intense longing to sleep. This time she slept a sweet dreamless slumber and when she awoke to the distant rumbles of the waking house, she wondered whether she had imagined it all.

She struggled to rouse herself from her comfortable bed that morning, her eyelids still heavy from lack of sleep. As the sounds of the house grew steadily more insistent, she could ignore the need to rise no longer, and with an effort she dragged herself from beneath the warm cover and rested her feet on the rug next to the four-poster bed.

Images of her and George making love the previous night

flashed through her mind and her skin burned at the thought of her wanton behaviour. What alarmed her even more was her longing to feel his arms around her again, as his beautiful hard body covered hers and he took her. A virgin when she retired for bed the previous night, it was surreal to awaken in the morning and know what consummation felt like.

She washed and dressed in haste, her linen shift sticking to her damp skin as she rushed into her plain gown, worrying all the while that she would miss breakfast and incur Cook's wrath.

It would be all right, she reassured herself. The countess and Olivia were still abed at this hour, and George would no doubt be out riding as usual. She closed the door quietly behind her and entered the hallway, intending to dart down to the kitchen unnoticed. She meant to fit her cap onto her mane of chestnut hair as she walked, to save precious minutes, but before she could do so, it slipped from her fingers and tumbled to the ground. As she bent to retrieve it from the cold wooden floor, she heard footsteps and raised her head. Her eyes locked with George's, who appeared unperturbed at finding her in such a dishevelled state.

'Good day, Caroline. Are you having trouble with your cap?' he said, an unmistakable teasing gleam in his dark eyes, as he stooped to help her. She noticed he called her Mistress Caroline when they were in company, but when he encountered her alone, he dropped the formality. Their hands brushed and a fierce current shot through her and she jumped. She could not stop a fierce blush steeling across her chest, up her pale neck and onto her cheeks.

Caroline couldn't hold his all-knowing gaze, so she cast her eyes downwards as if seeking her cap, wishing he hadn't loomed at her like a shadow out of nowhere.

He handed her the cap, holding on to the garment longer than needed, before releasing it into her hand.

'Are you all right, Caroline? You seem a little troubled. May I assist you further?'

Caroline raised her head and resolved to push through her embarrassment. 'I'm quite all right, thank you, my lord. I must hurry as I'm late for breakfast.' She bobbed a quick curtsy and almost ran down the corridor.

He looked after her and watched her disappear out of sight, wondering why he was so bewitched.

CHAPTER 9

The Cavendish School, Willow Wick - Georgiana (1721)

CAROLINE HUDDLED in the corner of the classroom in the old cottage where the children attended the village school, which was recently set up and funded by the Cavendish family.

'Attend to your studies quietly until I return,' Caroline's father said when he looked up from reading a note, a stern expression on his usually amiable face. He left his usual post at the front of the classroom and hurried out to respond to the latest school emergency.

Three tall and skinny, grubby looking boys taunted Caroline and chanted, 'Teacher's pet, teacher's pet', as they closed in and surrounded her, pulling at her petticoat, their dirty faces looming over hers as they pushed and prodded at her clothing and body.

The wiry, innocent young girl began to shake with a mixture of terror and revulsion, but she did her best to hold herself together so she wouldn't cry. She didn't want to give them the satisfaction of reducing her to tears, but she felt the emotion welling up within her and desperately tried to conjure other thoughts to distract herself.

Think of Mother reading to me on Sunday afternoons after church, turning the pages of the book slowly while I perched on her knee with one arm round her soft neck.

Caroline could still smell the comforting lavender scent of her dear mother when she recalled the maternal scene. Her father said her mother was watching over them and keeping them safe, so Caroline thought of her whenever she was scared or lonely.

Why were the boys so mean just because she was the teacher's daughter? She'd done nothing to antagonise them other than come to school, but they seemed to think she was special.

Caroline saw the door swing open and prayed it was her father returning. He would command them to leave her alone and would restore order with one sharp look. Her shoulders hunched over further, and her chest heaved as she realised it wasn't her father, but a tall boy with jet black hair and piercing blue eyes who entered with a swagger. She recognised him as a local boy, but she couldn't recall his name, not being in the habit of mixing with the village children. Caroline tried to shrink into herself further as if she might become invisible in the corner, out of reach of the boys' odious hands as they continued prodding her viciously. But alas, it was no good. They enjoyed goading her too much to stop of their own accord, and the atmosphere in the room had reached fever pitch. The onlookers, who were mostly boys, were either too scared or too weak to intervene, even though they pitied the newcomer's plight. They knew from experience how cruel the Knight brothers could be when the fancy took them, and none of them were about to take on the three brothers who had decided to make Caroline their prey for the day.

The blue-eyed newcomer strode over to the boys and pulled them off her, one by one. 'Leave the poor lass alone. Pick on someone your own size,' he hissed at them, clouting one of them round the ears, and pushing the others so they lost their footing. One brother raised his fists at her blue-eyed defender, but then thought better of it and quickly backed down, and she saw the fight go out of him. Like all bullies, they didn't do well when they received a taste of their own medicine. The boys turned away from Caroline and returned to their seats, cursing under their breath, and kicking some stones on the floor.

'Are you all right, Mistress? I must apologise for the behaviour of my oafish brothers. There isn't a brain between them, and they act before they think. They mean no harm, really.'

Caroline's breathing gradually regulated, and she straightened her petticoat, scowling at the boys who were already homing in on their next victim.

'You will have no more trouble from them. I'll see to it,' said her mystery saviour. Then he smiled the most charming smile she had ever beheld, and as she looked into his blue eyes, she struggled to breathe freely again. He stretched his hand out towards her, which wasn't grubby like his brothers' hands, and he introduced himself. 'I've seen you in the village, but we've never met properly. 'I'm Ralph… Ralph Knight. I'm the elder of that sorry lot you've been up against on your first day.'

She shook his hand, somewhat timidly, and returned his smile, grateful for his bold intervention, and intrigued by his gallant manner and breath-taking good looks. 'I'm Caroline,' she said.

Some of the children watching from their small hard

chairs tittered at the exchange, finding the new girl's awkwardness amusing.

'Return to your seat, Caroline, before your father comes back and threatens to give us all a thrashing. As for you lot,' he said, turning towards his brothers, his blue eyes flashing, 'If I see you lay a hand on her again, I'll skin you alive. Is that clear?'

Caroline saw it was certainly clear to everyone in the room that Ralph Knight was in charge, and his brothers wouldn't dare cross him. She settled back in her seat, relief coursing through her, grateful to have been rescued. She thought her defender must be a little older than her. It was difficult to tell with him being so tall, and she wondered why he was at school at all. Most young people of their class were out working, as she would be too if her father wasn't an educated man who could afford to feed her and put a roof over her head for a few more years yet.

Willow Manor, York - Present day

George and Eddie were called away after breakfast to assist the builders and Cara stole a few quiet hours to make some final edits to her book before she would send it to her editor.

She sat in the snug in a cosy armchair, a half-empty cup of tea on the small table nearby and her manuscript open on her computer. After combing through the text for more than an hour, her eyelids began to droop, and she fought to stay awake. Several unsuccessful attempts later, and she gave into the temptation. She wouldn't make any more progress on the book when she felt so lacklustre. A quick power nap would do her the world of good and so she set a twenty-minute alarm on her phone, pushed her computer aside and pulled the velvet blanket over her as she snuggled into the armchair. Her heavy eyelids were already closing to the hypnotic pitter-patter of gentle rain against the windowpanes, and the sound lulled her effortlessly into a deep sleep.

It wasn't long before Cara saw Caroline, the eighteenth-century version of herself. In the dream, she connected to the girl's emotions and thoughts. Her uncontrollable feelings for George, the master of Willow Manor, troubled Caroline. She was considering resigning her post because she was overcome by the situation and feared what she might do if she stayed.

I must not allow myself to think of him in such sinful ways. He is not my husband and can never be my husband. What is happening to me?

The girl wrung her hands together in prayer on her knees in what was obviously her bedchamber, and Cara recognised as the green room.

The young woman's lips moved as she prayed and although Cara couldn't hear her words, they echoed through the chambers of her mind as she slept. She was an observer, but they shared the same soul, which meant she felt her feelings and read her thoughts whether she wanted to or not.

Please, lord absolve me from the sin of my wanton weakness. Oh lord, help me turn away from the lure of the flesh and show me how to extract myself from this unholy bind in which I find myself. Why do I love him when our union is forbidden?

Caroline remained on her knees, her hands clasped tightly together as she quietly sobbed, and the tears spilled down her cold cheeks. She was wretched and didn't know what to do.

Oh lord, must I leave Willow Manor? Should I put distance between us so I may be absolved of my sin and tempted no more? Please give me a sign for I am lost.

Cara's eyes peeled open and the memory of what she had

experienced flooded her consciousness. All-consuming loss gripped her body and the agony in her heart reminded her of the trauma of when she couldn't be with George in their present-day life.

If what she had experienced was really happening in Georgiana, it meant there was a very real possibility of Caroline leaving Willow Manor before George fell in love with her and they committed to one another, which could lead to their past lives being rewritten.

A familiar face appeared in her mind through the foggy remnants of sleep, and she knew what she must do. She retrieved her phone from the table, stopped the alarm three minutes before it was due to ring, and typed out a one sentence text and pressed send. She took a gulp of the remnants of her lukewarm tea, dressed and raced into the hallway. She grabbed her denim jacket off the hook, her fingers closing over her car keys in the pocket.

Cara considered looking for George over at the centre to tell him where she was going, but decided that would take too long. She texted him instead, saying not to worry and she would be back soon. And then she tore down the long willow tree-lined driveway, her mind whirling with questions as she expertly swung her car out of the estate and onto the road that would take her to the city centre.

She hoped Sylvia would have time to see her or it would be a wasted trip.

Willow Manor, York - Georgiana

Caroline tried to sneak into the main kitchen unnoticed, but Cook spotted her immediately. 'Ah, there you are, lass.

You nearly missed breakfast, but I saved you a bowl. Take a seat.'

Caroline smiled gratefully at the short, rotund woman who exuded kindness, and sat down at the long table and bid good morning to the others who were finishing up. She was fortunate they were a friendly bunch and had accepted her into the fold even though she fell between the ranks—neither a servant nor a member of the aristocracy.

Caroline lingered at the table after the others left and ate her porridge as she fell into a pleasant daydream in the warm kitchen. Cook was busy clearing up and preparing her menus, ready to consult with the countess.

Caroline's mind drifted back to a few days earlier when she and Olivia had ridden into Willow Wick with George. The earl had stayed by her side, and she felt an inner glow as they rode into the village, despite her unease that they may bump into Ralph at any minute. George's calming presence made up for her trepidation and she pushed her fears aside and engaged with his witty conversation and gracious flirting with reckless abandon.

The connection between them was undeniable, and she was powerless to fight the magnetic pull that drew them to each other. The essence of her father's sobering words reverberated through her mind again—*our kind don't marry their kind,* but she allowed herself to enjoy the moment and stop fearing the future. Olivia cantered smoothly ahead as she liked to ride fast, and every five minutes or so she circled back so she didn't leave them behind.

By the time they reached the end of the footpath which cut through to Willow Wick, Caroline was giddy with love. George had shown himself to be everything she had imagined and more. He had entertained her with amusing stories from his visits to court and had a wonderful, self-deprecating way about him. He was confident without being arrogant and dashing without being ostentatious. The combination was a heady one and Caroline knew there was no going back. She loved him. She loved him from the moment he entered the library when he had interrupted her meeting with his mother.

She couldn't explain where these powerful feelings came from or why she felt them when she barely knew him. All she knew was that it was as though she had always known him, and now there was the chance for them to have a proper conversation alone, Caroline relaxed and her unease in his company dissolved. As they turned the corner and the village green came into view, she wished they could stay like this forever, and her heart ached at the realisation that they may not have the opportunity to speak privately again for weeks or even months.

What am I to do?

The question lingered in her mind, and she was so preoccupied that, at first, she didn't notice the tall, dark figure looming in the distance. Caroline raised her head, her mind still confused and her heart full of love for George, when she saw Ralph striding towards them across the green.

'Who have we here?' George said, glancing at Caroline.

'Just a friend of mine. Let me handle him,' she said. Then, realising her instruction might be construed as impertinent, she added hastily, 'My lord.'

Caroline drew herself up to her full height and sat straight on the horse as if it might give her the courage she needed.

'Caroline,' said Ralph, his tone stiff and showing no acknowledgement or deference to George. Olivia joined them and her horse's hooves thundered to an abrupt halt next to her brother, her cheeks flushed a becoming rosy hue in the blustery Yorkshire winds.

'Miss Olivia,' said Ralph, surprising Caroline by doffing

his cap in Olivia's direction, his attitude altogether more gallant towards the young woman.

'Good day, Master Knight,' said Olivia, inclining her head elegantly, all charming blushes and smiles.

'I didn't know you two were acquainted,' said Caroline, a sense of foreboding in her chest. Ralph had quite the reputation for being one with the ladies and had various liaisons, both with young women and older, more worldly ones, which Caroline heard about through village gossip. This was just one of the many reasons she had never taken him seriously as a potential husband... for all he swore his undying love to her, he had a roving eye, and she did not trust him. If it was up to him, they would have been married years ago—she would devote herself to raising their children and he would be free to go about his business as usual.

No, thank you.

'Are you well, Ralph? I must apologise for not looking in on you. Miss Olivia and I have been preoccupied with her studies.'

'I'm sure,' he said, his tone cold but polite. 'I don't expect you have time for the likes of us in the village now you're otherwise occupied at the manor.'

She guessed that if they were alone, he would sneer and mock her, but was keeping himself in check for the sake of impressing Olivia.

'Well, it's been a pleasure meeting you, Ralph, but we really must be on our way now,' said George. 'We have business in the village.' He clicked his heels against his horse's flanks and signalled to Olivia to follow him.

'Yes, excuse us. We are in rather a hurry,' said Caroline, dying to get away from him before he started chastising her for not seeking him out.

'You are excused,' he said, with mock gallantry, but she recognised the bitter edge to his words as he moved next to her after George and Olivia rode slightly ahead, leaving them to say goodbye. 'I will be seeing you,' he whispered, his height bringing him almost level with her shoulder. 'You haven't heard the last of me, so don't get too comfortable at the great house, my dear Caroline.'

Now they were alone, she heard the full force of his anger and saw his blue eyes flash. He reached upwards and whispered, 'I'm coming for you.'

Caroline twitched her reins and rode on towards the others without looking back.

George said, 'Well, he seemed like a thoroughly disagreeable fellow. A good friend of yours, is he?' His eyes narrowed as he assessed Caroline, who shifted uncomfortably in the saddle. 'And Olivia, how on earth are you acquainted with such a reprobate?'

Caroline didn't reply, and Olivia followed her example, so George was left without answers as the ladies rode on ahead.

Caroline was too embarrassed to try and explain her relationship with Ralph and would talk to Olivia when they were alone.

CHAPTER 10

Sylvia's office, York - Present day

CARA DROVE into a short stay spot near Sylvia's office in the city. She headed towards the usually plain door and noticed a bold new sign proclaiming *Sylvia's Psychic Services.*

The door chimed, and she entered the familiar cosy waiting room and was relieved to see it empty. Sylvia was probably in a client session, which was why she hadn't responded to her last-minute text. Cara paced around for a while, flicking through various women's lifestyle and spiritual magazines, too anxious to sit still for more than a minute at a time. After about ten minutes of trying to be patient, she heard sudden movement from Sylvia's office. She popped the magazine back onto the table and waited expectantly, her eyes on the office door.

Sylvia emerged with her client and waved at Cara, mouthing she'd be with her in a minute, as she saw the woman to the door.

'Hello, my lovely,' she said, closing the door, putting the latch on and turning round to face her. 'So sorry I couldn't get back to you earlier. It's been hectic. This is the first lull in clients since I arrived.'

Cara crossed the room towards Sylvia, and they embraced warmly, and Sylvia kissed both of Cara's cheeks. 'I hope you don't mind—I took a chance I might catch you in-between clients.'

'No problem at all. I'm always happy to see you and I have a break now, so your timing is impeccable. Let's go into my office, and we can catch up.'

Sylvia's room where she did her Tarot readings and psychic consultations exuded a calming energy which enveloped Cara immediately, and she settled into one of the shabby green chairs, her nerves melting away in Sylvia's soothing presence.

'Latte?' asked the psychic.

'Yes, please. I'm flagging a bit,' said Cara. 'I took a nap after a writing session, and then I had this weird dream and awoke in a panic and just knew I had to come and find you right away.'

'That sounds intriguing. What's going on?'

Sylvia brought the steaming cups of coffee over, placed them on her desk, and sat opposite Cara.

'Gosh, where do I start?' said Cara, grimacing. 'As usual, it's a confusing scenario.'

'Just start where you start and let's see if we can make some sense of it.'

'Okay, but don't say I didn't warn you!' said Cara, rolling her eyes.

'How are George and Eddie keeping, by the way?' asked Sylvia, coaxing Cara gently into her revelations.

'They are well. Eddie's staying with us, and he thinks I

discovered some kind of quantum wormhole in the Willow Manor library.'

Sylvia's green and gold-flecked cat-like eyes widened as she sipped her coffee. 'Tell me more…'

'Well, you know how I kept wishing I could time travel on demand, rather than be randomly transported to Tudorville at the whim of the vortex?'

Sylvia nodded encouragingly as she stared at Cara, who was her favourite client and had the most fascinating experiences of any with whom she'd consulted. 'Yes,' she said.

'Well, I stumbled onto what looks like a Tudor priest hole, but on the two occasions I went into it, the vortex appeared and I'm pretty certain I time travelled.'

'Goodness. And do you know what's going on in Tudorville?'

'That's just it,' said Cara, shaking her head. 'I remember nothing in the way I usually would. Instead, I'm having these weird vivid dreams about a different timeline altogether!'

'Which one?' said Sylvia. 'It crossed my mind that one day you may come in here and tell me you've been travelling to ancient Greece or Rome... I'm excited about the possibilities even if I only live the experience vicariously through your readings.'

Cara smiled. 'You and Eddie are far more excited than me and George. All we want is a normal life…'

Sylvia covered Cara's hand with her own and squeezed it gently. 'I know it must be tough. Sorry, I interrupted you as you were about to tell me about another timeline.'

'Ever since I went into this priest hole or wormhole… or whatever we want to call it, I've been dreaming about Georgiana.'

Sylvia's eyes widened again, and she paused with her coffee cup mid-way to her mouth. 'Georgiana… you mean the life where you were that young girl who went by a different name, and I spoke to her when I hypnotised you?'

'That's the one,' said Cara, her shiny hair tumbling over her shoulders as she jerked her head.

'Remind me of the name you used in that life,' said Sylvia.

'Caroline. Presumably named after Caroline of Ansbach, who was married to the future king, George II. Honestly, I don't even know what my surname was, but I'm having regular run-ins with that awful Ralph Knight. Oh, and I'm, or should I say, Caroline, is now governess to George's sister at Willow Manor.'

Sylvia shifted in her chair and gently rubbed her temples with her fingers. 'So, doesn't that mean things are unfolding as they should? We undid Ralph's hypnotic suggestion so that you would accept the job at Willow Manor, and you and George would presumably fall in love like in the original timeline. Or am I missing something?'

'I don't have much experience in time travel, other than my forays into Tudorville, but I'm worried the reason I'm suddenly dreaming about that other life is because it's a warning.'

'Interesting, yes I suppose that could be the case,' said Sylvia, resting her cup on the desk. 'Give me your hands, let's see if anything's changed.'

Cara tentatively offered her palms upwards, and Sylvia moved them towards the light, squinted and then fumbled about for her glasses with her other hand. 'Hold on, I'm as blind as a bat close up these days without my specs.'

Cara crossed and uncrossed her legs as she waited. On a previous visit, Sylvia examined her hands, and the psychic was amazed to see a splintered lifeline showing more than one life.

What will she see this time?

Cara gulped but tried to stay calm. There was no point in

getting in a panic. That much she knew... but it was far easier said than done.

'It's as I suspected. Your lifeline has splintered again on both palms. Look.' Sylvia steered Cara's palms back towards her and pointed.

Cara followed Sylvia's sparkly pink nail, which touched the edge of both lifelines, and she saw multiple little lines shooting off them both. She gasped and turned white, a chill shooting through her body. 'How many lives must I live?'

Sylvia turned Cara's hands back over before releasing them. 'I don't know. There are quite a few, but I doubt you will experience them all. There are many schools of thought in palmistry, but it doesn't show what will happen, only what could happen.'

Cara sighed, clasped her hands together, and rested her elbows on the desk. 'As usual, George and I are in a right jam. We were hoping it was all over and we could just get on with our lives. We're due to open the Tudor Heritage Centre soon, you know.'

Sylvia pursed her lips. 'Um, you will get on with your lives by the looks of it. The only question is, which ones! Sorry, it's not the reading you were hoping for, but it's better to know what you're up against.'

Cara studied Sylvia's face, seeking reassurance. 'Eddie wants me to go into the priest hole again. He and George went in to test it yesterday, but the vortex didn't appear. I think Eddie was a little disappointed. He says this is our chance to time travel on demand and he wants me to do some controlled experiments with him,' said Cara.

'I bet he does!' said Sylvia, shaking her head. 'He's nothing if not zealous in his quantum research. So, are you going to go through with it?'

'That's why I came, really. I don't know, but I thought a card reading might help to point me in the right direction. I feel rudderless on this one. My head is so noisy, I can't seem to quiet down enough to hear my intuition.'

Sylvia nodded, opened the top drawer in her desk and extracted two sets of cards. Cara watched as she shuffled and arranged the cards in her own unique way, and the vibrant coloured images of the Tarot and the Angel cards flashed before her eyes.

'Usually, I have no choice whether I time travel or not. This time, it seems like I may only travel when I enter the wormhole. Unless we count the dreams which I don't understand at all. I mean, am I time travelling in my sleep or is it just some kind of karmic memory being activated?'

'I wish I knew… As always, you bring me the most complex of puzzles in all my years in the business.' Sylvia peered at Cara over her reading glasses, which hovered on her nose. She continued to shuffle the cards and then lay them down on the desk.

'I'm not up on quantum physics, but by wormhole, I'm guessing the good professor means it's like a portal or, or… what are those stones called that the lead female character goes through in *Outlander*?'

'Standing stones,' replied Cara, with no hesitation. 'I read it recently. I only wish my experience was fictional!'

Sylvia smiled. 'I read it years ago but didn't expect to have a real time traveller in my office.'

'I didn't read the next book in the series yet because, although it's brilliant, it completely spooked me. I just wanted to forget all about it,' said Cara.

'Yes, I can understand why you'd feel that way. And it would be helpful it if were up to you to decide your future, but as you already know—it doesn't work that way.'

Cara nodded.

'It'll all be okay, don't look so glum, my dear. Now, what

do you want to ask the cards today?' said Sylvia, becoming business like.

'Two things,' said Cara, gently tapping the desk. 'I want to know whether I should enter the wormhole again and see if I time travel on demand. And, also, are the dreams just of me time travelling in my sleep, or are they merely karmic memories? I think if I can get some guidance, it will help me feel clearer on what to do about Eddie's request.'

Sylvia held the cards gently in her hands, almost like a loving caress, and her pink nails sparkled as she swayed. The room grew warmer, and Sylvia slipped into a light trance. Cara watched and waited, nervous that the reading wouldn't answer her two questions, but equally nervous that it would.

Willow Manor, York - Georgiana

Caroline opened her eyes to the sound of horses' hooves clattering beneath her window, so she threw the warm blanket off her body and set her feet down firmly next to the bed in the crisp morning chill. The unmistakable velvet tone of George's voice floated into the room. She rose quickly and crossed the short distance to peer cautiously out the window, standing to one side so he wouldn't glimpse her watching him.

Her heart jerked, and her pulse raced. Where was he going? She had heard no word of his plans, but judging by the carriage and his luggage standing ready, and his formal dress and fashionable wig, he was going further than York.

What if he was leaving indefinitely, and she had somehow missed the signs? No one would think to tell her. Why would they? After all, she was only the paid help, and George didn't know she was in love with him—not that her tender feelings would be of any consequence to a titled man like him. He no doubt had girls flocking to him and falling at his feet wherever he went.

Caroline drew back further behind the drapes, anxious not to be seen spying on the family, as Olivia and the countess stepped forward into the bright early morning sunshine and George embraced and kissed the cheeks of first one, then the other.

The scene beneath her window seemed to be a formal farewell, and she concluded it must be as she feared. He was going away for at least some length of time.

She stood, transfixed to the spot, watching him, unable to leave the window and race down to see him and throw her arms around him as she longed to do with every fibre of her being. Never had she felt her lowly station in life so greatly as in this bitter moment. She would have to watch her dearest love leave without being able to even bid him farewell, never mind kiss his lips like she did in her dreams.

So fierce were her feelings of shock and loss, she thought she might wretch. Caroline clutched her sides as she looked on, an icy dread strangling her heart as he stepped into the carriage and settled back, looking out at his mother and sister.

And then his dark eyes moved upwards towards her window, and she imagined he sought her out. He stared for a few seconds longer as she shrunk further into the shadows and continued to spy on him, her senses thudding guiltily.

Was he disappointed to have missed her? She shook her head and chastised herself for being fanciful. Then the carriage lurched forward and from her hidden position, she watched him go. Once he was further away, she moved back into full view of the window and stared after the carriage until it was a just tiny speck on the horizon. The countess and Olivia had long since re-entered the house, and she stood alone, her heart splintered into a million pieces.

One thought terrified her above all others.

How will I bear living in his house without him?

It was a bitter thought that hadn't crossed her mind until she realised he had gone.

CHAPTER 11

Sylvia's office, York - Present day

CARA SHRUGGED her arms out of her jacket, a wave of unbearable heat creeping over her as she watched Sylvia settle down for the card reading in her trance-like state.

Cara stared as the cards hit the desk, knowing it wasn't time yet. The glossy, colourful reverse side of the Tarot and Angel cards intermingled like a mystical tapestry and blurred in front of her eyes as the seconds passed. 'Now,' she said, her voice clear and firm. There was no hesitation—she just knew when it was the right card.

'Repeat your first question, please,' prompted Sylvia, her eyes still closed.

Cara drew herself up and rested her elbows on the edge of the desk. 'I want to know whether I should enter the wormhole again and attempt to time travel on demand.'

Sylvia flipped the card onto the top of the thick pile. Her head drooped forward slightly as she focused on the card, and then she raised her eyes to Cara. 'What do you know of this card?'

Cara studied the image. 'How apt.' She paused and considered the vivid picture of The Magician standing behind some kind of altar. 'Tarot scares me—I much prefer the Angel cards,' she said carefully.

'Don't be scared. The card is with us to help you. You chose it and it chose you. What do you think it desires you to know?'

'Is the magician supposed to be Eddie?'

The skin around Sylvia's eyes crinkled into fine lines and her eyes glowed. 'Seems so, doesn't it? And just look at the sign above his head.'

'It's the symbol of infinity.' Cara's words tumbled out.

'I'm not sure there could be a more suitable card to answer your question. The meanings are not always as straightforward to understand as this, but this looks like a no-brainer.'

'As though it's telling me to follow Eddie's lead into infinity?'

'Yep. In addition, The Magician is all about fulfilling one's potential, so I'd say you've got a green light from the cards to enter the wormhole under Eddie's guidance.'

'I almost wish I didn't! Who knows where it will lead?'

'Shall we answer your next question?' asked Sylvia.

Cara inclined her head and Sylvia continued flipping over the cards. 'One, two, three... Remember to hold the question in your mind and tell me when to stop,' she prompted.

A card slipped from Sylvia's hand, almost as if it had a will of its own. 'Here we go. We've got a runner,' she said. 'Better see what this one has to say. The wild cards are often the most enlightening because they are determined to be seen and heard.' Sylvia laid the card down so they could see it.

'Ah, lovely, an angel card,' said Cara. 'I like these the best.'

'Adriana is an oracle card from one of my favourite Doreen Virtue packs. I've noticed this card appears when someone is trying to run the show. Consider whether your karmic memory question is about you logically trying to gain control of the future, and in your case, your past too, rather than following your inner guidance.'

Cara sat up straight and stared at Sylvia. 'Oh God, I'm doing it again, aren't I? I never learn… I'm always trying to steer the ship by force on my own desired route.'

'Angel Adriana communicates through intuition, thoughts and dreams, so it's fitting for your question, although it doesn't give you a definitive answer like the first card. It's more an important reminder that you're not in control.'

'I'm always amazed at how I lose sight of it and fall back into my old habits.'

'Easily done, my dear. It's a side effect of being human,' said Sylvia, her tone light.

'Right, before I leave you in peace, is there anything else I should know?' said Cara.

'Let me just have a few minutes and see what comes up,' Sylvia said, closing her eyes and holding the cards as though she were communing with them. She began to sway gently once more, and the room heated up again, as Cara shifted in her seat.

After a few moments, Sylvia fell into a deeper trance. 'You are being called to relive the Georgiana timeline. We don't know why, but what you need to know will be revealed as you step forward into the unknown.' Then her body jerked, and her eyes opened wide as if in surprise. 'Everything happens for a reason. It might change nothing, or it might change everything,' she said cryptically. She took a sip of water from a bottle she kept on a side table. 'Was that any use to you?'

'I'm not sure,' replied Cara. 'It didn't answer my question about the dreams, but I feel calmer... as though a weight has lifted from my shoulders, and I don't really need an answer. You've reminded me again—that it's not all on me. I can just take it one step at a time as the path becomes clear.'

Sylvia smiled. 'And if that was all you ever understood, it is all you will ever need to make your remarkable journey easier. The challenge is in remembering it.'

'I'm realising that,' said Cara. 'Thank you so much for making time for me today. I know you're busy.'

'It's always a pleasure to fill in a piece of your magical, mystical puzzle. Please give my love to George and Eddie. And let me know how it goes. I can hardly wait to hear more about your adventures through the wormhole.'

'I will. And you must come and visit us. The grand opening will be soon, so look out for your invitation in the post.'

Cara left the office, feeling light, as though she had grown wings.

Willow Manor, York - Present day

When Cara got back to the house, she found George and Eddie eating buttered toast and drinking tea. 'Ooh, that smells gorgeous.' She took a bite of George's. 'I'm ravenous, I forgot to eat.'

'Let me pop a slice in for you,' he said.

'Thank you, darling. And what have you two been up to?'

They told her about the progress with the builders and

they sat round the kitchen table as they drank tea and finished their slices of toast.

'I went to see Sylvia,' said Cara, after she pushed her plate aside. She laughed out loud at the attentive look on Eddie's face. 'I swear your ears just pricked up!' she said.

'Well, are you going to keep us in suspense much longer?' he said, waving his hands about as he spoke.

'No, and you'll be pleased to hear that the cards pointed me clearly toward your wormhole experiment!'

Eddie grinned; his smile so wide it seemed in danger of splitting his face in two. 'Bloody fantastic! Thank goodness for Sylvia.'

'There was a definitive answer on the wormhole question, but it wasn't clear about whether my dreams are me actually time travelling in an alternative way, or whether they are just karmic memories.'

George reached for Cara's hand, and she flashed him a reassuring smile and squeezed his hand.

Eddie stared at her. 'Oh, is that what you wanted to know? I could have answered that if you'd asked.'

'Go on,' she said. 'I'm listening!'

'My research, as well as the findings of the great quantum brains before us, point to there being many versions of every possible timeline. So, the real question is, does it matter whether it's your dreams, your thoughts, or you travelling in the vortex? All those experiences are equal. They are all versions of the timeline, and while you may have preferences, in quantum terms, none are either better or worse.'

Cara shook her head and looked from Eddie to George. 'Well, I thought I understood it, but now I'm even more baffled! You?'

'Me too. I suppose that's what you get when you ask a quantum physics professor about time…'

Cara stood and stretched. 'Pass your dishes and then let's crack on. May as well get it over with.'

'Get what over with?' asked George.

'During the reading with Sylvia, I realised I don't have to make life harder by trying to decide what should happen. It's hard enough without me sticking my fingers in the cosmic engine.'

George frowned. 'And in this case the cosmic engine is…?'

'She means she's ready to go back into the wormhole,' said Eddie, not managing to hide his jubilation.

'He's right,' said Cara. 'My dreams and finding the hole all point us towards me being called to Georgiana. There must be something I'm supposed to do, and I don't want to let fear cloud my judgement so I ignore the warning signs. This could be our chance to help that version of ourselves.'

George ran his fingers through his hair and looked worried. 'I'm afraid I still don't understand what you two are hatching.'

'Think about it,' she said. 'Falling in love and being together when they were from such different worlds in the eighteenth century is against everything Caroline and George would believe possible. The rewriting of the karmic warrior's hypnotic suggestion seems to have worked or Caroline would have turned down the governess job like Ralph instructed, but we don't know what happened afterwards, do we?'

George shook his head. 'Can't we just leave it unfold on its own as it was supposed to? I mean, it's three hundred years ago.'

'No, because Ralph is still bent on destroying us and with Willow Manor derelict in Victoriana, I think he may have succeeded.'

George looked at Eddie. 'What do you make of all this?'

'Honestly, I don't know. Cara has a point, though. As I said, there are many possible versions of the same timelines. This could well be your chance to rewrite that one,' he said, scratching his shadow of a beard. 'Excuse me for a minute, I need to make a quick call. I'll be back soon, and you can let me know what you've decided,' he said, rising and crossing the room to exit the kitchen.

A few minutes later, they saw him pacing around the garden, phone pressed to his ear.

'He's a good sort—giving us space to decide together, even though he's so keen for me to do it,' said Cara.

'Yes, I'm not quite so keen,' said George, pulling her into his arms and kissing her forehead. 'You know I will back anything you want to do, but must you really do this?'

Cara stroked his cheek and kissed him. 'I think this is me being called to heal the Georgiana timeline for our Twin Flame mission. Do you remember Sylvia once said that until our souls are healed in all our past lives, we won't be left in peace?'

George sighed. He held her tight, and they stood like that in the comfort of each other's arms for some time before Eddie returned and they heard a discreet cough.

'So, what's it to be, Lord and Lady Cavendish?'

Willow Manor, York - Georgiana

The days and weeks passed but seemed like months and years for Caroline. She had no word of George other than the occasional piece of news she gleaned from Olivia.

They fell into a predictable rhythm of life revolving around lessons, riding and long early afternoon walks around the grounds. Olivia was young for social occasions and, with the master of the house away at court, the three women led a quiet, sheltered existence.

Caroline began dining with the family more frequently, upon the countess's request. 'You are such diverting company, dear Caroline. I would wish that you eat with us for we are a sorry, sad pair without my son to entertain us.'

And so, Caroline ate other meals with the servants downstairs as usual, but she was invited to dine with the countess and Olivia most afternoons for the main meal of the day. She didn't mind and began to rather enjoy the experience once she relaxed into the routine and grew more at ease as time went on. It was interesting to observe the aristocracy in their day-to-day routines, and she saw they were similar to her in many ways, beyond the idiosyncrasies of their class.

One day, the countess announced that she'd received a letter from George, and she would read it to them after they had eaten. Caroline's heart buffeted like a wild storm in her chest, and she struggled to swallow her food. The meal dragged on and on until finally the footmen cleared the table and they retired to the drawing room as was their custom.

The countess extracted the folded pages of parchment from a drawer in her desk, and when they all settled in their usual places near the fire, she began reading.

Dearest Mother

I pray all is well with you and you are in good spirits. I was sorry to be called away at such short notice. I hope the weather is not inclement. Here in London, we have been enjoying some rather fine days for the time of year, which is as well because the king is an enthusiastic hunter and I have become a regular in his party.

Whilst it is not unpleasant at court, I do confess I would rather be at Willow Manor and hope to have permission to return home shortly. I am told the king is keen to acquaint himself with the young nobles, so I pass much of my days with the other lords of a similar age. I trust Olivia is doing well in her lessons with Caroline, and that both young ladies are in good health and not straying too far from the estate. I urge them to be cautious on their outings and if they wish to visit Willow Wick, I think it best if they are accompanied by one of the grooms. I don't think I mentioned it before, but we met a most unpleasant man from the village when we rode together shortly before I left.

Pray beg Olivia write me, with news of her studies, for I feel remiss in my duties with my unexpected absence.

I passed your blessings to Queen Caroline as you requested and she bade me to send you the same, and said you are most welcome at court should you wish to attend. A game of cards awaits, so I must end here. Please write with your news and the latest of the estate as soon as you may.

Your loving son,
George

Caroline did her best to maintain her composure as though the letter meant no more to her than if she were to hear news of a distant acquaintance, but she was flustered as her ears strained for every word and paid attention to every inflection in the countess's voice.

'I do wish he didn't have to go away like that, and I hope he will be released soon,' said Olivia. 'I miss him so terribly.'

The countess smiled indulgently at her daughter. 'Court isn't prison, my dear, although it's true it can feel that way when you don't wish to be there,' she said. 'I imagine we will have your brother back with us in the not-too-distant future. Unless they have other plans for him, such as matching him with a wife in London.'

'Oh, how simply dreadful for poor George,' sighed Olivia. 'To have someone foisted upon him, rather than to choose his own wife.' She stuck her chin out and drew herself up in her chair. 'I mean to marry for love, not by royal decree,' she declared in a rebellious tone, shaking her blonde head.

'I'm afraid you have a lot to learn, my dear girl. You shall be matched in the same way your father and I were matched. We had a wonderful marriage and that is the way of things in our world.'

Olivia rolled her eyes at Caroline behind her mother's back, but Caroline wasn't paying attention. A violent chill swept through her body when she heard the countess's fateful words, and she was busy trying not to show she was shaking at the thought of George returning to Willow Manor with a hand-picked bride. She fought an urge to rise from her chair and flee the room to the solace and safety of her green chamber. Instead, she steeled herself to smile as though she hadn't a care in the world.

Never had she felt so trapped. What was she to do?

CHAPTER 12

Willow Manor, York - Present day

Eddie entered the wormhole first, torch in hand, with Cara and George bringing up the rear. George had stubbornly insisted on accompanying them, even though Cara would have liked him to watch from the library at a safe distance.

'I much prefer to call it a gateway or portal. Wormhole isn't a very attractive name, is it?' she said, wrinkling her nose at Eddie as they discussed the pending quantum experiment.

'I don't mind what you call it, my lady,' he said. 'Gateway may sound more appealing, but wormhole is the correct scientific term. More importantly, are you ready to begin?'

Cara was nervous and stalling to buy some time. 'Are you certain you won't stay out there, George? Perhaps it would be better to have an observer rather than both of you in the hole with me—wouldn't it, Eddie?'

Eddie shook his head. 'I don't mind either way, don't bring me into it!'

George said, 'I'm coming with you. Are you sure you want to do this? This is your last chance to pull out. You don't have to go through with it, you know.'

He wrapped his arms around her, and the solid warmth of his body comforted her.

She kissed him and then pulled away reluctantly. 'Yes, let's get started. The longer we hesitate, the more nervous I become.'

The air was musty and cold, and she was pleased she had remembered to wear a warm sweatshirt. She shivered at the thought of what may await her if the experiment worked.

'Okay, go ahead and touch the wall when you're ready,' Eddie said as they neared the back of the hole.

'It's incredible to think a priest must have hidden in here, terrified for his life,' said Cara, distracting herself from the fear she felt.

And then she reached for the wall. Before she could say another word, the vortex enveloped them like a bubble. The air grew colder, and there was a whooshing sound in their ears. Eddie tried to illuminate Cara with the light of the torch, but the force of the whirling vortex knocked it out of his hand and the sound of it bouncing on the hard floor reverberated through the dark space.

In the silence that followed, George whispered, 'Cara, Cara, are you there?'

'I'm here,' said Eddie, 'let's look for the torch so we can see what's going on.' He bent to his knees and scrabbled about. Several minutes later, the light flickered back on, and George saw Eddie rise, waving the torch. He shone it in the wall's direction and there was Cara slumped at the bottom.

'Looks like she's out cold again. Cara, my darling. Can you hear me?' George tapped her face gently with his fingers and embraced her as he prepared to lift her off the freezing ground.

Her head moved, and she groaned. Then her eyes opened, and she said, 'Did it work?'

'I don't know. Are you okay?' said George.

She nodded. She pushed herself upward with her hands, and George helped her to her feet.

Eddie said, 'My goodness, this is exciting. The vortex came, but it only took you. I could feel it! What do you remember?'

'Not much,' said Cara, as they stumbled towards the light through the crack in the bookshelves. 'I heard the vortex but after that, nothing.'

They stepped into the bright light of the library, rays of sunshine illuminated the room and the wall tapestry fabrics shimmered.

'Are you all right, darling?' said George, putting his arm around Cara's shoulders, relieved that she was still with him.

'Yes, I think so. Can we get out of here, though?'

They wandered out onto the terrace and after a few minutes when he saw she was all right, George went to make tea, and Eddie and Cara discussed the experiment.

'What do you make of it?' said Cara.

'Well, that is the third time you've entered with what appears to be the same result, so it's reasonable to conclude that one hundred per cent of the time, when you enter that wormhole…' He drew breath and smiled, 'Or, gateway—you automatically summon the vortex. It's extraordinary,' he said, shaking his head. 'And in our previous experiments, when the vortex appeared, you time travelled to Tudorville. I suspect you're correct that this time it's different—but we'll soon see what's going on—when your memory updates.'

'If my memory updates,' she said.

George set down three cups of tea and a plate of chocolate biscuits on the trestle table on the terrace. 'What does the professor make of the wormhole, then?'

'Well, my dear boy, it appears your wife has just time travelled on demand!' He took a sip of the piping hot tea. 'Where to? We're not one hundred per cent sure, but if I had to put money on it, I'd say there's a version of Cara just arrived back to Georgiana in the year 1729. This is the most exciting development in the TTS since I first began years ago.'

Cara sipped her tea. 'I haven't heard much about the Time Travel System for a while. I knew you were keen for us to discover a way to time travel on demand, but I didn't realise you were still working on the TTS. Of course, I should have known…'

Eddie looked puzzled. 'This is the opportunity of many lifetimes. I haven't even begun to digest the implications of what happened back there, but it already indicates there is more than one way to time travel.'

'What next, then?' said Cara, afraid to hear his answer but compelled to know what she was up against.

'If it's okay with you, I'd like to do it again, but this time you'll enter on your own so we can see for sure it's only you who triggers the vortex. We must remember we are time travellers too, so we could in some way be impacting the experiment.' He looked across at George and then back at Cara.

She nodded her agreement. 'Okay, when?'

'Not yet. Let's see what happens, if anything, because of today's experiment. I'd like to document your dreams and anything else that comes up for you. We are in virgin territory—everything counts and could be critical to our understanding of how it works.'

They finished their tea, and walked around the estate,

Cara and George explaining to Eddie their long-term plans for the house and the Tudor Heritage Centre.

'I'm excited to find out more about the history of the priest hole. I think we'll attract a lot of visitors. Old unsolved mysteries fascinate people. We could create some possible background stories to generate interest,' Cara said.

'I like that idea,' said George. 'I'll see what more I can find out and then let's jot down some potential angles.'

Eddie stopped abruptly and turned to them. 'There's something about the priest hole I didn't mention yet.'

They stared back at him.

'The vortex didn't take me, but I remembered something when I was in there,' he said.

'Don't keep us in suspense,' said Cara. 'What did you remember?'

'I had a clear vision of a Jesuit priest, and I knew him... I was helping him, in fact.'

Cara's eyes widened as she stared at him. 'Do you mean you, as in Tutor Edward from Tudorville, were helping a Jesuit priest to hide from the authorities?'

'The very same,' he said, nodding slowly, as if he didn't quite believe it himself. 'It seems we had a fugitive in our midst.'

Willow Wick, York - Georgiana

Caroline frequently distracted Olivia from riding into the village, with promises of a variety of entertaining endeavours in the house and out on the estate, but at least once a week, Olivia insisted they rode the horses into Willow Wick. Caroline ensured there was no set day for their outing so that Ralph wouldn't be able to predict when to expect them.

Sometimes there were menacing undertones when they met, although he was always outwardly polite, which she presumed was for Olivia's sake. She could tell he enjoyed toying with them both, and it was obvious Olivia admired Ralph. The young woman had developed a dangerous crush, and Caroline was even more wary than before. It was one thing fending him off herself, but quite another keeping him away from Olivia.

'He is so dashing and good looking,' said Olivia, one fine afternoon as their horses' hooves picked over the occasional craggy rock and clump of purple hued heather. 'The sight of him fair makes my knees go weak,' she continued, glancing at Caroline to gauge the effect of her words, a mischievous glint in her brown eyes, which reminded Caroline of George.

'You do like to torment me, so,' said Caroline. 'You know it's my responsibility to take care of you and if Lord Cavendish heard you speak in such a way, you would be confined to the estate, never to leave again. Not to mention, Ralph is only a farmer and is not a suitable match for you.'

Olivia tilted her head and smiled. 'You're right, dear Caroline. I shall keep my daydreams about Ralph to myself so as not to compromise your position.'

'What would be better is if you put a stop to those daydreams all together. They can go nowhere, and trust me when I tell you, he is not the good-natured charmer he appears to be. Stay away from him,' said Caroline firmly. 'He is a dangerous man.'

They tethered their horses by the square, and entered Talbot's, the haberdashery shop where Olivia regularly indulged her fancy for ribbons and buttons. Caroline hurried her in and out of the shop, avoiding conversation with old Mrs Talbot who could chat all day with very little encouragement, in an attempt to be on their way back to the estate, unseen by Ralph.

A short while later, they mounted their horses and joined the footpath. Caroline inhaled the fresh air and let herself enjoy the ride. Now they were on their way out of the village, it would be fine, and she could relax.

Then she blinked. There was Ralph, riding steadily towards them on one of his bulky farm steeds. 'Remember what I said. Please don't encourage him,' she hissed to Olivia. 'You'll get us both into trouble.'

Caroline's breathing was fast and shallow, and her heartbeat quickened as his large frame bore down on them.

Please God, let him leave us in peace.

She looked over at Olivia, whose cheeks had turned a rosy pink, and her eyes glowed with something more than just fresh air and exercise.

Caroline feared if he goaded her again, she would react like a bull to a red flag. She tried to ignore his underhand taunts, but the chances were, if he persisted, she would retaliate. She could not abide bullies and since she had dared leave the village and accept the position at Willow Manor without his blessing, Ralph had come dangerously close to behaving like his vicious brothers.

He drew his horse to a halt in front of them, blocking the path so they couldn't continue even if they wished. 'Good day, ladies. And what a fine afternoon it is. I must say, I'm pleased to bump into you again. Fridays, is it you ride into the village?'

'Good afternoon, Ralph. No, we have no such set schedule, as we cannot take leave of our studies frequently.'

'Of course,' he said. 'Your studies must be right important,' he said, inclining his head at Olivia, who, despite her pledge, dissolved into a bundle of simpering young female delight.

He turned his head and directed the force of his sharp blue eyes back to Caroline. 'It's been some time since I've seen you. I visited your father not long back, to ask for word of you.'

Caroline knew he meant this as a warning. If she didn't come and see him, he would seek news of her from her father, his former teacher. Her father couldn't abide him and would be unsettled by the visit.

'Oh, yes? I trust Father is well?' she said.

'He is well enough… for an old man abandoned by his only daughter, that is,' he said, his voice low so Olivia couldn't quite catch his cruel words on the wind, and he smiled at Caroline as though they were exchanging social pleasantries.

She drew herself up to her full height on her horse and spoke clearly so Olivia would witness the conversation. 'I have not abandoned my father, as you well know.'

'Aye, whatever you say.' He clicked his tongue and turned his head towards Olivia. 'You look particularly fine today, Mistress Olivia,' he said, directing the full force of his charm at the young girl who lit up beneath his intent gaze.

'We are expected back at the house,' said Caroline, her tone stern.

Ralph bowed his head and flicked his reins to direct his horse to move aside.

As Caroline passed by him, he said, 'If you are unwilling to visit me, I shall come to you. We have matters to settle,' he said ominously, his jet-black hair glowing in the afternoon sun.

Cara shivered, turned away abruptly, and tapped her booted heels into her horse's flanks. The mare needed no encouragement. 'Come on, I'll race you home,' she said to Olivia, who turned back for one quick glance at Ralph, before she followed Caroline, who had already set off at a fast canter.

As she rode, Caroline considered Ralph's intentions. He was clearly using Olivia to provoke her and try to make her jealous, but what if it was more than that? What if he had really taken a liking to the girl? Olivia was at a vulnerable age and although she was sensible in most matters, Caroline doubted she would be quite as sensible under the full blaze of Ralph's charms.

He knew how to turn it on when he wanted, which was one of the reason's she hadn't seen through his nature, to just how cunning and vicious he could be when he wasn't having things his own way. As long as she'd been available for him and didn't go against his wishes, he had been a caring and loyal friend, albeit with romantic intentions, which she had deflected. Until now.

Would he really have the audacity to come to Willow Manor, or was he using the threat to manipulate her?

One thing was certain, she must keep an even keener eye on Olivia because he knew she was her weak spot, and he wouldn't hesitate to exploit it.

CHAPTER 13

Willow Manor, York - Present day

George sat on the chesterfield in the library, carefully turning the delicate pages of the Cavendish history volume he had recently discovered. The paper was thin and tore easily, so he had to take his time.

Cara was emptying the boxes of books and restoring some order to the antique bookshelves. 'The only thing with tidying books is it's a never-ending job,' she said. 'Unless it's an official library with reference numbers and a system, it's tricky to know how to organise them.' She picked up a slim book and fanned her face. 'Are you hot? It's roasting. I'm going to open the windows.'

'It's a stunning day. We're not making the most of it huddled in here, but I must say it's good to have a dusty old manuscript in my hands again,' he said.

They continued reading and sorting in amiable silence for some time and Cara reflected on how right things were between them. She reorganised the books to the comforting sound of the rhythmic tick of the grandfather clock in the hallway that echoed through the open door. A feeling of deep peace descended upon her, and she was calm for the first time since the experiments with Eddie. She'd been back into the wormhole several times in a variety of scenarios under his guidance so he could get some solid data, as he called it. The vortex appeared every time she reached out to touch the wall.

Eddie and George had been back in several times too, alone and together, touching and not touching the wall. Eddie was in what she laughingly called *professor mode* and he was nothing if not dedicated and thorough, so she had followed his instructions, but she was relieved she could now get on with her other projects.

The professor had returned home the previous evening on the fast York to London train, eager to get into his lab and study his data.

'Listen to this,' said George, his finger underlining a section on a page of the old book.

Cara looked up expectantly, a heavy book in her hands.

'It was never proven, but is widely believed that Lord and Lady Cavendish were sympathetic to the Roman Catholic cause. They were suspected to have harboured priests in their ancestral home, Willow Manor in York, to protect them from being caught and charged with heresy by the Crown. In one particular case, a member of their household, their children's tutor, is said to have saved the life of a well-known Jesuit priest by hiding him in a priest hole, which has never been found. The tutor became a hero amongst the locals, many of whom were still for the pope, following the disastrous end to the Pilgrimage of Grace: the Tudor uprising against the Dissolution of the Monasteries and the reformation of the church.'

'Wow!' said Cara. 'Good spot. That gives us something tangible to say about the priest hole to generate public interest. The journalists will be all over that if we position it right,' she said, ever the savvy business-historian.

'You're right, it'll be brilliant for the centre. But even more intriguing is the reference to Eddie. It says he was actively involved in saving this Jesuit priest, which explains that weird deja-vu moment he had when we were in there.'

Cara nodded. 'And now I think of it, he disguised himself as a priest when we planned to break you out of the Tower of London in Tudorville, and he mentioned that his family had ear-marked him for priesthood. It makes sense he would have connections and be sympathetic to the cause.'

'Poor Eddie, he's not had an easy time of it over the centuries.'

'That must have been a dangerous time for all of us. Do you remember anything about it?' said George.

Cara shook her head. 'I don't recall a thing after I was lady-in-waiting to Jane Seymour, and it kicked off in the north with the Pilgrimage of Grace. As far as I'm aware, that was the last time I travelled to Tudorville, and I have no idea what happened to us after that. I'm keen to read that book. You mentioned there are other volumes?'

George peered at Cara over his glasses that had slipped down his nose at an angle. 'This is volume one, which means there are probably others, but I don't know how many or where they are.'

'What we could really do with is the volume that covers Georgiana so we can get a better idea of what went on after Ralph hypnotised Caroline.'

They agreed Cara would look for the other volume and George would reach out to a journalist about the priest hole publicity.

'Imagine if they knew the truth! That the priest hole is

also very likely a quantum wormhole to 1729,' she said. 'That would really attract the crowds.'

George shook his head. 'We'd never have a minute's peace again. Aside from the fact they'd think we are completely mad.'

'True,' said Cara. 'Our greatest secret is the one we must never reveal.'

'And talking of not revealing. Guess who's coming to visit soon? I didn't have time to tell you when Eddie was here and then I forgot.'

Cara raised her head from the shelf. 'Kate?'

'How did you know?' he said.

'Well, your parents live in York, so they're probably not going to come and stay. And Kate's been talking about coming over from Seville for a while now.'

Cara shoved the last book from the pile onto the shelf and clapped her hands together to dust them off. 'I'm done for today. Shall we go outside for a wander?'

George lay the heavy tome down onto the coffee table, ready to continue later, and then held his hand out to Cara. 'Come on, beautiful. Let's go and see what those builders are up to, shall we?'

They ambled across the lawn, admiring Swifty's handiwork, neither of them quite believing their good fortune. Not only had the universe somehow conspired to bring them together, but they were also the owners of their stunning ancestral home.

'When is Kate arriving?' said Cara.

'She's not sure yet, but she said she'd love to stay for a while if it's okay.'

Cara smiled. 'It's more than okay. You know I love Kate. If it wasn't for her, I'm not sure we'd even be together. Remember when I thought she was your wife when we met in Seville?'

'You were always so quick to presume the worst of me!'

'True, although you must admit you gave me plenty of reason to,' Cara quipped.

George's phone dinged, and he withdrew it from his pocket and peered at the message. 'It's Kate. She's arriving tomorrow morning!'

Willow Manor, York - Georgiana

Caroline awoke as first light seeped through the glass panes into her bedchamber. She pushed herself upwards and leaned heavily against the headboard, still groggy. The dreams were becoming more insistent—each night George visited her. Not the George she knew, but a different George from another time.

At first, she thought she was dreaming about him because she longed for him. The first dream had been so passionate when they had lain together, it was etched in her mind and she found herself frequently lost in the memories of their lovemaking when she was supposed to be concentrating on lessons with Olivia or discussing plans with the countess.

After several weeks of nightly dreams, it was as though a different life was unfolding as she slept. She dared not mention her experience to anyone, or she would surely be marked as a witch with powers to divine the future. When she was a young girl, Caroline witnessed a newcomer to Willow Wick, ducked on a stool in the waters of the village pond to test whether she was a witch.

She shivered at the cruel punishments meted out by the holy men on their witch hunts. Caroline hadn't believed the poor girl was guilty of anything other than having a birthmark on her breast. A sign of the devil, they said. What would they say if word got out that she was speaking about visions in her dreams?

No, I must keep this to myself, even if I am fearful for my sanity.

The previous night, she dreamt George was driving a fast green vehicle, the likes of which she'd never seen or even imagined before. She was alongside him in the dream, and it was obvious by the way they looked and spoke to each other that they were very much in love. And when Caroline thought of how George had touched her in the dream, she blushed.

She shook her head, as if trying to grasp at some newfound clarity, but her mind was still full of snippets and images of another life. A life she couldn't understand where her name was Cara. There was bizarre immodest clothing, they drank endless cups of coffee, and they each held a small object in their hands, called a phone.

What is the meaning of these visions? Have I developed psychic powers?

Caroline rubbed her tired eyes. Not only was she confused and exhausted by the nightly visions, but an intense yearning for George coursed through her, and she was never at peace.

They had made love, but it only made her crave him more. Images of their urgent lovemaking flashed through her mind. Her skin grew hot, and she thought it must surely be sinful, but just the thought of him inflamed her. She craved his hard body on hers and thought about how he made her cry out with joy. He touched her with his beautiful firm hands, with an urgency and confidence which had her begging him to wait no longer, but to take her.

In the dream, no class barrier divided them. They were man and wife, and equal in all things. He was her other half, and she was his. They were counterparts. They fit together perfectly, and as Caroline lay there on the cool sheets, in the glow of the early morning light, she realised one thing. By some strange sorcery or divination, she was Cara. Their beings were one and the same.

And she must never tell a living soul. Her visions must go with her to the grave or she would meet hers all too soon.

Caroline dozed for a short while, until the gentle sounds of the stirring house grew louder and more insistent, and then she forced her weary body to rise from the bed, and she washed with the sparkling cold water she poured into the bowl from the heavy jug that always stood on the chest in her chamber, ready for her morning ablutions.

Harriet was a conscientious girl who performed her duties with dedication and efficiency. Not for the first time since being in the countess's employ, Caroline muttered a prayer of deep gratitude. That morning, although she ached for George in body and soul, she reminded herself of her blessings.

As she dressed hurriedly in a freshly laundered shift and another recently altered cast-off gown of Olivia's, George's face loomed in her thoughts. Not the beardless George from another time, but the earl who was away at court.

She missed him more each day; more than she had thought it possible to miss anyone. When he had been at Willow Manor, just knowing he was there, and that there was the ever-present possibility of bumping into him at any moment, even though he was out of reach in every way, had been sufficient for her budding love. She had not expected more.

But now they were together in her dreams, their union had become real in her consciousness. It had living, breathing form to it. He was hers in the visions, and she was his. And now she felt his absence in a desperate, heart wrenching way that made her want to run from Willow

Manor, to escape the pain where she felt his absence in every room.

The days were endless without him, but she did her utmost to engage and entertain Olivia. She was a delightful girl with an optimistic spirit and despite their class divide; they had developed an uncommon bond. Caroline felt at home when they were together, not like a governess or a servant. She chastised herself that she should be content with her good fortune. But her heart ached more each day as his absence continued, and the only George available to her was the phantom of her dreams who, like a delirious pleasure, was ripped from her each morning when she awoke to the reality of another day without him.

She frequently remembered her father's sentiments: *Our kind don't marry their kind.*

Thoughts of George at court, eagerly being matched with a suitable wife to continue the noble Cavendish bloodline, plagued her.

She considered leaving Willow Manor, not able to contemplate being there when he returned with a wife. But she could not bring herself to leave Olivia. It would be cowardly to run away, and she felt a responsibility to the girl, at least while he was away. Besides, where would she go? She couldn't go back to the village where she would be at the mercy of Ralph's marital intentions. And deep in her heart, she knew she could not bring herself to resign her position and leave Willow Manor without seeing George. If he returned with a wife, she promised herself she would leave. She wouldn't be able to bear witness to his life with another woman.

If he returned alone, she resolved to accept their situation as it was and be content knowing he was in the same house, and it must be solace enough to be aware there was another life, and another time when they were together in mind, body, and soul.

And then the most unexpected thing happened. That morning at breakfast, Cook raised her head from the steaming pot to inform Caroline a letter had arrived. 'It is for you and bears the earl's seal.'

CHAPTER 14

Willow Manor, York - Georgiana

Caroline could barely summon the patience to stay and eat breakfast in the kitchen as though something momentous hadn't occurred. As soon as she reasonably could, without attracting undue attention, she rose from the table and wished the others a good day.

Once on the other side of the kitchen door, she flew up the stairs in a most unladylike manner, racing along the corridors towards the library. As she reached the door, she brought herself to an abrupt halt, steadied her breathing and then entered sedately. Olivia was already seated at the table, and Caroline's eyes strayed immediately to the silver tray upon which lay a tightly folded letter.

'Good morning,' said Olivia, glancing up from her book. 'There's correspondence for you,' she said, as if it was the most normal occurrence for her to receive a letter from the earl.

'Thank you, yes, Cook told me.' Caroline did her best not to show how flustered she was at the sight of the neatly folded paper.

'I expect my brother writes to enquire about my studies,' Olivia said, with all the natural confidence of a young woman used to being the centre of attention.

Caroline's heart lurched. Of course, he would not correspond with her for any reason other than his sister's wellbeing. Her mood plummeted as she realised the folly of her naïve romantic hopes.

The dreams had given her false expectations—she saw that now. She reached out and picked up the artfully folded paper and studied the bright red seal. Fortunately, Olivia had sunk her head back into her book and didn't notice how affected Caroline was by the sight of the paper with George's wax seal.

He touched this paper and addressed it to me personally.

She broke the seal and held the heavy parchment between her trembling fingers, imagining George writing to her in his elegant fashion from his rooms at Kensington Palace.

'What does my dear brother write?' asked Olivia, turning a page and briefly scanning Caroline, who still hovered near the table, the unread letter in her hand.

'I don't know yet,' she said, as she tried to conceal her agitation. She walked to the window and began reading, hoping to avoid Olivia's prying eyes. The pale early morning light washed over the ink, illuminating the letters on the paper as she read George's words.

Dearest Caroline,

Her heart thumped in her chest as she read the term of endearment, even though she knew it was simply a polite form of address.

I trust my letter finds you in good health and spirits, and that you are happily settled at Willow Manor. You and my beloved sister, Olivia, are ever present in my thoughts and I am sorry to have had to take my leave so early in your appointment. I fear I was remiss in not speaking to you before my leaving, to enquire whether there was anything you may need, but alas, they called me away to court without notice and I could not bid you farewell in person.

I would ask a particular favour with both yours and my sister's safety in mind. Please do not venture into the village alone, for there are untold dangers for young gentlewomen such as yourselves. If you must go, pray, do not tarry, and take one of the grooms with you as your escort. Bid them I give my blessing to accompany you whenever you should so desire to ride out or walk to Willow Wick.

I confess I fear for my sister and your good self after the rather alarming meeting with the Knight fellow. I do not wish to offend you with my request, as I understood him to be an acquaintance of yours, but my brotherly instincts warn me something is not quite as it should be regarding his intentions.

Meanwhile, I trust Olivia is engaged in her lessons and is keeping out of mischief. If it is not too much trouble, I ask you to write me by return with news of Olivia's studies and how you ladies are keeping entertained in my absence. I confess the days are becoming rather long and wearisome here in London, as I am a country gentleman at heart, and I miss the peace and harmony of Willow

Manor. I am hopeful to return in the not-too-distant future, but news from home keeps me cheerful.

If I may impose on you as such, please write to me, and my mother will arrange for the letter to be delivered to Kensington Palace with the next forwarding of my correspondence.

Sincerely and with my very best wishes,

George Cavendish

'Does he ask after me?' Olivia interrupted Caroline's reverie as she gazed at the letter, transfixed by thoughts of George at the palace. She wondered how he passed his days and, more importantly, with whom. Dare she hope he thought of her in the way she thought of him?

She shook her head slightly and took a deep breath. 'Yes, Lord Cavendish asks after you and bids us not tarry in the village and we may only travel with an escort.'

Olivia's eyes widened. 'Really? Whatever for? We've been riding without incident for months. That is simply unreasonable.'

'Unreasonable or not, he is the head of the family, and we must follow his thoughtful instruction.'

Caroline had been nervous about the potential visit from Ralph, but so far, he had not followed through on his threat. Nevertheless, she found herself on edge and always alert for his approach when she was out on the estate and thereabouts. What had once been a pleasant friendship had taken a sinister turn when he allowed his jealousy to dictate his actions towards her.

On one occasion, when she lingered at the stables alone

after an afternoon outing, the hairs on her neck stood on end and a fierce shiver ran down her spine. She turned abruptly, sensing someone watching her, but other than a slight rustle in the bushes, she saw no one, and dismissed her suspicion as fanciful.

Folding the letter and clutching it in her hand, she excused herself for a minute and dashed up to her bedchamber to study it further and savour it alone. The letter filled her with optimism and joy, and after tucking the letter away in one of her drawers, she left the room with a renewed buoyancy in her step.

Perhaps she dared hope her feelings were reciprocated, after all. Surely, a great man such as George would not take the time to write to her if he didn't care for her? Throughout the day, the letter stayed in her mind, always in her consciousness, and she glowed at the memory.

Willow Manor, York - Present day

George's sister, Kate, was due to arrive that morning and he whizzed off early to meet her at Leeds Bradford airport while Cara stayed at home to keep an eye on the building work.

She thought it would be an excellent opportunity to see if she could locate the Georgiana volume of the family history series. Cara was exhausted from a disturbed night which she hadn't mentioned to George, not wanting to worry him when he was so excited about Kate's imminent arrival.

The previous night she had a nightmare which had shaken her to the core. Caroline lingered at the stables, stroking the shiny chestnut mare she rode most days, oblivious to being observed. Then she saw her start and look around the stables. In the dream, the same visceral fear Caroline experienced gripped Cara, but unlike Caroline, she clearly saw Ralph watching the young woman from behind the shed at a discreet distance.

Cara wanted to cry out to warn her, but the words wouldn't form on her tongue, and then she awoke in a wild panic, her senses hammering. Her nightdress was damp, her skin hot, and she drew several deep breaths as she rested her head back down on the pillow, trying not to disturb George, who slept peacefully beside her. Her heart gradually returned to a slower rhythm, but her mind flitted manically from fearful thought to thought.

The nightmare showed that Ralph Knight hadn't given up on Caroline. She guessed he would continue to try and separate her from George and win her back. Cara tossed from side to side until the first hint of pink-hued daybreak splashed through the slits in the wooden shutters, casting shadows on the whitewashed walls, and the birds in the old oak tree outside their window began to stir and chirp. She lay there a while, trying to quieten her hectic mind, but it was clear she would not get any more sleep.

Cara swung her legs off the mattress and pushed her feet into her slippers. Grabbing her robe, she slipped through the bedroom door and went downstairs, treading carefully on the creak-prone staircase. She poured the boiling water from the kettle onto the tea bag and watched the golden colour seep into the water before adding a splash of milk. Then she carried her cup through to the snug and curled up with a blanket in the armchair near the window, sipped her tea and tried to make sense of the nightmare, which seemed more like a premonition.

Ever since she discovered the priest hole in the library, Cara found herself in a confusing new world. Knowing there was a wormhole in the library, which, if Eddie's conclusion was correct, would transport her to Georgiana on demand, presented alarming choices she didn't feel equipped to face. She pulled the soft blanket further over her legs and stared out of the window at the ancient willow trees swaying gently in the breeze.

She wondered how much of Caroline's story she had witnessed so far in her dreams.

Is this a sign for me to intervene, and if so, should I?

After breakfast when George left for the airport, Cara dressed quickly in a pair of pale green cotton trousers and a cream silk shirt, and entered the library, determined to look for the Georgiana history volume. After an hour of intensive combing of the shelves and nothing to show for it, she sank onto the comfy sofa and took a short break, her weary muscles aching.

She decided she needed a coffee and went to make one. George wouldn't be back for a while yet, so she still had plenty of time before Kate arrived.

As she stirred the coffee, her eyes fell to the row of cupboards that lined the floor of the old basement kitchen. An idea flitted into her mind— what if the volumes were stored in the kitchen cupboards, which were used to store so many household items from previous owners who hadn't wished to take them when they left?

She'd made lots of surprising finds in the past few months, and suddenly a thrill of excitement shot through her. Cara opened the sets of heavy wooden doors one after the other and hunted meticulously through each storage space. She had to stop herself from being derailed from her mission when she found various fascinating items, such as a pot that looked like a Georgian antique. She reached up to place it on the kitchen counter and then continued with her search for the history volume.

Just as she was losing hope and flagging again, her hands

touched a large wooden box. She pulled it out towards the cupboard entrance and impatiently wiped the dust from the top, revealing a shiny wooden surface as she fumbled with the clasp. At first it was stubborn and wouldn't open to her touch, so she grabbed a tea towel and increased the force, pressing carefully with her fingers. After several attempts, the clasp clicked, and the lock sprang open and triggered the part-shiny, part-dusty lid to bounce slightly, causing Cara to sneeze violently.

She lifted the heavy box out of the cupboard and onto the cold kitchen floor, moved to her knees and pushed the lid upwards and peered into the box. Rows of exquisitely bound books were snugly stacked inside, and she rubbed one of the spines clean with the tea towel to reveal the words: *Cavendish Family History, Volume III.* She dusted off the other books, but was disappointed to see there weren't more volumes.

Just as she was about to look through the book, she heard wheels outside and Cornelius barking frantically. She peered out of the window and saw George retrieving cases from the boot of his car, and Kate staring up at the house, a delighted expression on her pretty face.

Cara hurriedly shoved the books away, washed her hands and headed out the back door to greet her sister-in-law. Georgiana would have to wait.

But would it?

CHAPTER 15

Willow Manor, York - Present day

IT WAS lovely to have Kate with them in the family home. She was suntanned from her months in the Spanish sunshine and looked relaxed and as beautiful as ever.

'It's so good to see you both... and this place, you guys! It's unbelievable. I can see you've made significant progress since we stayed here for your wedding.'

Cara and George held their wedding at Willow Manor when it was still a hotel before they'd even thought that buying it was a possibility.

'You've made some subtle changes, but you've nailed it.' They were standing in the great hall, which retained its impressive Tudor décor, but would be a costly endeavour to maintain and update.

Cara beamed at Kate, and they walked arm in arm out the front door and onto the lawn, the easy camaraderie evident between them. 'I can't tell you how lovely it is to have you with us and to be able to show you everything. We're really excited about what we're doing here. I hope you can stay a while—we need your professional designer's eye.'

'Absolutely. I've just completed a couple of extensive projects in Seville and am ready for a much-needed break and a change of scene. I've been buzzing about coming, but the stars only recently aligned to make it possible for me to get away for more than a few days.'

What had begun as a brief trip to stay at Casa Cavendish in Seville, had morphed into a long-term stay when she'd attracted several high-net-worth, expat clients who wanted a designer of her calibre to create their dream homes in the sun.

'I don't know if you realise just what a legend this house has been in our family since we were kids. It's surreal to see you actually living here. I still don't know how you pulled off buying this place!'

Kate was even more enthusiastic than George, if such a thing was possible, and Cara loved her joie de vivre. Kate was also the most knowledgeable of the two siblings about their family history and Cara intended to discover anything that might help develop the Tudor Heritage Centre.

Cara smiled and changed the subject, carefully dodging Kate's roundabout question about how they raised the millions they needed to buy the estate. She would have to tread carefully to avoid getting into detail, but it shouldn't be too difficult. Cara planned to steer Kate into talking about the Georgian period and see what more she knew from her research about the family and the estate in the eighteenth century.

Previously, Kate told them that their ancestor, George Cavendish, from that period was a bit of a black sheep and had lost Willow Manor in a card game. And from George's time travel sojourn in Victoriana, he learned that legend had it that Willow Manor was haunted, and the history of the house was shrouded in mystery surrounding a fire. No one seemed to know exactly what had happened and, as was so often the case with bygone tales, they became more convoluted and inaccurate as the centuries passed.

So far, they knew Caroline fell in love with George in 1729, and that the Twin Flames married in 1840 when they were prominent figures at Queen Victoria's court. But what occurred in the one hundred and eleven years in-between?

AFTER DINNER, Kate retired to her room, saying she wanted to catch up with her husband, who was away on business, and pleading exhaustion from her trip and the early start.

Cara had been on edge all evening, not able to find a suitable moment to tell George about her earlier discovery. 'I found another volume of the family history,' she blurted out as soon as they wished Kate goodnight, and the door clicked, and they were alone in the snug, at last. 'In fact, I'm off to retrieve it now.'

She leapt from her seat and tore out of the room before George had a chance to respond. He continued to leaf through the pages of *The York Press*, wondering how she could possibly have found it in the short time he'd been out. He shook his head and chuckled. She was like a tornado when she was onto something. Returning with the volume in her hands several minutes later, Cara heaved it onto the low coffee table and a cloud of dust billowed off the cover, irritating the delicate tissue of their noses and causing them both to sneeze.

'Bless you,' they said in unison.

'I only found this. Guess which one it is.'

'Um, the Georgiana volume?' he said, stealthily deciphering the title on the cover, upside down.

'Oh, how did you know?'

'Let's not forget I'm extremely gifted with rare old manuscripts,' he said, his tone dry.

She rolled her eyes. 'You saw the name!'

'Okay, well, there is that… But more importantly, my goodness, you are quite the sleuth. Where on earth did you dig up this dusty old thing? I searched and searched the other day with absolutely nothing to show for my efforts. Which shelf did you find it on?'

'That's just it. It wasn't on a shelf. I found it in those bottomless old cupboards in the kitchen where I've found so many unlikely things since we moved in. They are like a magical treasure trove. I had a feeling it might be there—I don't know why, but the thought just came to me, so I hunted about when you went to get Kate. I've been itching to tell you all day but thought it best not to mention it until we've got our stories straight about what we know of Georgiana.'

Cara opened the book and pored over the contents page, moving her finger down and tracing the words as she scanned the page, looking for references to 1729. 'It's so clever how the past reveals to us only as much as we need at any given time. First, we found the reference to the priest hole just when we needed it, and now this specific volume which covers Georgiana.'

'Let's hope it helps us to put an end to all this. I really miss our uncomplicated, quiet life,' said George.

Willow Manor, York - Georgiana

In the seemingly endless weeks that followed, it was the knowledge that George had written her a letter that kept

Caroline sane. Even though it contained nothing to harm their reputations, she guarded the letter closely, not showing it to anyone, and the thought of it nestled in the drawer, awaiting her in the bedchamber was her heart-warming secret. At night, when she climbed into the cold four-poster bed after a tiring day, the letter gave her solace and warmed her gloomy heart. Each time she picked up the piece of paper, she felt an instant connection to George. A connection she had never experienced before, and one that she sensed went far deeper than any piece of correspondence could. Then sleep would seduce her like an insistent lover, and the night's dreaming would reunite her and George.

Caroline witnessed many scenes from their past and future lives of which she didn't understand the significance. It was as though, each night, she watched another clip of a never-ending film. The only common denominator was George. He was in most of the clips and even when she didn't see him directly, she sensed his presence in everything. She learned more about Cara and was convinced she was another version of herself. Caroline felt Cara's feelings and thought Cara's thoughts when she was sleeping. But when she awoke, all she could recall were snippets of the film. The intense dreams faded with each daybreak as she stirred in her chamber, and she awoke confused and bereft without George.

When would he return home?

She longed to see him again and the double life she led was like balancing on a cliff edge where any second, she was in danger of saying or doing something inappropriate and revealing her feelings for George either in her words or by the expressions on her face.

One day they were taking lessons in the blue room, which more recently had become one of Olivia's favourite spots in the house to pass the mornings. The room was exquisitely decorated, and the overall blue theme complemented Olivia's fine blue gown.

'If I didn't know better, I might imagine you dressed to suit the drawing room today,' said Caroline.

'And you would imagine correctly, my dearest Caroline. I confess I itch with the desire to get out into the world and am driven to frivolous pursuits such as matching my gowns to the rooms in the house. If there is not a clearer sign, I am in need of stimulation, then I do not know what is,' said Olivia, rising from her chair and pacing around the beautiful room like a swirling blue cloud.

Caroline contemplated her charge, not knowing what to suggest. She too was restless, but if George were to return home, she suspected that restlessness would diminish, and the joy would be restored to her aching heart.

'Where is it you would have us go, my dear Olivia?' Caroline asked, tilting her head to one side as she tried to assess Olivia, who was still flitting around the room and was now passing by the window looking out.

'I am so restless, I could scream. Whilst I adore your company and that of Mother, I long for horizons new. With my brother away for such a time, I find myself yearning to join him at court.'

Caroline was taken aback. If Olivia were to attend court, her position as governess would naturally become obsolete. It perturbed her to learn of the girl's discontentment and she worried it must be her fault and she was lacking in the abilities to entertain and engage her sufficiently.

Caroline knew little of court life, other than what she'd read in the occasional society pamphlet and what she'd gleaned from smatterings of conversation. The countess had served at court when she was younger, and it seemed a probability Olivia would do the same.

'Are you not still too young in years to attend court, my

dear, hence my position as your governess and companion? Perhaps, I misunderstood as I confess, I know nothing of court.'

Olivia let out a dramatic sigh and sat down heavily on a chair next to the window. One might think she bore the weight of the world on her petite shoulders, judging by her gloomy expression and distraught tone. 'No, I am sorry to say, you have not misunderstood. I am still too young to attend court. Well, as far as my brother is concerned. Of course, there are many young women my age already serving at court, but he will not allow me to do so. We have talked of this much in the past, but I mean to address the matter again upon his return.'

Caroline rose and crossed the room to Olivia and lay her hand on her shoulder. 'Never fear, your life lays before you like a rose about to bloom. You cannot hurry a rose to bloom, for it requires its budding phase. I am certain, knowing how Lord Cavendish cherishes you, all will unfold just as it should and you shall attend court in due course when the time is right,' said Caroline.

But vague promises and distant prophecies would not rally Olivia, who was in unusually low spirits today.

'Come along. Let us take the horses out and blow the cobwebs away. We both need some fresh air,' said Caroline.

Olivia jumped up immediately, her eyes glowing. 'Please say we may ride into Willow Wick. We haven't done so in such a long time. I feel that will be just the tonic I need.'

Caroline's stomach tightened as she considered the prospect of riding into the village. What would happen if Ralph came upon them again? She shook her head and reminded herself she must not live her life dictated by her fear of him.

'Very well, but we must do as your brother bade us, and have one of the grooms accompany us. The earl warned us to heed Ralph Knight, and I fear he is not mistaken in his concern.'

By the time Caroline had finished her sentence, Olivia had already flown out of the drawing room up to her rooms to shed her blue gown and change into her riding habit. Caroline closed the door behind her and went to change into the countess's old habit, which she had kindly given to her.

Caroline was grateful for their generosity, but occasionally the unexpected thought flitted into her mind: *What would it be like to receive new gowns made especially for me, like a noblewoman such as Olivia? Or as George's wife, Lady Cavendish?*

She bit her lip. The servants would call such lofty ideas getting above her station.

No one must know I think such fanciful things, or I would be forever ostracised and banished from the estate.

CHAPTER 16

Willow Manor, York - Present Day

CARA, George and Kate paced around the display cabinet, appraising the *Tudor Kings' Manuscript* from all angles. The builders had done an incredible job, and it was hard to believe the centre had been a neglected old barn.

'It's the pièce de résistance!' said Kate. 'It lends such credibility to the centre. Shows you're not just interested in Tudor history but have real background and familial ties to it.'

The manuscript had been the pride of the Cavendish family for centuries, ever since George Oliver Cavendish had commissioned it for Henry VIII in 1536.

'Indeed,' said George, as he studied the display, to spot any minor changes it might need.

'The centre is taking shape,' said Cara, beaming at George. 'I'm so excited it's coming together. It seems an age since we first presented the plans and got started.'

George reached for Cara's hand and squeezed it, while Kate went to check out the various exhibits in more detail.

He said, 'It's not been long, but in some ways, it does seem like we've been waiting for it to be ready forever…'

'You've done the most amazing job,' she said, reaching up to kiss him. 'And the best thing is I can see you're loving it.'

He nodded. 'I am. I think I may have found my dream job and am looking forward to developing this place. We'll hire a small team to support us in the day-to-day running, so we can focus on the more interesting aspects.'

'Wonderful. That means I can assist when needed, but will have time for the launch of my new book and for my client work. I've neglected my consultancy during the past few years, but I feel the urge to run with it again.'

George said, 'I'm so pleased it's all coming together for you, Dr Bailey… I mean, Dr Cavendish, or will you go by the name Dr Cara Bailey-Cavendish for your work?'

'Bailey-Cavendish has a lovely ring to it, don't you think?'

'It does. Will you work from here or would you prefer to return to your office in the city?'

She shook her head. 'I'll work from here. As a Tudor and Elizabethan specialist, it would be crazy not to make the most of the opportunity to have my office on an authentic Tudor estate. My clients will love it. Besides, it will be brilliant working near each other but both having plenty to keep us busy with our various projects.'

George pulled her into his arms. 'Perfect. I want you to do what's right for you, but both of us being based here at the house is brilliant. It was your idea even before we bought the estate, if you recall?'

Cara nodded. 'I do. I imagine I'll need to travel for client assignments and the occasional conference like I used to, but it shouldn't be often, so most of the time we'll be working here together.'

They walked around the main room of the new centre and caught up with Kate. 'What do you make of it all?' said George.

'I think it's amazing. What's the story with this priest hole? I see it says we can view it in the library. I don't remember you mentioning that!'

George shifted his weight from one shoe to the other, and Cara stayed quiet, letting him handle the sensitive topic. He always knew what to say. It wouldn't do for them both to blurt out different versions of what had happened in their effort to avoid saying the unsayable.

'Cara discovered it recently, quite by chance, when she was organising the books in the library. The shelf lurched backwards to reveal one of those infamous priest holes so common in the Tudor and Elizabethan eras.'

Kate's eyes gleamed. 'Goodness. I want to see that. Show me, please!'

George and Cara exchanged a discreet look. Kate wasn't someone who could be brushed off easily, and they both saw how excited she was by the unusual discovery. They may as well deal with it now—as if it wasn't anything out of the ordinary in a Tudor house.

'Okay, let's walk back to the house and you can check it out. I'm afraid the idea of it is significantly more exciting than the reality… it's just a dark tunnel that leads nowhere, but come—it's fitting you should be our first visitor to check it out,' said George.

Apart from Eddie.

George and Cara exchanged another look as they crossed the yard and headed towards the back of the house, through the kitchen and up through the maze of corridors, and then arrived outside the heavy wooden library door.

'Have you seen this room yet, Sis?' asked George.

'I don't think I have unless I saw it when we were here for the wedding?'

George shook his head. 'No, I shouldn't think so.'

He opened the door and beckoned for Kate and Cara to enter ahead of him. Kate's face was animated as she surveyed the library. 'This is absolutely divine. What a simply gorgeous room. I can't believe I haven't been in here before,' she said, spinning around like a manic dreidel, only stopping to study the names of the tomes on the floor-to-ceiling shelves, and then crossing to gaze out of the tall windows. After a few minutes appreciating the view, she turned and said, 'I cannot tell you just how much I love this place. And this room feels like home. I can't put my finger on it, but do you ever have that feeling you've been somewhere before even though you know you haven't? This is how this house feels to me. And this room even more so. Deja-vu is the only way to describe it.'

George and Cara looked at Kate, and then at each other.

'Do you know what I mean?' said Kate. 'Did you feel it too when you first entered the house, George?'

'A little, yes. It seemed familiar. I put it down to all the stories we've heard about the house since we were kids. Those things enter our consciousness more than we realise.'

Kate nodded and then switched her laser focus to Cara. 'I don't suppose it was the same for you, with the estate being fairly new to you?'

Cara nodded. 'Living here gives me a lovely feeling of being connected to history. It's certainly the perfect home for a historian,' said Cara. 'Of course, I don't have the same long-standing ties to it as you two. I am new to the Cavendish fold, but I already feel very much at home,' she said carefully. 'It's such a beautiful house.'

'It's only natural you'd feel something after hearing so

much about Willow Manor over the years,' said George, turning to Kate.

'Yes, that must be it. Although, I do wonder about deja-vu. I read an article recently about past lives and how when we have that odd feeling of having been somewhere before, it's because in a former life we have. Woo-woo, I know, but that stuff fascinates me,' said Kate, with a wry smile.

'Me too,' said Cara.

George raised an eyebrow at Cara and swiftly changed the subject. 'Ready to see the tunnel? Remember I warned you, it's just a black hole without much of anything to see, but imagine for a moment, if you will, the Jesuit priest, rigid with fear, concealed in the walls of this beautiful room, praying for his life and that of his protectors.'

'You do know how to set the scene. I got chills at the thought of that poor priest. What happened to him? Did he live?' she asked, barrelling a cannon of questions at her brother, who was used to her endless curiosity and took it effortlessly in his stride.

'We're only just discovering more about what happened. I didn't even know there was a priest until we found this hole. I found a volume of family history which refers to a Jesuit priest who was hidden by our ancestors' tutor. Local hero, as far as I can tell, so it sounds like his actions saved the priest from being discovered, but we don't know for certain.'

'We don't know all the details yet… if we ever will,' said Cara. 'These historic matters are notoriously difficult to get to the bottom of as they become entwined with people's different versions of what happened.'

Kate's interest only intensified, and her eyes shone as she processed the information, which alarmed Cara, but made perfect sense. If she wasn't interested in the family's heritage and history, she wouldn't have bothered to find out all she had.

'Okay, get ready for a bit of jiggery-pokery,' said George, as he raised his hand and pushed against the section of the shelving which concealed the priest hole. He then pushed his weight against it, and they heard a noise as the shelves slid from their usual position and swung open to reveal the black hole.

'Wow!' said Kate. 'How on earth did you find this, Cara? It's so well hidden.'

Cara gave her a potted version of what she'd been up to and how she'd fallen on the shelves when they'd swung open.

'Can we go in?' asked Kate, excited as a child.

'I knew you'd want to!' George replied. 'Hang on—where is the torch?'

'Ah, yes, we need the magical torch without which we do not enter. I warn you, though, it's musty and freezing in there. Are you sure you want to, and wouldn't rather just poke your head inside? I can flash the torch so you can see the walls and ceiling from here,' said Cara.

Kate turned to her sister-in-law and clasped her hand. 'You're not getting off that easily. Come on, let's go in together.'

Before Cara could come up with a reasonable excuse not to follow, Kate tugged her by the hand and pulled her through the gap until they were inside. Kate had taken the torch and was shining it up and down and around as they entered.

'You are going to make a lot of money with this place. It's fabulous! I can almost sense the poor priest in here, shaking and terrified of being discovered at any moment. How brutal.'

She pulled Cara along behind her, one hand in hers and the other on the torch. 'Let's go right to the end,' she said.

Cara didn't reply. Without causing a scene which would only draw more attention to their desire to hide something, she couldn't think of a way to extract herself from Kate's determined progress towards the end of the priest hole.

Cara approached the wall as slowly as she could without stopping. The words *gateway* and *wormhole* ran through her mind with each step she took towards her potential fate. She peered backwards over her shoulder, trying to see George, but the shadows obscured his face. She felt his hand touch her back and pat her reassuringly.

'Take it slowly,' George said. 'It's easy to trip in these small spaces.'

Cara inched forward, her hand limp in Kate's, the pressure of her booming heart so intense she feared it would explode in her throat and choke her. She struggled to swallow and to breathe. 'I think I'm having a panic attack,' she gasped.

Willow Wick, York - Georgiana

It was a particularly warm day, and the sun glinted across the green hills and golden wheat fields, showing Yorkshire at its most captivating. Caroline and Olivia cantered down the footpath, enjoying the fresh breeze which took the sting out of the hot noon sun.

The cheerful groom, who was only too happy to have a break from his routine and be out for a ride, followed a way behind to keep a watchful eye on them but to give the illusion they were alone. Whenever Caroline spotted him, she was reminded of how thoughtful and caring George was. Another brother could have easily overlooked the finer details of protecting his younger sister and left it to his mother, but not George. He was cut from a different cloth than most, Caroline realised. Her heart was full of him and though she hadn't seen him in person for what seemed like forever, she now knew him intimately from her detailed dreams which had shown her their life together in a distant future where they were in love and perfectly suited. She had decided to stop worrying about how strange it all was, and to just enjoy the experience. It was her secret, and she hugged it to herself as they rode.

But how she missed him in her day-to-day life when she could not see him in her dreams, and he was far from Willow Manor at the Georgian court.

Sometimes when they rode into the village or pottered about the estate, she sensed someone watching her and couldn't help but wonder if it was Ralph. He still hadn't fulfilled his threat to visit her at Willow Manor, but she feared he would not give up easily. She knew him too well—he would have a plan, and she was certain it wouldn't be one she liked. For that reason, she was all too pleased to have Taylor, George's groom, as a chaperone, and she shivered slightly, despite the heat, at the thought of Ralph spying on her.

As they rode, her thoughts switched to her father. She visited him as often as she could, but explained she wished to avoid Ralph. He assured her he was occupied with the school and his books, and she must not worry about him. He always enquired after the countess's health, and she could see how proud he was that his daughter was in residence at Willow Manor. 'I can't quite say why, but it seems right and fitting that you be there,' he said one Sunday morning when she made a brief visit to the cottage alone. 'You were always different from the others. Destined for greater things. Your mother would be so proud to see you have become a fine lady,' he said.

Olivia's words broke the spell of her introspection, and she looked up to see her waving excitedly in the direction of a carriage and horses moving at a steady pace on the track in the distance. 'It's the carriage in which George travelled to London,' she called, her voice high-pitched and squeaky with excitement. 'George is home! George is home!'

Caroline was overcome with conflicting emotions. Feelings of joy swirled in her chest that he was home, but she dreaded the implications of facing him every day as though nothing untoward was happening between them.

As far as he was concerned, nothing was happening between them… Part of her yearned to flee to her father's cottage and avoid meeting him. While part of her; a more insistent part, desired to turn around immediately, return to the house to behold his handsome face and bask in his all-consuming presence.

Olivia drew her horse to a halt as Caroline, who had fallen a little way behind, joined her. 'Are you certain it's Lord Cavendish and not someone else visiting?'

Olivia nodded, her eyes shining. 'It's him. I know it's him. I could make out the crest on the side of the carriage. Only the immediate family use the crested carriages and Mother is at home today.' She pulled on the horse's reins and expertly turned around.

'Whatever are you doing?' said Caroline. 'We must carry out our errand.'

The countess had tasked them to deliver a basket laden with Cook's pies, bread, and pastries, to a sick tenant and their family in the village.

'May I please be excused? I am simply dying to greet George upon his return.' Olivia's cheeks were flushed, and she found it difficult to sit still in the saddle. 'Let us have Taylor deliver the basket with our blessings, and we may return to the house immediately. If we ride fast enough, we may even make it before George arrives and he will be delighted to see us waiting for him.' Olivia relaxed the reins on the horse's hot neck and clasped her hands together in a sign of a prayer. 'Please, please, Caroline.'

'Very well. I have an idea,' said Caroline. 'We must deliver the basket personally, but you turn back, and Taylor will accompany you, and I will continue on to the village. I will make haste and be back in no time.'

Olivia considered only for a second, for she was too distracted by the thought of her brother bearing news and fancy gifts from London to resist.

They parted ways and Caroline continued along the footpath alone, her emotions crashing through her as she contemplated seeing George again after so much time had passed.

Is it possible to have such vivid dreams of another life with him, whilst he has no such feelings for me at all?

As she approached the village, she noticed the bushes sway to the left side of the footpath, as though someone moved through the thickets. She stared at the spot, heart thudding and the blood racing through her veins. She knew who was there before he appeared.

Ralph stepped out from the bushes and moved to block her way.

CHAPTER 17

Willow Manor, York - Present day

It was freezing in the priest hole and Cara shivered, as much from the cold as from her fear of the vortex claiming her while Kate was there.

'Are you okay?' said Kate, turning back to Cara, squinting to see her face. 'I didn't know you had panic attacks.'

'I don't usually,' said Cara in a muffled voice. 'It's this confined space. You carry on if you like, although there's not much more to see.'

'No, it's okay. Let's get out of here. I could make out the wall, so I think we've just about reached the end, anyway. I'll come back and explore some more another time.'

Cara exhaled, relief flooding through her. They had avoided reaching the wall by only a few seconds.

George jumped down into the library and, ever the perfect gentleman, turned to help Cara and then Kate to clamber slowly down onto the plush carpet.

Cara threw herself onto the nearest chesterfield and fanned her face with her hand. 'I don't think I'll join you next time if that's all right! I felt like I was losing it in there. I've never liked confined spaces, but today it really freaked me out.'

'My poor darling,' said George. 'Come on, let's skedaddle and take a walk to blow the cobwebs away. It's bloody damp in that tunnel. I can only imagine how dreadful it was for the persecuted priest unable to move a muscle for fear of being caught.'

As they took a walk around the grounds, Kate stooped to pick up a fallen bunch of lance-shaped willow leaves and twirled them in her hands as they walked. 'You know that strange feeling hasn't left me. I kept expecting something significant to happen in that tunnel.'

'And it did!' said George. 'Cara almost had a panic attack...'

Kate shook her head. 'No, I mean something else. Never mind, I can't explain it.'

They walked to their favourite riverside local pub for lunch and watched the boats drift by on the sparking water as they ate.

'It really is an idyllic spot, isn't it? No wonder our ancestors thought it was a good place to build the family home. I could get used to this,' said Kate.

'I'm so pleased you like it. You know, you are welcome to stay for as long as you fancy,' Cara said.

'Be careful. I might just take you up on that, what with Rick away on business for the foreseeable future. It's lovely having your company and there is something comforting about Willow Manor. I know I keep saying it, but it really feels like home.'

'That's settled then,' said George, pushing his plate aside

and arranging his knife and fork to signify he had finished eating.

'What's settled?' asked Kate, pausing over her cheese and onion quiche and crispy coleslaw.

'You're staying on for a while. We can certainly do with you help in the run up to the grand opening.'

They admired the cerulean blue sky and sipped their drinks and relaxed in the ambiance of the sun-drenched riverside terrace, surrounded by shrubbery and artistically arranged pots stuffed with bright summer flowers.

'With weather like this, how can I decline? It's almost like Seville,' said Kate.

They laughed, all knowing that even during the British summer, it was liable to be dull and rainy the following day. Kate offered her full services to assist them with the grand opening and they chatted and made plans to divide up the long to-do list as the big day approached.

Kate said she'd especially love to be involved with anything to do with their family history, and so they decided they would talk about what else she might know that could help them, while George was overseeing the final steps with the builders in the centre, that afternoon.

'I must also give Eddie a quick call,' said George.

Cara looked up. 'Everything okay?'

'All good. Just wanted to run a few things by him. He made a few interesting suggestions when he was here.'

Kate looked intrigued. 'How is Eddie? We really hit it off at your wedding. He's so lovely.'

They chatted for a while longer, not wanting to leave the sun trap by the peaceful, meandering river. Finally, George stood. 'Come on, you two. I must get back to see the builders before they call it a day.'

On the way home, they passed a sign that pointed to a footpath which led into the nearby village of Willow Wick.

'We've not been that way yet,' Cara said. 'We should check it out and take Kate into the village when we have a chance.'

'I'd love that. Willow Manor was at the heart of Willow Wick back in the eighteenth century,' said Kate. 'Many of the villagers depended on our ancestors for their livelihood and were tenants in their cottages, and from what I could glean, it appears there was a thriving community, and the family even funded a school for the local children which was far ahead of the thinking of the day.'

Cara stopped in her tracks. 'I'd like to hear more about that and make some notes later,' she said.

She saw herself riding along the footpath into Willow Wick, and a vision of Ralph flooded her mind and panic shot through her.

Kate touched Cara's arm. 'Are you okay? You look a little pale again.'

'I think I must be coming down with something,' she said. 'I don't feel quite myself today.'

Back at the house, Cara and Kate settled down in some stripey deckchairs in a shady patch of the garden, and Mrs Lightfoot brought them a pot of tea and some home-baked scones.

'My goodness, I can see I'm going to have to watch my weight while I'm here with you lot,' said Kate. 'These scones look scrumptious,' she said, slicing one in half and spreading it with butter and a spoonful of strawberry jam.

Cara poured them both tea and opened her notebook, ready to quiz Kate. 'Please, tell me all you can about your ancestor, George Cavendish, who was head of the estate in the eighteenth century—around 1729. He inherited the title of earl when his father died.'

In between mouthfuls of delicious scone which crumbled on her tongue, and sips of hot tea, Kate regaled Cara with what she could recall about the house and its inhabitants. 'So, as I told you before, this particular George has a reputation as having been a bit of a black sheep.'

'Remind me why exactly,' said Cara, her pen scratching the paper of her notebook as she scribbled furiously. 'What did he do?'

'I think it may have been more about what he didn't do. He let the side down, as it were.'

'Oh… in what way?'

'Well, I don't know all the details, and I don't know how we would find them, but my understanding is that he fell in love with a servant who was employed at Willow Manor—she may have been a governess or something like that, so not quite one of the servants, but not an aristocrat either.'

Cara scrawled as fast as she could to keep up as Kate talked. 'What about him burning the house down? You mentioned something about that, didn't you?'

'Yes, that's right. Again, I don't know how or what, and the original house still stands, so he obviously didn't burn it all down.'

'But why on earth would he want to burn his own house down?'

'There are various versions of the legend I've heard over the years. Some say he was so heartbroken over his lost love he vowed to burn it down and didn't want to live without her.'

A chill ran through Cara as she thought of the George and Caroline, she'd seen so much of in her dreams recently. It sounded like they were headed for doom, even though Sylvia had overwritten Ralph's menacing hypnotic karmic warrior spell. Perhaps this was the life when they destroyed each other with no one else's help…

Cara prompted Kate to continue and asked a lot of questions to see what she might have overlooked. Every word was of consequence in helping Cara to solve the eighteenth-century puzzle.

'What was that thing you said about George losing the estate in a card game?'

'Um, that's part of the legend, too,' Kate said, pouring them a refill from the large china teapot. 'You know how legends are—big on drama and small on detail!'

Cara smiled and sipped her tea.

'Have you spoken to my parents about it? They may know more, although they just left for an extended Caribbean cruise, so we won't see them for a while!' Kate said.

Cara thought of George's parents. They were a lovely couple who had welcomed her into the Cavendish family as though she had always been a part of it. 'Yes, we saw them to say goodbye, but they were in a bit of a rush, so I didn't get a chance to pick their brains this time.'

Kate continued, 'Ancestor George is said to have been playing cards in the village, when his arch enemy turned up and taunted him, so things got heated and he went all in. Gambled the house—and lost…' She shook her head. 'Imagine having to live with that. No wonder he turned to drink, and the estate fell into ruin. Reputations were everything for noble families in those days. I imagine the disgrace finished him and the family at the time.'

'It sounds awful.'

Kate continued, 'Maybe he tried to burn it down in a fit of despair, but failed?'

A dense gloom descended over Cara, and she realised she was very likely experiencing the karmic weight of those tragic events. When she was affected by the past, it seeped into her soul and consumed her every feeling.

One thought ran through her mind like a relentless ticker tape as she shifted on the deckchair and stared up at the blue sky.

Who was George's arch enemy at the card game?

WILLOW MANOR, York - Georgiana

OLIVIA GALLOPED across the fields with Taylor following closely behind and they arrived to see George's carriage in front of the house, already vacated. She handed her horse to Taylor and ran into the house, clutching the skirts of her riding habit so they wouldn't hamper her progress. She saw one of the maids as she fled through the downstairs hall. 'Where may I find the earl, Harriet?' she cried, only slowing down enough to catch the girl's reply.

She knocked, and without waiting for a response; she burst into the blue drawing room. 'George, George,' she cried. 'You are home, at last! We spotted you on our way into the village and I insisted we turn around immediately and abandon our errand.' Tendrils of golden hair escaped from her riding hat as she bobbed her head about.

'My dear girl,' he laughed, embracing her, and then holding her at arm's length. 'Let me have a good look at you. You have grown much in the short time since I saw you last,' he exclaimed.

'Short time? It was too long and wearisome without you, brother. I couldn't wait to see you and to hear all about your adventures at court.'

'Pray go and change, my dear,' said the countess, 'and then we shall take tea and hear your brother's news.' She signalled for Olivia to do as she bid. Olivia hesitated and moved towards the door with an unconcealed sigh.

As she approached the door, George called out, 'I trust you returned in the company of Mistress Caroline and one of the grooms?'

'Taylor escorted me like you instructed Caroline, but she continued onto Willow Wick to deliver Mother's basket as we had originally intended.'

George's dark eyes narrowed. 'You mean to say you and Taylor left Caroline to ride to Willow Wick and back, unaccompanied?'

Olivia's lip trembled. She couldn't abide it when her brother was displeased with her. He was slow to anger, which was just as well because he had a fierce temper when provoked. 'Caroline insisted. She didn't want me to ride back alone, and she said she must complete the errand for Mother.'

The countess interjected. 'It's not safe or proper for her to ride alone, but in this one instance in the name of charity, we may overlook it,' she said, imagining her word would be final.

George towered above them, his formidable height, and broad shoulders in his white shirt and coat, filled the window against which he stood. 'No, Mother, I'm afraid it won't do. I sent implicit word the ladies were not to ride without a groom, and they have ignored my instruction. I shall ride out now to find Mistress Caroline, for it is far too dangerous for her alone. She is under our protection, after all.'

The countess stared after him as he swept from the room, and Olivia scurried out, tears rolling down her face. She hated being out of favour with her brother and now she was genuinely scared for Caroline's safety. What had she done?

George strode to the stables, not bothering to change out of his fancy London clothes. He commanded Taylor to saddle his black stallion and leapt onto its back, the groom at his heels. They galloped out of the estate and thundered across the field, and joined the footpath to Willow Wick.

'We may need to search for her in the village. Let us split

up—you make haste to the family's cottage and see if Mistress Caroline is there. And I'll go to her father's, by the green, and see if he knows her whereabouts.'

Taylor nodded and soon after disappeared from the footpath as he entered the village. George continued at a slower pace, looking and listening carefully for anything untoward. He had an ominous feeling, and he believed in following his instincts. Something wasn't right—of that much, he was certain.

And then he heard a muffled cry. It sounded like a woman, but he couldn't be sure. He pulled on the horse's reins and drew to a sharp halt, stroking the horse's neck as he scanned the area from which the noise had come. And there it was again. He was certain now it was a woman's voice, and he dismounted stealthily from his horse and tethered the stallion to a nearby post. He walked with long, careful steps in the voice's direction.

Then he saw Caroline. She was wedged against the bough of a huge ancient oak tree, and a tall black-haired man stood in front of her. George edged closer, and saw that Caroline saw him over the man's shoulder, so he put his finger to his lips to urge her not to alert her captor. Then George moved forward and grabbed the man deftly from behind, and he was taken off guard and almost fell backwards.

As he suspected, the man was Ralph Knight.

'You!' said George.

'What the devil are you doing?' Ralph snarled, cursing as he tried to shake George's powerful grip off his back. Caroline took the opportunity to move away from the tree and beyond Ralph's reach, as she stepped swiftly behind George.

'Go home, Caroline. Don't say a word of this to Olivia and my mother. I will handle this unfortunate incident.'

'But what of Nellie, my horse? She took off in a fright and I must find her.'

'Fret not. I will bid Taylor look for her. You go home,' he said again, more sharply this time.

Caroline hesitated and shook her head. 'No, I should not leave, my lord. Let us try to resolve this misunderstanding peaceably with Ralph,' she said. Her chin jerked upwards as she stared into George's dark eyes and directly forbade his order. 'I feel sure he meant no harm.'

George removed his hand from Ralph's back and the two men glared at each other.

Ralph spat on the ground and continued to stare at George. 'Just because you're an earl, it does not mean you may attack me.'

'And just because you're a man, it does not mean you may attack her. If you so much as look at her, you will answer to me and I will not let you off so lightly again.'

Ralph spat on the ground again, and then turned to Caroline. 'Heed what I said, or you'll be sorry, Mistress Caroline,' he growled.

CHAPTER 18

Willow Wick, York - Georgiana

As they emerged from the bushes, Caroline's horse was nowhere in sight, and nor was Taylor, the groom. George helped Caroline up onto his horse and made sure she was all right.

'You've had quite a shock,' he said, his deep voice soft as velvet. 'Hold on to me tight.' And with that, he spurred the horse on, and they cantered all the way back to Willow Manor.

Caroline was in the throes of conflicting, tumultuous emotions. Still shaken by her run-in with Ralph, who had been more aggressive than she had ever known him, she was overcome with joy as she clasped George around the waist and held onto him as they swooped through the fields toward Willow Manor.

She thought of her dream the previous night when he had been in her bed and they had made love, first tenderly and then feverishly, as they abandoned themselves to their mutual desire.

I must not reveal my love for him, or my position will become untenable.

The thoughts and feelings churned within her as she wrapped her arms around him all the way back to the house, savouring every second of their closeness. She was embarrassed he had come upon her in such a compromising situation and worried he would think ill of her.

They entered the estate and trotted into the stables, the horses' hooves clip-clopping and echoing in Caroline's ears. She was flooded with disappointment that their solitary time was about to come to an end. But he reached for her, and his strong hands held her waist, as he carefully set her down before he too dismounted. No one was around, and for a brief time, they stood opposite each other, neither knowing what to say. Any previous awkwardness from before he left for London seemed to have dissipated in the long absence, and Caroline felt like they had known each other forever.

'I am sorry you had to go through that. I meant what I said. If that scoundrel so much as looks at you again, pray tell me, and I will make certain it's the last time he troubles you.' He fired off his instruction in staccato like fashion, his expression dark and his brow furrowed.

She watched his lips move as he formed his words.

Then he stumbled and paused for a few seconds and moved his eyes away from hers as if looking into the distance. 'Unless, of course, I was thoroughly mistaken, and you should wish for the attentions of that Knight fellow,' he said, his rich voice now hitting a lower melodious note. 'In which case, I must apologise for my intervention. I confess, it only now occurs to me I may have misinterpreted the situation and I feel rather foolish.'

A sardonic smile touched his full lips, and his embarrassment touched her all the more deeply as it was in such stark contrast to his usual assured manner.

He added, 'Perhaps you did not wish to be saved, and my intrusion was unwelcome…'

Caroline blushed beneath his probing gaze.

Is that truly what he thinks of me?

She raised her head slightly, gathered all her courage and, with as much poise as she could muster, said, 'My lord, I assure you I am not in the habit of cavorting with gentlemen in the thickets.'

She saw the glimmer of a smile cross his handsome face before he grew serious once more. 'Ah, just as I thought, Mistress Caroline. If I have offended you, I apologise—I realise I may have been rude and for that, I am sorry. Not that I would call that fellow a gentleman.'

Caroline's heart lurched and clattered in her breast. 'I thank you for your concern and assure you I am most grateful for your timely intervention. However, I am quite certain Ralph meant me no serious harm. We have been friends since we were children.'

'I see,' said George, his dark eyes becoming unreadable. 'Even so, I must warn you of the dangers of allowing yourself to become entangled with a man such as he.'

Caroline bristled. 'When you say, "A man such as he", am I to interpret you mean a man of the lower classes, my lord? We are not all fortunate to enjoy your level of society.' Her cheeks flamed at her own impudence, but she did not check herself. Despite the obvious class disparity, she felt equal to him and that she must speak up.

George straightened to his full height, and said, 'You may interpret what you wish, Mistress Caroline, but I assure you I do not allude to his class. What I meant is that blackguard is a member of the Knight family. I have been informed they treat their women poorly, and they have been stealing game from our estate since I was a boy. My gamekeeper has had more than one run-in with him and his brothers in this past year alone.'

'I see,' she said. 'I confess I had no knowledge of that and must apologise for the misunderstanding. Please excuse me.' She inclined her head, wishing the ground would swallow her up and take her out of this excruciating situation, and then she gathered her skirts and fled the stables as fast as she could without running and losing all appearance of ladylike decorum.

Taylor appeared in the stable yard leading Nellie, Caroline's missing mare, as George stood staring after her retreating back, regretting what seemed to be his unwitting knack for insulting her. He wondered why he cared so deeply what she thought of him. What strange spell did this governess hold over him, and why did she haunt his dreams?

He feared he wasn't in control of his senses when she was around. But lord how he had missed the sight of her when he was away at court, even surrounded by an endless supply of beautiful, high-born women. He had found none of them to his taste and was no closer to finding a suitable wife, which his mother had made clear must be his highest priority. As the latest Earl Cavendish, he had a duty to perform and a noble lineage to continue. His wild desires had no place in his life, and he resolved to get a firm hold on himself. Such lustful feelings and attraction for Olivia's governess, no matter how charming and graceful, would not do at all.

George's fate was decided for him long ago; his future mapped out, and with a troubled heart, he made his way into the house to greet his mother and sister properly.

Fortunately, Caroline had made it to her chamber, unseen, and no one witnessed her distress. When she closed the door behind her, she removed her riding boots, ran to her bed, and threw herself upon it. And then she let the tears flow. The pent-up emotion from the past weeks and months as she had grappled with her feelings for George erupted and shook her whole body. She allowed the violent emotions to overcome her usual composure and to take their course. She knew not how long had passed, until she quieted, and her tears slowed and then ceased, leaving her face pink and wet, and her heart still sore.

Giving way to the storm of distress lent a certain cathartic release, and her spirits lifted slightly, as though renewed. She lay on her bed, clasping a piece of the green counterpane, wondering whether coming to Willow Manor had been a huge mistake and she should return home to the cottage and resign herself to living a simple life with her father. But the mere thought of leaving George and never speaking to him again, which would surely be the outcome of retiring her post, made the tears bubble in her eyes anew and her breast heave.

No, I do not have the strength to leave. Not yet, anyway. I will pull myself together and accept that I am only a governess in his eyes, and he was merely showing the kindness any gentleman would for a lady in distress.

Caroline could not bear the bleak thought of the empty days stretching out before her, turning into years, with no sight of him. Being in the same house and dreaming of him would have to be enough for her aching soul. She vowed she would force herself to leave if staying became unbearable, but as it was, he was home and darts of joy shot through her as she realised he would be present at Willow Manor every day, once again. The realisation hit her that despite all the gossip; he had returned without a wife.

How could she leave him now?

Willow Manor, York - Present Day

The date of the grand opening was confirmed, and the press coverage booked. Kate rolled up her sleeves and was busy making the final touches to the centre. Cara was going through the motions of ticking off her portion of the to-do list, but her mind wasn't on the job. She remembered Sylvia's warning to be present, but she found it increasingly impossible as she grappled with her dreams and the events of Georgiana.

Will we ever be left in peace to enjoy our life?

After many conversations with Kate, she had managed to piece together an understanding of sorts of what may have happened in 1729. There were still enormous gaps in her knowledge and her mind constantly reverted to them like a tongue probing a tender tooth. After the priest hole debacle with Kate, she had avoided entering again, but the thought was never far from her mind, that she could try to time travel on demand to Georgiana to intervene if George and Caroline were in danger of resetting the timeline.

Why would I be given the chance to time travel on demand, if not to use it?

Eddie had texted her several times to ask whether she had travelled through the wormhole again, and she sensed he was disappointed at her reluctance to embrace the opportunity more enthusiastically.

She loved having Kate on their business team and enjoyed her company immensely, but they had to watch their words when she was around and avoid discussing anything that would alert her to their strange circumstances. Cara dreamt nightly of Georgiana and remembered snippets of Caroline's life at Willow Manor at odd times of the day. She was confused because, so far, she had no reason to believe that George had been an irresponsible gambler or drinker. From what she learned, he indulged in the occasional whisky or glass of wine with dinner, but he was no profligate drunk.

'What's the eighteenth-century version of me like, then?' asked George one night when they settled into bed.

'Funny you should ask. I was just thinking earlier about how charming he is. The description of a cad, a drunkard and a wild gambler doesn't match, at all.'

George smiled. 'I have to confess to being rather pleased to hear that! I didn't like the idea of being some ungrateful, drunken wastrel. It didn't sit well with me.'

Cara stroked his hand and ran her fingers down his arm. 'Well, I don't know how things took such a disastrous turn. There must be a misunderstanding because I can't see such reckless behaviour in his character.'

'So, what you're saying then is that I'm just as wonderful in Georgiana as I have always been?'

She rolled her eyes.

He removed her book from her hands, pulled her further down the bed, and kissed her.

'Pretty much, but you want to watch that gigantic head or you won't be able to get through the door, never mind the priest hole,' she laughed. George dropped tender kisses onto Cara's neck.

'I thought you were tired and getting an early night,' she said.

'I am… but I have a bit of energy in reserve, and I know just how to use it.'

Cara trailed her fingers across his chest and down his body until he shivered. 'You don't look at all tired, to me,' she said, raising an eyebrow.

They made love until they were both spent and satisfied, and drifted off to sleep in each other's arms.

Cara slept, and the church clock struck six and she saw a heartsick and confused George in her dreams.

She stayed in bed later than usual that Saturday morning, exhausted from her restless night, feeling like she hadn't slept at all. The dreams were becoming more urgent, and it was like she was living two lives—the busy one in the present day, and the emotionally charged one where she was Caroline.

George rose early and went down to the kitchen. 'Good morning,' he said, when Eddie answered his call. They were both early risers and had a habit of catching up in the mornings when they had time. 'Ah, Lord Cavendish himself, I was just thinking about you and wondering how it was all going at the centre.'

'I've been meaning to catch up with you and tell you about our discovery, but it's been crazy here, trying to make the deadlines for the opening,' said George.

'Ooh,' said Eddie. 'What discovery?'

George could hear the eagerness in his voice. Eddie loved nothing more than a new discovery, which George supposed was the motivation for his becoming a quantum scientist.

'You know how when you were in the priest hole, you said you had a sense of deja-vu?'

Eddie said he did and added that the feeling had lingered, and he still wondered whether he too might have been present in Georgiana. 'After all, we've been together in several lives. Why would I not be in that one too?'

'That is quite possible, but what I found points to something simpler,' said George.

'I'm all ears—go on,' said Eddie, making a show of holding his rather large ears and peering at George through the screen after switching to video call.

'I don't recall whether I told you I found a book of the family history, but anyway, I found a reference to you in it!'

'To me—how so?' said Eddie, his eyes widening.

'The book mentions a tutor to the family in the Tudor period.'

'Gosh, how exciting. If I'm not mistaken, this is the first time we've found something to prove my existence in Tudorville.'

George nodded. 'Correct. I hadn't thought of it like that. I was just thinking that no wonder you had a karmic memory of being in that priest hole. But you haven't heard the best of it yet,' said George.

'I'm listening… still all ears,' said Eddie, who was in a jovial mood that morning.

'You, my friend, have gone down in the history books as a local hero, no less! You apparently saved the Jesuit priest's life…'

Eddie sat down on a hard wooden chair in his lab as he absorbed the news. 'How bloody fantastic. I must say, it's good to know we did something useful between all this flitting about between timelines and dodging the endless disasters coming at us.'

George poured fresh coffee into his cup and raised it to the screen. 'Can I get you one?'

'I'd love one—you make the best coffee. I must invent a way to send coffee through the phone line. Now that would change the world! But never mind that now. Where can I get a copy of this book that proclaims my former self a Yorkshire hero?'

'Ah, yes, well… about that.' George ran his hand through his hair and continued, 'When I said "books", it's more accurate to say "book" as it's a volume of the one-of-a-kind Cavendish family history.'

Eddie rolled his eyes. 'I see. Just my luck, I would be proclaimed a hero in a book that was never published.'

CHAPTER 19

Willow Wick, York - Georgiana

THE NEXT DAY dragged by as Caroline went about her duties and deliberately stayed out of George's way. She needed time to think—not that he made any effort to seek her out. She wouldn't blame him if he avoided her, after the uncomfortable and embarrassing scene that occurred between them in the stables.

They only met when she joined the family for dinner, which had become somewhat of a routine for the three women when George was in London. Now he was back, Caroline was concerned he would think her presumptuous and overreaching her station, but she did not wish to risk offending the countess, so she attended as usual.

'Olivia and Caroline have been most accomplished in their studies while you were away,' said the countess after they took their seats at the table, with George opposite her, and Olivia and Caroline on either side.

George raised his head and Caroline felt his eyes on her. She had no appetite, such were her nerves at dining with him again, but she went through the motions as though her entire world hadn't spun out of control and crashed upon his return. His dark eyes appraised her, and her cheeks burned as he studied her with his infuriatingly confident air, dashing as ever in a white ruffled shirt, elaborately embroidered waistcoat, and velvet breeches.

She thought him the epitome of assured elegance, which only unnerved her further.

'Yes, so I understand from Olivia,' he said, sipping his wine. 'And Mistress Caroline was kind enough to reply to my letter, detailing the books and subjects they have been studying with such dedication.'

Caroline tried to steady her hand while she raised her glass to her lips. Her other hand gripped at the skirts of her gown, out of sight, beneath the table. She hoped the undercurrent of irony in his voice, so apparent to her, went unnoticed by the countess, but Caroline saw Olivia watching them with unabashed curiosity.

'Perhaps, if they weren't quite so occupied riding back and forth to the village, my dear sister may have been even more dedicated to her studies,' he continued.

'George,' Olivia interjected. 'Pray do not be so harsh. I have made significant progress. Is that not so, Caroline?'

Caroline looked at him once more and their eyes clashed as though privately duelling. 'Indeed, you may rest assured, Mistress Olivia has been most attentive to her lessons in your absence,' she said.

'I am pleased to hear it,' he said, turning his attention to the rich selection of food on the serving plates, before he sought to entertain them with anecdotes of court life and the antics of the German born King George and Queen Caroline.

'How curious that you should both be named after the

king and queen,' remarked Olivia, looking from George to Caroline.

'It is merely a fashionable coincidence—George isn't named for the German king. He's named after your ancestors and continues a prodigious family tradition, going back hundreds of years. My memory fails me as to when the first boy in the family was named George. Your dear father would have known, of course.'

'Would it be in the family history books, Mother?' asked George. 'If father would have known, then I too should acquaint myself with the finer details of our lineage.'

The countess nodded and smiled; the pride etched on her face. She looked from Olivia to Caroline. 'I think it would be a worthy use of your time to study the family history with George.'

Caroline reached for her wine and took a large glug to fortify her nerves. If the countess knew of the tension between her and George, she imagined she wouldn't be so keen to throw them together in the name of their precious Cavendish lineage.

They ate and Caroline gradually calmed down and forced herself to appreciate the many lavish dishes which appeared before them like a display of England's finest foods. No sooner had they finished one serving, more were presented and piled onto the table by the immaculately dressed footmen.

Caroline felt queasy and had to draw on every reserve of composure to act as though it were normal for her to dine with the family. As much as by some strange twist of fate, her dreams taunted her with a different and most wonderful life where she was George's wife, she knew that could never be the reality in this one. The conversation washed over her as she reflected on George's earlier comment. She smiled and nodded her head at appropriate times, as though she were attentive, following Olivia's example.

Although she had thought George chivalrous when rescuing her from Ralph, he now seemed displeased, even angry. She didn't think it would be obvious to the others, but she sensed his moods keenly, almost as though an invisible cord connected them. She didn't understand it but thought it must be because of her dreams.

Caroline finished eating and prepared to take the first opportunity to excuse herself. She had longed for George's return, but now he was here, being in his presence was uncomfortable. She feared that his mother or sister, who were both quick witted, would observe her confused emotions and put two and two together to reach the dreadful conclusion that they must never reach, or she would be disgraced. Her father would never forgive her, and for all she wasn't of noble birth and heritage, her father had instilled in her a certain pride and care for their reputation.

She thought ruefully that he had often remarked she must take extra caution because she was poor at concealing her feelings and they were written all over her face for any fool to read.

Her mind had drifted off as she wondered what she could do to make future dinners easier to endure, without revealing her complicated feelings for George, when she noticed all eyes suddenly upon her.

'What say you, Mistress Caroline?' George said.

Caroline gulped. 'I beg your pardon, my lord—would you be so kind as to repeat the question? I confess my mind had wandered elsewhere…' she stuttered.

'I trust your mind was not pre-occupied with unpleasant acquaintances?'

'Whatever do you mean, George? Why would Caroline think of such a thing?' said the countess.

Caroline shook her head. 'No, my lord. It's simply that I have a headache and was thinking I might withdraw to my chamber.'

'In that case, my question is of no consequence. By all means—let us all retire. I am still weary from my journey, and with the house party descending upon us shortly, there is much for you ladies to do, and you must be fully rested. I know how you adore preparing for grand festivities such as these.'

House party?

She regretted not paying attention, for now she was caught off-guard and did not know to what he alluded.

Olivia chattered away, almost bouncing out of her chair, her cheeks pink and her dark eyes shining. 'I simply cannot wait. Thank you, dear brother, for arranging this. At last, we will have some company and entertainment from London, and it shall be almost as though I am at court.'

'Your court days shall come faster than you imagine,' said her mother, patting her hand. 'It is not wise to wish your life away, for I assure you the years pass soon enough.'

Caroline's stomach flipped, and nauseous waves rolled through her gut. The details of the pending house party were what she missed when she had been daydreaming.

'Mistress Caroline looks perplexed, so I shall repeat my news,' he said, turning his full attention to her. 'We are to have a house party from London to stay with us here at Willow Manor. As you see, Olivia is thrilled at the prospect, as I trust are you. I imagine it will delight you to meet my London companions and be introduced to court society.'

Caroline tensed beneath his enigmatic gaze, sensing he was mocking her once again, and wishing she could flee the room without appearing rude. She composed herself as best she could, not wishing for him to see he had affected her to such a degree.

'I am certain it will be quite lovely for you all. Olivia has longed for such a lavish social occasion. I, my lord, am but a humble governess and am not prepared or destined for court circles, as I'm sure you appreciate. I shall be only too pleased to eat dinner in the kitchen with the servants.'

She was relieved that her words had somehow assembled themselves coherently and been delivered in a sensible manner, despite her thudding heart.

'Oh no, may Caroline not join us? She is my lady's companion, after all, not only my governess. It would be most unfair for her to miss out on all the fun when it is usually so dull here,' said Olivia.

'Quite so,' said the countess, eyeing her daughter fondly. 'I am certain your father would approve of you learning the ways of society, Caroline, and it will prepare you to secure a future role once our darling Olivia marries.'

Olivia looked startled. 'It is some years before I will marry, Mother, but even when I do, I mean to always keep Caroline at my side as my companion.'

'Then it is agreed. I'm afraid you are not off the hook with such ease, Mistress Caroline, humble governess or no. If I am to suffer through another social whirl in the name of entertaining Olivia in my country seat and making her ready for court, then you shall not be excused either!' George said. 'You are, as Olivia says, her companion, so it is only fitting you should be at her side.'

A wicked smile played over his lips as he enunciated his clipped words, and Caroline had an unpleasant feeling he was teasing her.

She flushed and her cheeks burned as she tried to swallow.

Why did he taunt her so? He must see how uncomfortable she was at the prospect of a house party.

She didn't have any answers, but suspected he found her a

quaint, amusing distraction after the sophisticated circles he moved in at court. Caroline retired shortly after, pleading a headache, and returning to her chamber, desperate for solitude. She hadn't lied; her head was pounding and the muscles in her face ached from playing her part of engaged dinner companion for what had been an exhausting two hours.

That night she dreamed of a different George and awoke abruptly and pulled herself up in bed to rest against the cold wooden headboard, the sheet covering her chest, as the vivid images of another life flitted through her mind. The dark stillness of the midnight hour unnerved her even more, and she was tormented by the now familiar fear of the unknown.

She sat contemplating her fate, wondering what was to become of her. A wave of sickening dread swirled through her as she realised that not only did she not belong at Willow Manor, but she did not belong in Willow Wick either. She seemed not to belong in this life, or in the future life she dreamed about, which became more real with every passing night.

I am lost.

Willow Manor, York - Present Day

The grand opening was approaching fast, and the Willow Manor crew worked every hour to meet the deadline. Cara and George did numerous interviews with the press and radio, and Kate styled new exhibits about the various Tudor features on the estate, and she had a wonderful time plundering local antique stores for pieces she thought would help set the scene.

Cara and George had a rare break alone in the city and nipped for a coffee after one of the interviews.

'It's a shame we don't still have the Hampton Court interview about the Tudor Kings' Manuscript, isn't it? That would be fantastic publicity to highlight for the opening.'

Cara looked blank, her overworked brain tired and sluggish to respond. 'Aye—why don't we?'

George raised an eyebrow. 'It was all lost in the great timeline reset.'

'Oh yes, how could I forget? Mind you, at least we still have the manuscript. That is the jewel in the Cavendish crown and now we have a more impressive setting than your workshop for people to appreciate it.'

George referred to the dramatic events after they first met in the present day. Because of a misdirected time-travel experiment, George had disappeared. After a lot of confusion and heartache, eventually they were reunited.

Cara felt a stab of guilt about the upheaval to his life when he had lost the career that he so adored, but she reminded herself that if it hadn't happened, the odds were that they wouldn't be together now.

'And let's also not forget Kate! We wouldn't have her if it weren't for the great timeline reset…'

George nodded. 'True. Life wasn't as good without dear Kate.'

'Talking of Kate… The priest hole is going to be a sensation. People love heroes and mysteries. And she has done a marvellous job with the exhibit. She is having an excerpt of the piece about Eddie and the priest blown up and displayed, along with some other pieces, about the reformation and fate of the catholic priests of the day. That will point people to explore the library where the family history volumes can eventually be on display too,' said Cara.

'A cunning plan,' said George, taking a last swig of coffee and offering Cara his hand. 'Shall we get back? Lots to do and all that…'

She accepted his hand, and he pulled her gently to her feet.

'I'm still studying the Georgiana volume. I'd like to keep that back for now, if that's okay,' Cara said as they exited the coffee shop.

'Of course. The Tudorville volume can be made available, and as we have found no others yet, anyway, I don't know quite why we're referring to them as volumes! We only have two… unless you found some in those bottomless cupboards that so intrigue you?'

'No, I haven't had time to look again. I wonder if the others were lost or sold over the years, as surely they would be in the library if there was a collection.'

They chit-chatted all the way home, and George's parents called from the Caribbean to tell them they were having a wonderful time and to wish them luck with the grand opening.

The line crackled, but they could just make out George's father's voice. 'I forgot to say we have some family books for you. We found them in the attic the other week. Had forgotten all about them—they've been up there for years.'

Cara and George looked at each other. 'Which books, exactly?' asked George.

The line fizzed and crackled and the connection died before they could hear his reply. George called back several times, but the line refused to connect, and they heard a beeping noise.

'Damn it!' he said, and they jumped into George's pride and joy; his olive-green Porsche and hit the road back to Willow Manor.

CHAPTER 20

Willow Manor, York - Georgiana

THE DAYS FELL into a predictable rhythm after George's return and the house hummed with the news of the imminent arrival of the house party.

When Caroline entered the warm, homely kitchen for breakfast, she noticed an air of excitement amongst the servants.

'Harriet and Ruth, all the chambers must shine and look as gleaming as a royal palace,' said Mrs Burton, the housekeeper. 'I won't have Willow Manor falling short in the estimations of these grand folk. They shall return to London with only fine things to say of us... and needless to say that goes for the fayre at table, too, Cook.'

Cook glanced up from stirring her huge pot of broth. 'Have no fear, we shall feed them so well they will roll all the way back to London!'

'Good to hear. This is our first chance in many a year to

show off Willow Manor in all its glory, what with the late earl, God rest his soul, confined to bed and unable to entertain in his final years,' said Mrs Burton.

Caroline could see the housekeeper relished the challenge of impressing the visitors, and wished she were as excited at the prospect of the peaceful house being invaded by upper-class strangers. She turned her attention to her porridge, idly letting the servant's chit-chat wash over her as she thought about the upcoming intrusion and wished there was a way for her to avoid it.

'Prepare the blue chamber with the view of the river for Mistress Charlotte,' continued Mrs Burton, instructing the chambermaids.

'It's such a beautiful room, perfect for a future countess,' said Cook, a mischievous glint in her eyes as she seated her heavy frame at the table with a sigh.

'Aye,' said the housekeeper, 'and if the rumours are true, we shall have a new mistress soon enough.'

Giggles rose from the end of the table.

'What tickles you silly lasses?' asked Cook.

'We were just saying that the blue room is near his lordship's,' said Harriet, bursting into another fit of uncontrollable giggles.

'And you two don't have the sense you were born with,' said Cook, rolling her eyes.

Mrs Burton chastised them for being inappropriate and dispatched them to their labours instead of making idle chatter and bringing shame on their God-fearing household.

Caroline's porridge had lodged in her throat, and she found she now had no appetite. Her stomach churned, and she wanted to cry out, but she did her best to appear unconcerned by the romantic revelations concerning George's soon-to-be-bride.

'What's eating you, lassie?' said Cook, who Caroline

noticed was more astute than most. 'You're awfully quiet this morn and have a sour face, most unlike you. What's troubling you?'

Caroline assured her she was merely a little under the weather and quickly excused herself to prepare for lessons.

Her thoughts were spinning, and she wondered what she had done to deserve such unhappiness and to find herself in this impossible situation. There seemed no way out of this bind, short of resigning her post, but then she would have to leave Olivia and never see George again. She did not want to return to Willow Wick, but where could she go?

She entered the library and sank into a velvet-covered chair near the window through which the morning sunshine streamed. This was such a beautiful room, but she did not see or appreciate it today. Her mind kept repeating the name: Charlotte, Charlotte, Charlotte. Who was this Charlotte, who the servants seemed certain would be the next Countess Cavendish? And how had she missed the nuance of it when they were talking about the house party arriving?

Her stomach lurched again, and she let her head fall into her hands, and her elbows slump onto her knees. Tears pricked at her eyes, and she sniffed and groped for her handkerchief. It wouldn't do to fall apart when Olivia may enter at any moment. No, this was her secret to bear, and she must take her feelings for George to the grave. That was that—she would be a governess-spinster and when Olivia had no need for her any longer, she would seek a new post far from Willow Manor. No man would be a match for George Cavendish in her tender, bruised heart—of that much she was certain.

'Good day, Caroline,' boomed a familiar voice from the opposite side of the room. She lifted her head and started; nervous needles prickled her skin when she saw George rise from a chair in the corner, brushing his hand down his breeches, as if to remove a piece of fluff.

Caroline had noticed that was a habit of his, and she stared at him, her heart racing. He had been there all along, and the knowledge he had witnessed her emotional collapse crushed her further.

'Are you quite well, Caroline? I must apologise for startling you. I did not wish to disturb you and then it was too late to make my presence known,' he said. His dark eyes showed concern, and it took every drop of Caroline's willpower not to fall apart and let her tears flow. She found it somehow more difficult to keep her feelings from him when he was gentle and kind.

He continued, 'I have not had the good fortune to see you alone since my return, and I therefore haven't had the chance to thank you for your letter. I want you to know how much I appreciated your correspondence, and I apologise if I seemed ungrateful when I mentioned it to Olivia.' He dropped his head and avoided her eyes and then met them again swiftly, as if he'd made a decision. 'I was homesick, you see. Rather silly for a grown man, I know, but I much prefer York to London life, and your account of your days with Olivia cheered me.'

'I am pleased of it, my lord,' said Caroline, inclining her head slightly and then looking away. His dark-eyed intensity overwhelmed her, and she knew that for him it meant nothing, but to her his words were everything. He was waiting for his beloved Charlotte while she was in danger of reading what wasn't there into his polite address.

'I wondered if perhaps you are a little homesick, and that's what ails you? I couldn't help but notice your distress,' he said. 'Please do not take my comments about you dilly dallying in Willow Wick to heart—they were fuelled only by my distaste for the Knight fellow, and my concern that he harbours ill intentions.'

'Think nothing of it, my lord,' she said. 'You are most kind.'

'I would not have you suffer so because of one of my foolish remarks made in the heat of the moment—if you wish to visit your father, please do so with my blessing.' He looked into her eyes as if trying to read her soul. 'Please do have a mind to ride with one of the grooms to ensure your safety,' he added. 'We mustn't have you ladies riding about the countryside unattended.'

'Thank you, my lord. I am grateful for your concern and will visit my father at the earliest convenience, as you suggest.'

She was not homesick but was relieved about the misunderstanding. It would be unbearable if he knew she was falling apart over him, and she would put them both in an untenable spot.

'Right, that's settled then,' he said, looking at her and still making no move to leave.

'I must prepare for my morning with Olivia.' Caroline inclined her head and excused herself after what seemed like an age of awkward silence.

'Of course,' said George, bowing. He reached the door, turned abruptly, and then hesitated.

Caroline flicked through the book she had pulled from the shelf, not seeing a word, her senses crushing her ability to focus. She felt his eyes upon her and looked across at him. 'My lord?'

'Um… nothing,' he said. 'Nothing at all. I wish you a most pleasant day.'

He disappeared through the door, and the clip of his boots on the wooden floor grew distant until the room was silent.

She was alone with her raging heart.

Willow Manor, York - Present Day

Cara sat in the snug with the Cavendish family history book open on her lap. There was finally a lull in her schedule for her to concentrate on the volume she'd dug out of the kitchen cupboard.

Kate had gone into the city to look for some antique pieces and do some errands, so she would be out for most of the day, and George was overseeing what he called the final touches to the centre.

'Aren't final touches supposed to be *final*?' She'd remarked the other day with a wry smile.

George shook his head. 'I know, I know... You would think so, but the place never seems to be finished! There's always more to do for this opening.'

'I think that's what we've signed up for,' said Cara, 'so I suppose we'd better get used to it.'

George glanced at her, concern in his dark eyes. 'Once the new staff are trained and we've been through the inevitable teething phase of a new operation, we'll go away somewhere lovely for a break. Would you like that?'

Cara hugged him and said she would like that very much. She knew George was excited about the centre and it was wonderful to see him back to his old self and so engaged in his work again, but they could do with a break. She reassured him that holidays could wait while they launched the centre.

The intrigue built within her as she turned the pages of the exquisitely bound blue book. She'd only managed to read a few pages and now that she was about to lose herself in the old volume, she was excited.

The embossed gold lettering on the cover said it was Volume III and covered the Georgian period. The book George had found was Volume I, which covered the Tudor period and contained references to the Jesuit priest and Edward. So, if this was Volume III, presumably Volume II would cover the Stuart period. Cara wondered whether that was one of the books George's parents had mentioned, but for now she was content to have the Georgiana book in her hands and a bit of peace amid the recent mayhem to study it.

She read the introductory section on the family background and learned that the Cavendish family of Willow Manor, York, was related to another noble branch of the Cavendish family, whose family seat was *the* Chatsworth House.

Cara made some notes and then chewed on her pen. That was the house they'd used as Pemberley in one of the film adaptations of *Pride and Prejudice*. So that was why the Cavendish name had sounded so familiar to her when she'd first met George. And he wasn't one to name drop, so she'd never put two and two together. The book explained that the family descended from Sir John Cavendish, who took his name from a village in Suffolk, where he owned an estate.

There were references to the earl, William, and the countess, Margaret. The book also referenced their son, George, and daughter, Olivia, and she turned the page and held her breath in anticipation of finally discovering what happened to George and Caroline. All she had to go on so far were the snippets relayed to her by Kate and the rumours George had picked up in Victoriana.

But the page was blank…

She flicked over again, taking care not to let her impatient fingers damage the delicate old paper. But there were only more blank pages.

What the heck?

She turned some more pages, but the rest of the book was impossible to read. There was faint text on many of the pages, but it had faded to such a degree that it was illegible, and the pages had turned a dark yellow.

Cara had been counting on this book to provide the answers she needed to fill in the gaps about what happened to the family and the house between 1729 and 1840. She'd been hoping she would find that George had married Caroline, and all had worked out for the best following Sylvia's undoing of Ralph's hypnotic rewrite.

She flicked back to the first half of the book and read about the lives of George's parents and grandparents.

George entered the room. 'Hello, darling, I thought I'd pop in to have a bit of lunch with you.'

Cara looked up. 'It can't be lunchtime already?'

'I'm afraid so—an early one! How's it going with the Georgiana research?'

She ran her hand through her tousled hair. 'Terribly,' she said, sighing.

'Oh?'

She pointed to the blank pages and then flicked to the section with the faded text.

He squinted. 'I can't see a thing, other than blank discoloured pages.'

'Here, use my specs, she said, balancing them on his nose. Perhaps you can shed some light on why this might have happened, given your manuscript experience.'

'Lucky, I didn't forget everything when the timeline reset,' he said, peering at the pages.

'Looks like age damage to me—it's not been properly stored. Not surprising with it having been stuck in that kitchen cupboard for goodness knows how long, and who knows where it was before that?'

'But what about the blank pages? How do you explain that? Seems very odd…'

'I don't know, darling. It does seem odd,' he said. 'I think I'm too hungry to be useful right now, though!'

'Nothing new there,' she said, laughing. 'Let's make some sandwiches and sit out on the terrace.'

They munched on their sandwiches and drank tea, while Cara filled him in on the interesting highlights in the book.

'Did you know your family is related to the super wealthy Cavendish family of Chatsworth fame?' she asked.

He nodded. 'Yes, of course. Distant relatives, but hundreds of years ago I think we were closer.'

'You never thought to mention it? I feel like such a dimwit.'

He laughed. 'It never occurred to me. We live in completely different worlds. They kept their titles and wealth and we faded away from the aristocracy so there's no genuine connection anymore.'

'In that case, I imagine you also know that a George Cavendish from the other family branch was the biographer of Thomas Wolsey?'

He paused between bites, then nodded. 'It sounds vaguely familiar, but I must have sort of forgotten.'

'My goodness, you come from such lofty stock. You don't even think it's a big deal, do you?'

'No, I suppose I don't,' he laughed. 'I suppose that's why I'm so pleased we have Willow Manor back in the family. We may be the poor relations but at least we've got our family home back.'

'It was a relief to read that your ancestors weren't all named George! Your father in Georgiana was named William, which is a refreshing change…'

'Well, we can't all have the same name. George in the Georgian period is confusing enough!'

'I'm going to see what Sylvia makes of the faded text in the book. It seems like a strange coincidence that we can't read the exact section that we need to check how things turned out after the hypnotism.'

'You worry too much,' he said, touching her hand.

'Maybe so, but that's easy for you to say—you're not having crazy dreams about a past life. Caroline and George are not on track to marry; they've not even kissed as far as I can tell. I don't think he loves her in this version of events. I must find out what happened before it's too late, and we can still try to avert disaster.'

George nodded. 'I know I don't remember but I would put money on the fact that he loves you.'

'Let's hope you're right,' she said.

'Is there anything I can do?'

'I don't think so—unless you can talk some sense into the former version of yourself. Honestly, I wish I could shake him and wake him up to the truth,' said Cara, biting her lip.

'Can't you tell him what's really going on and explain that he mustn't marry Charlotte?'

Cara sighed. 'If only—but what would I say? "Oh, by the way, I'm your wife from the twenty-first century, and if you don't marry me instead of Charlotte, we're going to lose our future together?" He would probably think me quite mad with jealousy and I'd only drive him faster into her arms.'

'I see the difficulty—although didn't you tell me we had a similar conversation when George was getting into all sorts of trouble during the Pilgrimage of Grace?'

'Yes, but I was your wife then, not a lowly governess in your household. You trusted me—it was different, and you still assumed I must be a witch!'

George wrapped his arms around Cara, and she leaned on him and relaxed into his solid warmth.

'So, what are you going to do, darling?' George said.

'Well, I am not letting that bloody karmic warrior get the better of us. He predicted he would rewrite our destiny and I'm beginning to fear he pulled it off… We must find a way to stop him.'

CHAPTER 21

Willow Manor, York - Georgiana

CAROLINE STIRRED AT FIRST LIGHT, groggy from a night of fitful, anguished sleep. Anxiety had overcome her, and she could not drift into the usual vivid dreams of her other life with George, such was her apprehension about meeting the woman he would surely marry.

The fear of falling short in her efforts to conduct herself suitably in society with his dark, all-knowing eyes upon her plagued her, and she could get no respite from her cascade of troubling thoughts.

Rising early, washing, and dressing hurriedly in the cold early morning chill, she went down to the kitchen for breakfast, meaning to avoid the house party and disappear before they arrived. After barely touching her meal, she sought Olivia out to excuse herself from greeting the party on the grounds of being unwell. She hastily retired to her room before anyone could question her further.

Her body was fit, but her mind and spirit were bruised to the core, and she didn't know how she would muster the strength to get through the coming days.

During breakfast, the servants had been all a-chatter, like excited birds at feeding time. The thrill of imminently having such esteemed guests in the house was palpable and they questioned how many of the party would bring their personal entourage. Harriet and the other young maids whispered and giggled about the possibility of meeting a handsome beau from one of the London households. Their wild imagination soon had them swept away into wedlock and moving to the big city with their new loves.

Their whispers and giggles grew louder until Cook tut-tutted and called for order. 'Hush, you silly lasses. We'll have no more of this nonsense, or whatever will they think of us?'

CAROLINE WATCHED DISCREETLY from the safe harbour of her chamber window as the house party swept down the majestic willow tree-lined drive, in a parade of impressive coaches and carriages, and halted in front of the Tudor-style country manor house.

As soon as Caroline lay eyes on the beautiful young lady in a sumptuous golden gown, her red hair curled and pinned elegantly beneath her lace cap, and elegant backless mules peeping from beneath the hem of her gown as she descended from the coach, Caroline knew with sickening certainty that she must be Charlotte, George's prospective wife.

She knew even before George appeared and advanced towards the coach. Her insides lurched as he bowed and kissed the young beauty's hand. They then turned as one when he gallantly offered her his arm and escorted her into the house, gaily chattering and laughing as they walked; a trail of finely dressed figures following closely behind the couple. George cut a dashing figure in his long, fitted coat and fashionable wig, and Caroline withdrew from the window, a sharp pain eviscerating her heart, and a sickness pervading her entire being.

Sylvia's Office, York - Present Day

Cara sat in Sylvia's room in her usual spot, watching her flip through the heavy buckram bound volume.

'So, this is supposed to cover the Georgian period, but there's nothing legible after around the time when the karmic warrior intervened?'

'That's right,' said Cara.

'Hmm,' she said, holding the faded text up to the light in an attempt to decipher some of the words. 'It's almost as if your permission to access the book has been revoked. I wonder whether it's a result of the timeline reset from when he hypnotised you.'

'I thought so too, but George thinks I'm overreacting. I don't know if it's logical, but it just seems like too much of a coincidence that the text on the pages I most need to read now to find out what happened immediately after that time, has disappeared.'

Sylvia studied Cara over her spectacles. 'My instincts tell me something isn't right. Would you like to ask the cards for guidance?'

Cara nodded. She coughed to clear her dry throat and then rose to pour herself a glass of water before they began. She had mixed emotions when it came to the cards—they had guided her correctly and helped her profoundly in the past, but she found the readings nerve-wracking as she never knew what outlandish thing she would be called to do next in her quest to fulfil her Twin Flame mission.

'Are you time travelling again?' asked Sylvia.

'Yes, and no… not in the usual way, but I am having incredibly vivid dreams and I know things about Caroline's life I couldn't possibly know any other way. . . So, if there is such a thing, I seem to be time travelling through my dreams as I told you last time. I think I travelled on demand via the priest hole too, when I did the experiments with Eddie, but we can't be sure.'

'Every time I think your story can't get any more intriguing, you come in here and casually drop something like that into the conversation.'

Sylvia shuffled her cards, and Cara waited, heart drumming and nerves fluttering wildly, causing her to feel nauseous.

'You know the drill,' said Sylvia, raising her gold-flecked eyes to Cara's. 'Are you okay? Sure you want to do this?'

'I'm not okay—but yes, I'm sure! We need all the help we can get to figure out what the hell went on in those critical years. It occurred to me that just because Willow Manor reappeared after we reset the timeline following the hypnotic curse, it doesn't guarantee we lived happily ever after, does it?'

'No—good point. As I recall, all we know is that the estate reappeared after we rewrote the timeline and instructed Caroline to fall in love with George, and not marry Ralph. On reflection, I don't think I told you to marry George because I was concerned about the potential repercussions. So, as it is, you may or may not have married him,' said Sylvia, still holding the cards.

'Yes, and I tried finding out who George married via the records office, but they couldn't find any documents. The whole thing just keeps getting more and more mysterious.'

'Okay, well, this is as good a time as any to ask the cards for help. Have your question top of mind and be ready to tell me when to stop,' said Sylvia, accustomed to instructing her clients step-by-step, even though Cara knew what to do.

Several seconds passed as Sylvia dealt the assorted cards onto the table, and Cara signalled for her to stop.

Sylvia flipped the card over. 'Ah...' she said.

'What?' Cara moved her head closer to study the card. 'I don't think I've seen that one before: The Hierophant. He looks like some kind of priest.'

Sylvia nodded. 'It's a major arcana card from the Tarot, and is the masculine counterpart to the High Priestess, sometimes known as the pope or the teacher. This looks like the perfect card for you on numerous levels.'

'In what way?' said Cara.

'What's your question for this card and let's see.'

'I don't have a specific question—I just wanted to show you the family history book and ask for guidance on what to do.'

Sylvia's eyes narrowed as she studied Cara's. 'And the card you get is that of a high priest!'

Cara nodded but remained silent, waiting for Sylvia to elaborate.

'I would normally say that's an obvious sign for you to enter the priest hole again, but as you already access Georgiana through your dreams, it may only be symbolic of the timeline. Let's not jump to conclusions because there are many facets to this card.'

'Thank you,' said Cara, her chest tight as she tried to calm herself by breathing steadily as she waited to see her fate.

Sylvia pointed to the two figures who knelt in front of the priest. 'This card is about tradition, and when the card is upright like this, it symbolises marriage. More accurately, it could indicate some type of arranged marriage. Now if it was reversed, that would mean the rejection of family values, but in this case, it would indicate a compliance with duty and tradition.'

Cara nodded again. 'George is expected to marry a woman of his class, not a governess… obviously. The servants were talking about how they think he's soon going to marry this woman he knows from court, called Charlotte.'

'I see,' said Sylvia, her eyes narrowed, and she twirled her spectacles between her fingers.

'Sometimes my dreams are fuzzy, and I don't remember much in the morning, but others, it's incredibly vivid, and I remember detailed conversations. The last one I recall is that Caroline is dreading a house party arriving from London because she can't bear to witness George falling in love and marrying another woman. She's in a terrible bind!'

'Do you see the karmic pattern repeating itself from when you met in the present day? George is with another woman but is in love with you. It's classic Twin Flames; they fall into the same trap of running from their heart's desire, over and over until they truly learn the karmic lesson and heal, by not allowing their need for approval to determine their actions,' said Sylvia.

'I just don't know what to do.'

'Your dreams sound fascinating. You talk as though that other life is unfolding for you now—is it really that tangible?'

Cara took a sip of water. 'It's the weirdest thing; in some ways it's even more disconcerting than when I time travel in the vortex because then I am awake and more or less understand what's going on. But now… it's like I have another whole life playing out in my subconscious at night, but I'm merely an observer. I can't influence what happens like I used to. I just have to watch it happen, which is a hell all of its own. And to confuse things even more, Caroline dreams about this life, which is her future life.'

'That must be confusing,' said Sylvia. 'So, the significance of this reading could be that George and Charlotte are currently destined to marry, but that doesn't mean it can't change.'

Cara pulled a face. 'I know we're together in this life, so maybe it's greedy and selfish to expect to be with him in every timeline—maybe I should just let it go however it wants to go, but it's so painful to watch him with someone else.'

Sylvia covered Cara's hand with her warm one, and her green and gold cat-like eyes radiated empathy. 'It's not greedy and selfish to want to be with your ultimate soul mate. And besides, there's an even bigger problem if you ignore your heart in your attempt not to be selfish,' she said.

Cara's expression brightened at the thought of not having to suffer through George marrying Charlotte and witnessing Caroline broken hearted and cast aside. 'Is there?'

'You two are Twin Flames, and it is your destiny to be in union. Without that, terrible things happen. I know this only too well from my own journey, as do you.'

Sylvia closed her eyes.

'George marrying the wrong woman could be why he had a breakdown and gambled Willow Manor in a card game and tried to burn it down in an act of total self-destruction. If he ran from Caroline, the other half of his soul, and chose his duty over love, he will most certainly have struggled to bear it. Twin Flame love is a soul deep connection and no matter how long and far someone runs, it cannot be denied or disconnected.'

Cara's eyes welled with tears and her chest was thick with emotion. She sniffed and shook her head. 'Sorry, I don't know why this affects me so—everything is fine with George. He's at home at Willow Manor,' she said with a watery smile.

'Don't apologise. Your soul carries the weight of your past lives, which is why it's critical that you heal and resolve the past karma of every timeline whenever you are given the opportunity. Remember what Ralph told you? He said he was burning in karmic hell because of his desire for revenge.'

'I remember, but I don't understand how that helps us heal.'

'We don't know what happens when you choose a different path and what the impact on his life would be, but what we do know, is the life that's unfolding in your dreams, looks destined for disaster and that won't help any of you.'

Cara winced. 'So, what should I do?'

'You know, as tempting as it can sometimes be, I must not tell you what to do. I can only show you the paths open to you, so you may follow your intuition about the best one to travel.'

Sylvia pointed to the crossed keys on the Tarot card. 'The keys represent the balance between the conscious and the subconscious minds, and the unlocking of mysteries for the Initiates to reach the next level. It's a rite of passage for you and George to fulfil your appointed roles. Let us not forget that you are multi-generational Twin Flames which brings the added complexity of hundreds of years.'

She touched the book as if trying to glean answers, and then shook her head and stared at Cara, her eyes widening. 'What am I talking about? You two have been connected for *thousands* of years.'

Cara stared at Sylvia. 'How do you know?'

'I feel it through the energy of the pages.'

Sylvia closed her eyes, her hand still touching the pages of the book as she began to speak in the staccato-like tone Cara recognised from previous readings.

'Your souls were present at the time of the Jewish Second

Temple when Jerusalem was ruled by the Romans,' Sylvia said, blinking as she emerged from the vision.

Cara's stomach knotted as Sylvia revealed her revelation.

'What on earth was all that about?' Cara asked.

'That was the most intense vision I've ever had. I saw the high priest in the Temple.'

The reading had come to an end and Cara left the building in a daze. Her future and her past flashed before her eyes.

CHAPTER 22

Willow Manor, York - Georgiana

Caroline and Olivia sat next to the window doing their needlework in the blue drawing room, when George's head appeared around the door.

'Ah, there you are. I was just telling Charlotte about the wonderful progress Olivia has made since you came to us. Do you mind if we join you for a moment?'

Without giving her time to reply, he turned and ushered Charlotte in, whose red curls framed her beautiful, heart-shaped face. Caroline reluctantly laid down her needlework on the window seat and Olivia did the same, and they stood simultaneously to greet their visitors. Olivia's cheeks were rosy with delight at the unexpected attention, while Caroline's grew pink with the strain of suppressing her feelings. The last thing she wished for was to be singled out by George and his soon to be betrothed, but she must be courteous.

'Good afternoon, my lord... Mistress Charlotte. I trust you are enjoying your stay at Willow Manor, and it is not too quiet for you after life at court.' She curtsied as they approached, and directed her comment to Charlotte.

The young woman smiled in return and inclined her head, seeming genuinely pleased to seek them out. 'How kind of you. I must say, Willow Manor is quite as delightful as dear George promised me. He said I would fall in love with the estate, and his prediction has already come true.'

Caroline attempted a smile, but it was more of an awkward grimace, and she prayed they wouldn't notice how ill at ease she was in their company. A mottled blush spread up her neck to her face and she longed to flee the room, but she stood firm and replied, 'How wonderful. I am not at all surprised—the estate is one of the most beautiful for miles around.'

Charlotte continued, 'Lord Cavendish tells me you are still quite new to the position of governess but are doing splendidly.'

Caroline's cheeks burned hotter, and a trickle of perspiration slid down her spine beneath her tight garments. 'How generous of my lord, to say so,' she stuttered, trying to keep herself together but fearing she was failing terribly and making a complete fool of herself.

Charlotte turned her attention to Olivia, and indicated they should sit, and then they discussed the perils of needlework and Charlotte admitted she was a poor seamstress and her talents lay more in the musical arena.

'You simply must play for us,' said Olivia, and George agreed, showing rather too much enthusiasm for Caroline's liking.

He was clearly very taken with Charlotte, and who could blame him? Of course, George would admire such an elegant woman of his own class, and no doubt he would marry her in due course. How could it be otherwise? Caroline's spirits sunk like a heavy anchor, and she went through the motions of resuming her needlework, doing her utmost to look poised and unaffected by the happy couple's presence, while inwardly she crumbled.

Charlotte and Olivia continued to exchange pleasantries, and she stabbed at the cushion cover she had been tasked with mending before cautiously raising her eyes. Her breath caught in her chest as her eyes met George's and she saw he was examining her with some curiosity.

'Mistress Caroline, you seem not quite yourself. I was sorry to hear you were unwell.'

'I am much recovered my lord, thank you.'

Her cheeks burned and her thoughts spun faster than her needle, as she reasoned he would, of course, be used to the effect he had on women, so it was nothing strange for him to see her nervous. He no doubt found it a dreadful bore to have young women swooning over his every word and would be relieved to have met his match in the confident and accomplished Charlotte.

Caroline straightened her shoulders and resumed her sewing with a vengeance, praying they would soon leave them in peace, but George was not done with her yet.

'I didn't realise you took your needlework so seriously,' he said, raising one eyebrow, his smile lighting up his eyes.

Caroline's heart pounded as he continued to appraise her, and he seemed in no rush to stop. Charlotte and Olivia continued their conversation about music, until Charlotte rose, almost reluctantly, as if she could quite happily spend all day talking to Olivia.

'We must leave you to your needlework, but I look forward to seeing you at dinner. Perhaps dear Olivia, we may play together?'

'That's settled then,' said George. 'And on another occasion, Mistress Caroline shall join you at the pianoforte. I have heard she plays like an angel.'

Caroline opened her mouth to protest, but then she saw the gleam in his eyes and knew he was teasing her.

'If only that were true.' Despite her determination not to encourage him, he had a knack for disarming her when she least expected it.

Charlotte smiled and said, 'I'm sure a little practice is all you need. I was fortunate to play for my dear sisters who had to endure many an off-note in my quest for improvement.'

Caroline found herself warming to Charlotte's easy manner and sincere remarks, despite her anguish. As they took their leave, no doubt to join the rest of the house party, she told herself it was just as well because if the servants were correct, Charlotte would soon be the new mistress of the house and her new employer.

Barely a moment after the door closed, Olivia whispered to Caroline over her cushion cover, 'What do you make of Mistress Charlotte?'

'She seems a fine woman,' replied Caroline, wondering how to distract Olivia so they wouldn't spend the rest of the morning talking about Charlotte.

'Yes, but do you think she would make a good wife for my brother?' Olivia asked, her eyes probing Caroline's in earnest.

'I have no experience in these matters, dear Olivia. What do you think?'

'I think I would be happy to have her for my sister,' she declared, looping and tying her thread with impressive precision. 'But if the truth be known, I would rather have you for my sister,' she added, her face splitting into a mischievous grin.

Caroline squeezed Olivia's hand. 'You are a very dear girl,' she replied, choking back the emotion to check the tears that threatened to fill her eyes. 'How would you like to go for a ride, just you and me?'

Olivia's eyes lit up, and they tidied their needlecraft away briskly and went to their chambers to change.

After Caroline dressed in her riding habit, she glanced out of the window and spotted Charlotte and George in the courtyard, headed in the direction of the stables, and she immediately regretted suggesting they go for a ride. She decided to delay a little before going down, so they wouldn't bump into the lovebirds again. It was more than she could bear.

Willow Manor, York - Present Day

Cara and George sat in the blue drawing room. 'This needs a complete overhaul,' she said, touching the faded blue paper on the wall. 'It looks as though they have decorated it in various shades of blue over the years. This room was a stunning shade of blue in Georgiana, but I recall it was much darker in our Tudorville days.'

'Makes sense—the style was more formal and sombre then. I'll add this to our extremely long list of rooms that need a complete overhaul,' said George dryly.

'Good idea, darling.'

George's phone rang. 'Hello Professor,' he said, and then paused for a minute, and sat down on one of the chesterfields as he listened to Eddie. Cara continued touching sections of the wall and poking about the room, trying to get a vision for how to bring it back to life and restore it to a more modern version of its former glory.

'Yes, she's right here with me. Her phone must be off.'

George passed his phone to Cara, and she walked to the

window and gazed out at the lush gardens, spotting Swifty and Cornelius in one of the flower borders.

'Thanks for calling back, Eddie. I tried to reach you after I visited Sylvia, but I think you must have been in class.'

She told him about Sylvia's strange vision when she touched the book.

'I've decided it's time to attempt to time travel on demand again. I've had enough of observing from my dreams— I must take a more proactive role, or I'll go bonkers.'

'I think that's a smart decision,' he said.

'Hmm, I thought you might.'

'What in particular are you aiming to do if you reach Georgiana?'

She filled him in on the faded pages of text in the family history book.

'It sounds as though you've created quantum time loops and the timeline is resetting again,' he said.

'That's more or less what Sylvia suspects.'

'Oh yes, what else did she say?' he asked.

'She reminded me that when we rewrote the timeline after Ralph Knight's hypnotic curse, she was careful not to instruct Caroline to marry George, but only to take the position... just because Willow Manor reappeared, doesn't mean that they lived happily ever after, does it?'

'Ah, I see. Why didn't she specify you marry?'

'Because we don't know whether we were supposed to marry.'

He clicked his tongue, and she imagined the professor's brain turning the problem around and assessing it from all angles. 'I wonder if you might meet me in Georgiana,' he said after a few seconds of silence that seemed longer as she waited.

'That would be nice. Have you been having dreams too?'

'No, it's only that we are in the other timelines together,

so there's a high mathematical probability we'd be together in this one too.'

Cara chuckled. 'Maths or no maths, what it really comes down to, is you don't like the idea of missing out, do you?'

'You've got me. I can't stand it!' He paused, and then continued, 'I also don't like the idea that you are alone there without an ally.'

'That's so sweet, Eddie. I would certainly prefer to have you with me, but I haven't noticed anyone resembling you in my dreams, but who knows—maybe you'll surprise me if I manage to travel through the priest hole this time.'

'Wormhole…,' he laughingly reminded her.

'It sounds so unappealing!'

'Okay, well I will take heart in knowing you are not entirely alone—George will be with you.'

'Um, unfortunately he's busy courting another woman, which is one reason I have to go!'

'Oh lord, not that again.'

They talked a bit longer about the possible vagaries of time travel, and she promised to keep him in the loop.

'Good luck,' he said before ringing off.

She felt George's eyes on her. 'When are you going?'

Cara walked towards him, and he opened his arms and held her. 'I think I need to do it soon. Things are moving fast in Georgiana. If I am to stop them marrying and make you realise we should be together, I am up against it.'

'All right, but please promise me one thing…'

She moved her head from the comfort of his embrace and raised her eyes to his. 'What?'

'Promise not to hold it against me if the 1729 version of me does something to hurt you. Remember, I have no control over what he does.'

She nodded, and her eyes shone. 'I promise—I learned my

lesson last time. You're right, it's unfair to hold you accountable for choices you made in a different life.'

'I can say on behalf of all versions of George Cavendish that we never mean to hurt you. Sometimes we are just complete arses!'

She laughed through her tears.

He crushed her tightly against him and they stood as one for several minutes. Cara wished she could stay like that forever, in the safe cocoon of his strong arms. But then she eased away gently, wiped her eyes, and said, 'I think I should go now.'

George nodded. 'If you're sure you want to do this, then yes, we may as well get it over with. Hopefully you'll retain your memory, and when you return, you'll know what's happening there.'

'I only plan to check what's going on. I'm hoping things are farther ahead than in my dreams, and something stopped George from marrying Charlotte. If things are going in the right direction for them to fall in love and somehow be together, there's nothing for me to do.'

George tilted her chin upwards. 'And if they're not going in the right direction?'

'Then I can only hope I'll have the consciousness and memory to know I have to act to put things right.'

George helped her into the priest hole and handed her the torch. 'Shall I come in with you?'

She shook her head. 'Better not—just in case. We don't want to risk the vortex taking you too, or who knows where we'll end up? Maybe in ancient Jerusalem!'

She kissed him once more and stepped further into the passageway, before turning her head and calling, 'I love you.'

'I love you,' he replied, his voice echoing through the cold, hollow space.

He waited at the entrance, watching the light from the

torch grow dimmer, and after a few minutes he heard the familiar whooshing sound, and a chill touched his skin and he shivered.

'It's working,' she called, her voice faint as the vortex encircled her and the noise filled her ears.

And then she was gone.

CHAPTER 23

Willow Manor, York - Georgiana

Cara found herself sitting next to Olivia on one side and a ruddy faced man she didn't recognise, on the other. The table was laden with delicacies and judging by the appearance and high spirits of the guests; they were already merry on wine.

She looked around and saw George at the head of the table. He was deep in conversation with Charlotte, but she was seated too far away to catch their conversation. She saw Charlotte touch his hand as she talked, and her red curls fell seductively, framing her radiant face.

Before Cara could remind herself not to stare, George raised his eyes directly to hers and she froze, caught in the act. Surely, he would read her expression and realise she was in love with him. His lips formed the ghost of a smile, and he raised an eyebrow, before turning his full attention back to Charlotte, who was enraptured by his company.

The jolt reverberated through her entire being. Not this

again… why did it keep happening? Why must she and George keep performing this heart-breaking dance? If this was to fulfil their Twin Flame mission, why must she be in this position where he was loved by another woman?

Her feelings merged with Caroline's, causing her mind to swim and her heart to pound uncontrollably. She wished she could flee the room, but that would draw too much attention, which was what she most needed to avoid.

She took a deep breath and told herself she had chosen to come back to Georgiana. She had chosen to time travel on demand, and she knew what to expect, so she mustn't let her feelings overwhelm her. She had a job to do, and it must begin with seeing what was going on and from there she would decide what to do, if anything.

Stay calm, Cara. George is your husband, and he loves you. This is just a blip in the timelines, and this is your opportunity to fix it.

George's face loomed in her mind, and she saw the love in his eyes before they parted in the library, and she entered the priest hole. She vowed to pull herself together, even as the trauma of the past stirred in her soul and ripped through her heart, creating a painful conflict which she feared must show on her face.

George's eyes sought her out again, but she quickly averted hers. He mustn't see her looking devastated—it could serve no useful purpose now. If he was going to fall in love with her so they could fulfil their Twin Flame destiny and reach union in every timeline, it wouldn't come from pity and from her seeing her as a shadow of her true self.

'I understand you are the governess to young Olivia, my dear?' said the ruddy faced man at her side, raising his glass to his lips, and giving her a lascivious smile.

She shuddered, and out of the corner of her eye, saw George staring at her, more openly this time.

An idea entered her mind, and she leant into the ruddy faced man and whispered in his ear.

The man laughed and moved closer to her, brushing her elbow as he talked and refilled her glass. She deliberately avoided George's eyes, but she knew they were fixed upon her.

So, this was how she must play the game to get his attention in this life. If she had to bet on it, she would put her money on him having more feelings for her than he had let on. He had seemed so formal, polite—even stilted in what she had seen of him in this life, but here was her George: a flesh and blood male. She risked a glance in his direction and saw he was still looking at her, and there was a fiery disapproval in his eyes.

Could the lord of the manor already have feelings for the lowly governess?

Cara needed to keep her edge if she was to discover what the state of affairs between them truly was, and so she turned back to the ruddy faced man, named Charles, and she flirted with him demurely. It was a delicate balance; she needed to keep George's attention but avoid attracting the countess's. She was just a governess and was supposed to be setting an example for Olivia. Mind you, in those days, a woman's only role was to secure a good husband, and so perhaps she was setting a more helpful example for Olivia than she would like.

Either way, sweet Olivia deserved a much younger man, and so did Caroline, for that matter. Charles must be sixty if he was a day, and far too old for her, but she noticed that didn't deter him.

'Are you married, Charles?' she enquired, to keep the conversation going and remind him of his duties. 'Alas, no,' he said, taking another huge slug of wine. 'My dear wife passed away last year, and I am alone. I must confess I find it a lonely life.'

His eyes showed he would be more than open to the company of a young woman such as herself, and she drew back a little. He leaned into her again, and she had to force herself to play the game. She glanced in George's direction and pretended to be looking at the other guests, but in that second, she glimpsed the thunderous expression on his face.

Okay, welcome back George. He clearly had feelings for her—the mark of jealousy was all over his handsome face.

Now she must find out how far their relationship had developed. She guessed they weren't yet intimate. Charlotte was also casting glances at her—the young woman was no fool and must have noticed there was something going on between them. She turned back to Charles to press her advantage. She would see how far she could push George. That was the only way she would know how far things had gone between them and how deep were his feelings for Caroline.

Time travel on demand was now proven to work, at least in one direction. Last time, she had travelled to Georgiana and returned, presumably through the vortex, with no memory of what happened. She was conscious that she could potentially be swept away to present day at any moment, but there was also the chance that she may be able to travel on demand to return whenever she wished.

There was only one way to find out, but she had more to do first and intended to make use of every moment when she was here as Cara, and not at the mercy of her dreams, having her heart broken as she came to terms with the tragic reality of the class divide between her and George in the eighteenth century.

She risked another look in George's direction and her heart hurt when she saw he appeared to be absorbed in deep conversation with Charlotte, who was laughing and giddy to have regained his full attention. Caroline continued the flirting charade with Charles, but she knew instinctively that George had withdrawn and would not look over at her again.

She knew him inside out, whatever timeline they were in.

Charles was disappointed when her interest in him abruptly diminished, but he continued to try and capture her attention with tales of his magnificent house in London and how he was certain she would adore his children. He even ventured so far as to hint she might wish to become their governess, rather than Olivia's.

Caroline's painful thoughts attacked Cara's mind as the young girl became more and more distraught at the realisation that George would be with Charlotte. Cara's logical mind told her to stay calm so she could succeed in carrying out her mission, but she feared she was fighting a losing battle against Caroline's volatile emotions, and she would break down at any moment.

This must be what it's like having a split personality...

Caroline was questioning her violent reaction and hating herself for her jealousy of Charlotte, which gnawed at her like a disease. Caroline had never experienced such intense feelings before, and everything was spinning out of control. She wished she had a good reason to dislike Charlotte, but she seemed like a lovely girl, which made Caroline feel even more ashamed.

She confronted the truth: she despised Charlotte and wished never to see her again. It was too painful seeing her with George.

THAT NIGHT GEORGE dreamt of Caroline. Again. He woke in the darkest, most silent part of the night, before dawn seeped into the sky, and he thrashed about in his bed, unable to fall back to sleep. Caroline's sweet face monopolised his mind and the thought of her with Charles, the wealthy industrial baron, filled him with hopelessness. He didn't know the baron well; a friend of a friend had invited him to join the house party, but he knew enough of his reputation to know he wasn't the sort to be tied down by family duty. He had made his money in the colonies, and George suspected he wouldn't think twice about taking Caroline as his mistress, if she were to oblige him.

He wondered why he cared so deeply. Why did a lowly servant girl from a questionable background haunt his dreams every night so he could know no peace? It was as though there was some kind of an unspoken bond between them, and he was helpless to break it. His duty was to marry Charlotte and make her his wife, as everyone expected. He had no doubt she would fulfil the role of the next Countess Cavendish perfectly, and she was bright, and he was fond of her. Perhaps over time his feelings for her would grow, but he didn't love her—he wasn't inflamed like he was when Caroline entered a room. Her mere presence touched him in a way he had never known, and much less expected. He'd thought love was for saps and he would find a good woman to marry and carry on the noble line in the Cavendish way. But since she had appeared in his life like an ocean of loveliness, he could think of little else—he was bewitched.

George remembered the day when her letter arrived for him to Kensington Palace, and he rushed to his rooms to tear open the correspondence like a parched man desperate for a drink.

He shook his head and then rose quietly from the edge of the bed and fumbled about in the bottom of his bedside drawer and extracted the letter. He had lost count of the number of times he had read it, so what was one more if it gave him some shred of comfort?

My dearest Lord Cavendish,

I received your letter with pleasure and may assure you that all is well with Olivia. She has taken to her studies more enthusiastically than one could hope, and we have been reading Oedipus Rex together daily, as you recommended, and we have found ourselves most enthralled by the day-to-day life of Ancient Greece. If the play continues to hold her interest, we may have even read all of Sophocles' works by the time you return.

We also ride most days for exercise and fresh air, and the weather is reasonably fine. Please have no fear for her safety. I shall ensure we take a groom with us when we ride off the estate towards Willow Wick or further, as you instructed.

Everyone is well here, but as no doubt they have told you, your company is sorely missed by your mother and sister, and I am certain you will hear from them soon, if you haven't already.

Be well, your lordship, and know that your sister is in good hands,

Blessings,
Caroline

And what of you, dear Caroline? Did you miss me too, or was that letter merely a function of your duty to your employer?

The thought plagued him still; sometimes he imagined he detected admiration and even love for him in her eyes, but after this evening, he had lost all hope and was tortured by the thought of her with another man. He didn't blame her—

how could she love him when she saw him sworn to another, and out of reach entirely to a woman of her station?

The truth was, he hadn't been able to bring himself to ask for Charlotte's hand in marriage. His mother had been dropping the most unsubtle hints ever since she'd arrived, and she clearly approved of the match. And yet, as perfect as their union would be on paper, he couldn't tie himself to Charlotte while his heart was so clearly Caroline's.

He sighed at the impossible dilemma in which he found himself, folded the letter and tucked it back into the drawer beneath his monogrammed silk handkerchiefs, and away from prying eyes.

George rose from the bed and pulled the curtain aside to reveal the first signs of a glorious dawn spreading across the Yorkshire valley. The sky held a hint of gold, with a splash of vibrant pink sprayed across the horizon like a painter's watercolour. The sun would soon be up, and sleep was no friend of his, so he dressed briskly in his riding breeches and jacket, splashed cold water on his face, and left the room, shutting the door quietly, careful not to wake anyone.

He craved some time alone and would go for a long ride before breakfast when the house party would buzz into life, and Charlotte would seek him out, no doubt expecting a proposal on the last day of her visit. He sighed again and walked down to the basement level to find his leather riding boots, which he left outside the kitchen door, ready for a quick exit to the stables. As he bent to ease his foot into one of the boots, he heard a faint noise coming from the kitchen, and raised his head to listen. There it was again.

He thought it must be one of the servants but decided he had better check no thief had found their way into the kitchen under cover of night. George left his boots where he'd found them and crossed towards the kitchen door, turning the handle slowly, and pushing the door open a crack before peering into the still room. He cast his eyes about and saw no one. As he had thought, not even Cook was in the kitchen at this hour, and the fire hadn't been rebuilt yet for the day but glowed gently with the remains of the night's embers. Just as he was about to back away and close the door, thinking he had mistaken the wind for someone in the kitchen, he noticed a hunched figure in the chair in the far corner. His eyes adjusted to the early morning meagre light, and he realised who it was. His heart flipped wildly, and he knew not what to say, and so he hesitated, trying to gather his words, and as he did, she raised her head, saw him, and jumped to her feet.

'Oh, my lord,' she cried, her misty grey eyes widening as they studied his face. 'I did not mean to disturb you… It's only that I couldn't sleep, and I thought this would be a quiet place to sit before the house awakens.'

On closer inspection, he saw her eyes were puffy and swollen. 'I did not mean to disturb you, either. I too could not sleep and meant to go for a ride, but I heard a noise and thought I had better check all was well.'

She was distressed by him seeing her upset, and she hastily wiped her eyes.

'I do not wish to pry, but are you all right, Caroline? It pains me to see you in such distress.'

She busied herself patting her messy hair and straightening her petticoat, hoping to distract him from the state of her face. George moved a step closer, and he saw her cheeks were flushed, and her eyes shone with the residue of tears. That's what the sound was. He longed to comfort her but held himself tightly in check.

She raised her innocent tear-stained face to his and his resolve crumbled as they stumbled towards each other like an unstoppable hurricane. As he pulled her into his arms, his lips found hers, and they kissed, first tentatively, then harder as she returned the force of his kiss. Moments passed as she stood locked in his embrace, and they clung to each other.

Then he released her suddenly, and she almost lost her balance. He reached to steady her so she would not fall, and muttered in a hoarse voice, 'Please forgive me. I know not what came over me.' He gazed upon her face once more, before turning sharply and exiting the kitchen.

And then all she was left with was the sound of the back door closing and a storm of emotion swirling through her as she tried to make sense of what just happened.

CHAPTER 24

Willow Manor, York - Present Day

When Cara had entered the priest hole and raised her hand to touch the wall, the vortex appeared on demand.

She'd been grateful to see George waiting for her when she groped her way back through the passage and emerged, squinting into the daylight.

'Thank goodness,' he said. 'There you are—let me help you down.'

Cara lowered herself into his arms.

He held her tight and stroked her hair. After a few minutes, he asked, 'Did it work?'

'It worked... all right. The vortex came for me, and I don't think I blacked out afterwards. How long was I in there, roughly?'

'Only about five minutes. I was just about to come in and check what was going on, but thought I'd better give it a chance and not risk messing anything up.'

'Let's go for a walk,' she said.

They strolled through the estate, the afternoon sunshine bathing their faces and soothing Cara's restless thoughts.

Kate was busy in the barn, which was now transformed into the major portion of the Tudor Heritage Centre. 'I can't believe how amazing it all looks,' said Cara. 'You've done an incredible job in the few weeks you've been here. Thank goodness you came on board.'

Kate led them to the Tudor Kings' Manuscript, and memories of George first kissing her in his workshop in The Rambles, proudly showing her the manuscript, whizzed through Cara's mind.

Throughout the rest of the day, she experienced flashbacks of Georgiana. She saw Caroline at a lavish house party dinner, and then she was in the kitchen and George kissed her unexpectedly. It was a sweet, forbidden kiss, and the memory of it brought tears to her eyes. After that, it all went a bit hazy.

That evening, Eddie called to see whether she'd ventured back into the priest hole and was thrilled to hear she had succeeded to time travel on demand.

'This is such a tremendous breakthrough,' he said, his voice booming through the phone as if he were in the room with them.

'I don't know,' she said. 'Hopefully my memory will update again soon, and I'll know what's going on.'

'Now you can choose *when* you go. Don't underestimate the power of this fresh development. It puts you in control.'

'I don't feel in control. Besides, Sylvia says we're never in control,' she reminded him.

'And she is right—well… sort of. But you are in control of when you go.'

'But what about when I come back? I've been wondering about that.'

'Um, I suppose it'll come clear to you soon.'

'Let's hope so,' she replied. 'Just when I thought I understood how it works, I'm thrown into a completely new time travel system.'

Cara went to bed that night, exhausted, and fell into a deep sleep. The dreams soon came, and this time she saw Caroline in the kitchen sobbing, then trying to reach her chamber unnoticed, but when she heard sounds of the house party approaching, she ducked into the blue room for cover so she wouldn't meet anyone in the hallway. Tears streamed down Caroline's face as she sobbed on the sofa, praying no one would come in and see her in such a state before she could get back to the solitude of her room.

Caroline didn't feel like she could stand any more heartache—something must change because she couldn't live like this any longer. George had made it clear he had feelings for her, but it was equally clear that they had no future. He had given into his heart for a blissful second, but then fled from the kitchen. Caroline's thoughts flooded Cara's consciousness as she slept and she tossed about the bed, overcome by dread of a lonely future without George, or worse still, a future where she was a servant in his new wife's household.

Cara felt a hand on her forehead and opened her eyes to see George perched next to her, and the bed sloping sideways beneath his weight.

'Wakey-wakey, sleepy head. I've been waiting for you to wake up for ages,' he said. 'Were you having a bad dream?'

She stretched, her eyes bleary from sleep, and then pushed herself up against the headboard, plumping up a pillow to lean against. 'I feel dreadful. What time is it?'

George raised his watch in the air and made a theatrical sweep with his arm. 'It's gone ten.'

'Gosh, I haven't slept that late in years. I was dreaming...

about Georgiana.' She rubbed her eyes, and said, 'Any chance of a coffee? I am totally zonked.'

'Yes, of course, but first, I wanted to ask whether you may have seen Cornelius?'

She smiled and reached up to kiss him. 'Good morning.' She nodded. 'Yes, dear Cornelius. Don't worry, it's me, or at least I think it is—I remember going through the priest hole.'

George deployed their secret time travel code, which they used to check whether one of them was aware they were time travelling.

'That's a good enough start. I didn't know what to expect this time,' he said. 'I'll go and get you some coffee.'

She placed her hand on his arm. 'Wait for me, I'll come down with you, darling.'

He pulled her silk robe off the hook on the door and held it out for her to slip her arms into and then captured her hand and they walked down the sweeping staircase together.

After the stressful dream, her heart flooded with gratitude that they were together now; married and blissfully happy at Willow Manor.

A lot could happen in a couple of centuries.

'In Georgiana, you kissed me—well, Caroline—in this kitchen,' she said. 'It's funny, it's not even all that different down here apart from the modern equipment and units.'

'I suppose the fire didn't destroy the kitchen,' he said, handing Cara a piping hot cup of coffee, made just the way she liked it.

'I still know nothing about the fire. We haven't reached that part of the timeline yet. And the way things are going, Caroline will leave Willow Manor with a broken heart. It's an impossible situation: a governess and an aristocrat falling for each other.'

'Remember that impossible situations are our thing...

we've come through them in other lives, and if I had to bet on it, I'd say we'll come through it together in this one too.'

'Talking of betting, I keep expecting to see eighteenth-century George gambling his fortune away, but so far he's played a few harmless rounds of cards with the house party, and that's about it.'

George made them some toast, and they sat in companionable silence drinking their coffee in the cosy, warm kitchen, each lost in their own thoughts as the sunbeams splayed a colourful pattern on the whitewashed walls.

'Do you have to go through the wormhole again, do you think?' George asked after he took his last bite of wholemeal toast and jam.

'I'm still dreaming about Georgiana and also having memory updates, so the time travel on demand seems to be working—thank goodness.'

George sighed. 'My poor darling—your head must be spinning.'

'It is a bit! Caroline was crying in the drawing room. I dreamt about that a while ago, if you recall, so that was a premonition and now it's come true.'

'Maybe it'll all resolve itself,' said George.

'That would be nice, but I've got a feeling in the pit of my stomach that it won't be quite that easy.'

Willow Manor, York - Georgiana

Much to Caroline's relief, the guests departed, along with Charlotte, and the house was restored to its usual peaceful equilibrium, but unfortunately her state of mind was not.

She had said goodbye to the house guests the evening

before they were due to leave, so she would not have to witness George taking leave of Charlotte.

Olivia sighed as she turned the pages of the book she was reading. 'Sophocles doesn't seem nearly as engaging now.'

Caroline brushed away a lock of Olivia's hair, which had escaped and fallen over her eyes. 'You will soon settle back into the normal rhythm of life—it's bound to feel a little slow after all the recent excitement.'

'A little slow? It is positively dull,' said Olivia, sighing again even more dramatically.

'We will finish our studies in one hour and then we may do as you wish. Let us do whatever you would like this afternoon,' Caroline said, taking pity on her bored companion, and wishing to cheer her.

'You are very kind, but it is not in your power to give me what I wish for, for what I wish is to be at court in London. I do not see why I cannot be when there are other girls my age serving at court.'

'I suggest you speak to your brother about this matter because, as you rightly say, it is not within my power to transport you to court.'

Olivia leaned closer to Caroline and whispered, 'I will talk to my mother… my brother would keep me here, closeted like a little girl to keep me safe, forever, if he had his way.'

'I fear he will have his way, for he is head of the household. If I were you, I would consider how to broach the matter with him, if this is what you truly desire.'

Olivia resumed reading, and then raised her head, and said, 'I know what we shall do. Let us ride into Willow Wick and spend the afternoon in the village.'

Caroline did her best to conceal her feelings about Olivia's request, for in truth she had known that were she to give her the choice of what to do, she would most likely choose such an outing, even so, her mind raced, and her hands grew clammy at the possibility of meeting Ralph again.

She had not seen him since the day George rescued her when Ralph had cornered her on her way into the village. Caroline would not be kept prisoner on the estate for fear of him, but still, she readied herself for another unpleasant encounter, for there was no other type since she had come to work at Willow Manor and dared to go against his wishes.

She laid her book on the table and looked out the window. 'Very well, it's a fine day. Let us ask Cook to prepare a picnic and we shall make an afternoon of it if that is agreeable to the countess.'

Olivia rewarded her with a beaming smile, and the rest of the hour passed quickly, and Olivia hummed, distracted from her previous melancholy at the promise of a ride to the village, and an afternoon picnic.

Caroline was not so easily distracted from her own melancholy and her mind flitted back over recent events. She yearned to be alone with George after the passionate kiss, to try and make sense of what had happened, but she had resolved to be distant and refused to look at him while Charlotte was staying. Each time he entered the room, she found a reasonable excuse to leave, taking care not to appear rude to the other guests. One morning before Olivia joined her for lessons, he sought Caroline out in the library, and they were alone for a rare moment.

She turned to leave so he would not see the tears in her eyes, and he reached for her, and whispered, 'Are we destined to live this miserable existence apart?'

The pain in his dark eyes destroyed her already tender heart, and she recoiled.

'I had not thought to repulse you. I am sorry you find my touch so deeply distasteful.'

Caroline's temper flared at the unfairness of the accusation.

'It is I who finds *you* repulsive, my lord? It is not I who fled the kitchen without a word—it is not I who is betrothed to another.'

Tears streamed from her eyes and her throat ached as she hurried from the room and didn't look back. She felt his eyes on her as she rushed to her chamber to try to regain her composure.

In her bedchamber, Cara's consciousness took over, and although she felt the weight of Caroline's sadness, she was fully aware of what was going on and realised the enormity of her task.

How the heck was she supposed to unite Caroline and George and give them a happy ending?

CHAPTER 25

Willow Manor, York - Georgiana

Cara remembered her present-day life and knew the vortex had swept her back to 1729. Her next Twin Flame mission was becoming clearer to her now that she had the advantage of accessing Caroline's consciousness in real time.

That night, as she prepared for bed in the familiar green bedchamber in what was both her past and future family home, she thought about the events of the day. In an impassioned moment when it slipped her mind that she was now a governess in the eighteenth-century, she had accused George of caring more about his reputation than he did about his happiness.

'You would rather be miserable and uphold your family's honour than honour your true feelings.'

He recoiled as if she'd bitten him, and then she saw the light dawn in his dark eyes, and he hung his head and didn't deny it. After a few seconds, he straightened his shoulders.

'You are correct, Mistress Radcliff. You see right through me to my despicable weakness, and I have no defence,' he said, reverting to a brusque biting formality.

It was obvious he was in despair too, but she must get a handle on her emotions. Outbursts like that would only complicate matters for Caroline and be considered subversive, given her lower status.

Or would they? Perhaps hearing the bitter truth was exactly what the lord of the manor needed to jolt him into facing how he felt about her and not allowing his ego to dictate their future.

Before she had entered the priest hole, Sylvia had reminded her on the phone that one of the most painful Twin Flame patterns was for one twin to run from the other when their feelings became too intense for them to bear.

'They call them *The Runner*. I think we discussed it before when you first fell in love in the present day. It can be one or both twins running from the power of the connection, which is why Twin Flame relationships are prone to be so emotionally messy and complex before a couple reaches union.'

Cara didn't know what to do for the best. On the one hand, her newfound ability to travel on demand was a gift to enable her to hack into the time system so that Caroline and George could find a way to be together despite the class divide. On the other, she must tread carefully, or who knew what she would mess up in the process? Other people's lives, as well as their future lives, were intertwined with theirs—it wasn't only them to consider.

From personal experience, she knew that timeline resets were a double-edged sword and had consequences—both good and bad, so she would need all her wits about her if she were to rewrite the timeline and not destroy their future along with it. This would be her most audacious timeline reset yet, and as she lay on the bed in her cold bedchamber, she feared she was not up to the task.

. . .

THE DAYS BECAME weeks and George avoided her every time they were in the same room. Cara found it increasingly difficult to live Caroline's life where George acted like a stranger. She knew from the talk below stairs that he was corresponding with Charlotte, and the expectation in the house was that they would soon marry.

It was hellish to sit and listen to the servants in the kitchen, and so she retreated into herself, and spent most of her free time walking around the estate, wondering if it would all be over soon, and she could go back to living just one life with George.

On one such occasion, she hastened into the grounds before dusk fell, clutching the folds of her cloak around her to shield herself from the chill in the air. The green leaves on the willow trees had turned a golden hue, and winter would soon be upon them. She sighed—it wouldn't be as easy to escape the confines of the house as in the summer when she had taken to walking for miles through the fields and along the river. It was the only thing that kept her sane through the hard weeks as Cara struggled with her past life in Georgiana. And as she walked, she reviewed her impossible situation, as she so often did.

It was incredible to her that she was back at Willow Manor in yet another timeline, and everything seemed so different and yet strangely the same. The house at least was a constant through the timelines, which comforted her, until she remembered that soon that wouldn't be the case if she didn't do something to stop George heading full force down his path of self-destruction. She had noted the gradual changes in him—what had been his light and sunny demeanour had grown troubled, and she heard the servants remark in whispered tones on the dramatic difference in his manner.

Cara tried to beg off the family dinners as much as she could, but sometimes, she had no choice but to attend or she would seem rude and churlish. The previous day, they had dined together and even the countess had commented on George's out of character behaviour.

'Really George, must you drink quite so much at this hour? We haven't even eaten dinner yet... you seem not yourself since the house party.'

'I am perfectly well, Mother,' he assured her and took another gulp of whisky.

Cara glanced at him, hoping he wouldn't see her watching him, but his eyes were already upon her, and she could see he was somewhat inebriated.

'I shall leave for court again shortly, so you won't have to put up with my dissolute ways,' he said.

'And shall we have the pleasure of dear Charlotte's company upon your return?'

'I do not know my plans yet, Mother,' he replied between mouthfuls, not being drawn so easily into pleasantries.

'Perhaps a happy announcement will be made soon?' she continued, undeterred.

Cara thought the countess must assume his sour mood was because of being separated from Charlotte, his heart's desire.

'Do you intend to marry her?' Olivia asked.

George let out a quick burst of laughter, but the humour didn't quite reach his eyes. 'I adore your forthright manner, my dear Livvy. It is an uncommon trait for a woman to say exactly what she means, rather than beating around the bush. If only more women had the same gift,' he said, his eyes passing over Cara for the briefest of pauses.

She looked down at her plate, her heart beating wildly and nausea threatening to overwhelm her.

Is he accusing me of not speaking truthfully?

They had avoided each other, and now he was lashing out. Cara couldn't make out this eighteenth-century version of George at all. He had seemed cold and unfeeling following their passionate kiss in the kitchen. It was as if he disliked her, and she didn't know how to reach him, and so she had distanced herself further, but she was acutely aware that the clock was ticking and that avoiding him would not bring them together. Seeing him lash out now made Cara realise that the avoidance was a protection measure.

Of course—it's classic George. Why didn't I see it?

Cara chastised herself for her blindness. She'd been so caught up in her own feelings and vision of what needed to happen that she'd overlooked reality.

She walked and walked until dusk turned into night and the autumn leaves were coated in darkness and the stars sparkled in the dark velvet blue sky like an artist's canvas.

Cara was in the unique position of knowing what was happening in the present day and in this timeline, but although she was no longer merely an observer, she still felt impotent to influence George. She had too much of Caroline's demure eighteenth-century consciousness to be bold enough to risk the wrath of the family.

Something rustled behind her, and she jumped; the fine hairs on her skin standing on end as a frisson of fear ran through her body and the adrenaline kicked in.

She took a deep breath to calm herself—it was probably only the sound of the birds in the trees, or perhaps a squirrel burrowing down for the night. But then she heard his voice.

'Caroline—is that you?'

She started and turned to see George approaching quickly.

'Whatever are you doing out here alone in the dark?' he said, coming to a stop next to her.

'I enjoy walking around the estate—I find it difficult to be cooped up indoors.'

'Indeed. As do I. I was just taking an evening stroll and I caught sight of—well, I thought my eyes must deceive me because no sensible young woman would be out at this hour unescorted, but no... there you are in all your stubborn independence—refusing to be tamed. I must confess I both admire and despair of this trait of yours in equal measure.' He shook his head.

A fierce blush stung her cheeks, and she was grateful he wouldn't be able to behold her face clearly in the darkness. She had Cara's awareness, but still the fact remained that she was a young and inexperienced woman: gauche in the ways of romantic love and overwhelmed by George's witty sophistication and superior birth. She did not know how to reply and shuffled awkwardly from one foot to the other, but this was the most he had said to her in weeks. His hard shell of an exterior had partially cracked, so perhaps this was her opportunity to reach him.

'I will return to court,' he continued before she could speak. 'I must tell you what is in my heart, Caroline, for we will not have this chance to speak openly before long.' He wrung his hands as he spoke and then let them fall loosely at his sides. The moon had risen and cast shadows across the hollows in his cheekbones.

She stared at him, not knowing what to expect, her senses crashing and overwhelming her as she waited for him to speak again.

'I have faced an inner battle these past months... ever since you first came into my life like an angel.' He raised his head to meet her eyes, and it was as though he reached into her soul.

She shivered.

'You are cold,' he said, and removed his cloak and draped it around her shoulders, covering her cloak, before she could refuse. She was cold—and then she was hot—and then cold. She knew not what she was as she waited for him to reveal what was in his heart. Memories of them together in the past and the future enveloped her like a storm cloud until she was disorientated and knew not what to do or say.

He continued, undeterred. 'I love you, Caroline. I do not know how it happened or why it happened… what curious spell you have cast over me to make me love you so utterly and completely when in some ways we barely know each other.'

Cara bowed her head as the tears slid from her eyes and cascaded down her cold cheeks, unbidden. She knew what was coming. They had been in this conversation before when they fell in love in the present day. This was deja-vu in reverse time.

He loved her, but...

She knew only too well where this was going, and the pain shot through her as she realised she would be powerless to stop him once he made up his mind. His will was ironclad when it came to his duty. He clearly saw Charlotte as part of his duty to his bloodline, and what could she—a lowly governess—say to dissuade him from his noble cause?

George, we will be married one hundred and eleven years from now, as well as three hundred years into the future, and we were married two hundred years ago, and it's likely that we've shared multiple past lives and were together two thousand years ago…

No—that would not work! He would think her completely deranged and she couldn't risk that happening in the eighteenth century, no matter how much she trusted him. History had not been kind to women with mental illness or those who bore any uncommon trait or mark of uniqueness. She could be accused of being a witch, or perhaps even worse; mad, and committed to a mental asylum. Not that she thought George was the sort of man to allow something evil like that to occur, but she wouldn't risk putting them both in such a precarious position. He was not his usual, steady self, and who knew what he might do?

'You were astute when you accused me of caring only for my reputation. I have thought of little else over the past weeks and have tried to find a way out of this dark hole I find myself in, but alas, there is no way out. We are from different stations in life… and we are simply not meant to be together. Fate merely taunted me with the possibility of you, while simultaneously coming between us.'

He kicked the earth with his leather boot, sending a stone hurtling across the ground and down to the bubbling stream that ran through the estate.

'Our classes do not marry. It is not only my reputation and that of my family I seek to protect. It is yours too. Society will never accept us. Your own as well as mine would shun you. I cannot do that to you.'

He extended his arm to touch her face, and the tears seeped onto his fingers. 'My words have made you cry…'

She sniffed and wiped her eyes, trying to compose herself. 'I am sorry to have caused you such distress. It was never and will never be my intent—I hope you know that.' Her emotions took over, and she spoke without checking herself.

George took a step closer to her and before she could say another word; he ran his finger across her lips and pulled her into his arms and his lips were on hers and he kissed her harder and deeper than the kiss they had shared in the kitchen. He let himself go, and she returned his ardour with abandon. Their kiss was sweet and familiar—like coming home, as the centuries of passion connected them.

'Why do I feel like we've done that many times before?' he said, when he gently pulled away but still held her in his arms, unwilling to sever their connection.

We are Twin Flames—our souls are destined to unite in every shared timeline, thought Cara.

She couldn't overcome her reluctance to bare her soul, and the words died on her tongue. And she remained silent.

Willow Manor, York - Present day

Cara and George breakfasted on the terrace in the early morning sunshine. Mrs Lightfoot said they would need all their strength for the grand opening and she surprised them with a full English breakfast.

'What an amazing housekeeper! Everyone could do with a Mrs Lightfoot. Where did you find her?' Kate asked.

Cara looked at George and smiled quizzically. 'We were lucky. She's our gardener, Swifty's mother, and she just fit right in.'

Kate buttered a piece of wholemeal toast, and looked from George to Cara, and said, 'I had *the* weirdest dream last night.'

'Oh, yes?' said Cara. 'What about?'

'Well, it was the strangest thing. It must be this house giving me ancestral delusions of grandeur!'

George raised his eyebrow, scrambled eggs on his fork, mid-mouthful. 'Go on... should I be worried? Are you going to usurp me as lord of the manor?'

Kate laughed. 'In the dream, you were my older brother, George—just like now, but my name was Olivia... I think it was the Georgian period that you keep asking about, so it must be in my subconscious.'

The eggs stuck in Cara's throat. She took a sip of orange juice and exchanged a look with George. 'Go on…'

'Well, this is the really bizarre bit. You were my governess, or some sort of lady's companion. And you were called Caroline…'

CHAPTER 26

Willow Manor, York - Georgiana

Cara heard noises below her window. She moved the curtain aside and saw one of the Cavendish carriages being prepared for departure. George had told the family he would leave for London to return to court and would be away for some time. She knew by their expressions they were overjoyed at the prospect of him asking for Charlotte's hand in marriage.

The household was wracked with nervous anticipation, from the servants below stairs to the elite above, as if everyone sensed their future hung in the balance and great change was imminent. What George did next would determine the course of all their lives, even if they didn't fully comprehend to what degree and how their future would be tilted towards disaster if he took the wrong step.

George had sought her out before breakfast and told her he would leave that morning. 'I must apologise for my reckless behaviour. You seem to have some strange power over me where I cannot account for my actions, but nevertheless it is neither just nor fair to lay my behaviour at your feet. There is no excuse, and I intend to get a hold of myself, therefore I shall leave for court as planned.'

This could be her last chance to get through to him to stop him from triggering the destruction of everything he held dear, so she took a sharp intake of breath and summoned all her courage. She must overcome Caroline's feelings of inadequacy regarding his social status, and risk losing face, or they would lose each other and Willow Manor.

It would be a senseless path of suffering for them both, and the downfall of everything he longed to protect. The thought of him sleeping next to another woman for the rest of this life, while Caroline was imprisoned in a miserable union with Ralph, jolted her to overcome her fears.

'Forgive me, for I must speak up, or it shall be too late, and we will both pay a heavy price,' she said.

His dark eyes were full of longing as he assessed her earnest face, which had become so beloved to him in the few months since she had appeared in his world, and he had questioned everything about who he was and what his future held.

'Go on,' he said. 'Of course, please speak freely.'

'I would have you know that my feelings for you are as ardent and true as those you professed to me last evening.' She hesitated, but pressed on.

'And as such, I ask, how would you allow your happiness —our happiness—to be forbidden by an archaic class system? A system which will crumble and is destined for decay whether or not we allow ourselves to be happy?'

They stood in the shadows of the corridor a few steps

from her door, where he had intercepted her before she went downstairs.

He stared at her as if she were speaking in foreign tongues, and the tears threatened to engulf her again as the emotion flooded into her throat.

She continued, 'I would beg you to consider what I have said before you rush into this doomed marriage. For it will be doomed—I can't say how I know, only that I do, and I am sorry to be the one to have to tell you so.'

His face was concealed in the shadows, but when he stepped into the light, she gasped. He looked as though he had been struck, and the sorrow she caused him was more than she could bear.

'Why do you speak so, Caroline? Has jealousy brought you so low that you would curse my impending marriage like some evil divining witch?'

His voice was quiet so they wouldn't be overheard, but his tone was harsh and unrelenting.

She looked at him and the tears spilled from her eyes and rolled down her hot face. 'As you wish, my lord. It was my duty to warn you, but it is, of course, your decision. If your reputation matters to you more than being true to your heart, then so be it. There is no more I may do or say.'

He grasped her arm and pulled her back to face him as she moved towards her chamber. 'I think it is obvious to us both that I love you. But it is no good… I cannot do it. I will not bring shame upon my family for my own selfish desires.'

'I see, so you are ashamed of me…'

'Caroline! That's not what I meant, and it is cruelly unfair.'

'Perhaps it's not what you meant, but it is what you inferred, my lord.'

She tugged her arm and freed herself from his grip, looking at him one last time before closing the door firmly behind her, and turning the heavy silver key in the lock. He looked like a broken man and her heart twisted in agony as she stood with her back against the door.

Had she broken him by coming from the twenty-first century to deliver a message with which he was not equipped to deal?

She threw herself on the large four poster bed and pulled the green counterpane over her head and sobbed silently. She lay like that for hours and was grateful Olivia was engaged with her mother today, for she had not the strength to face her and pretend all was well.

She was filled with intense feelings of loss and dread, and her chest heaved so she could barely draw breath. Then the room began to spin, and she saw flashes of her past and future. Images of her and George together in different timelines filled her consciousness until she could no longer think straight, and her head seemed like it would explode. And then she heard a familiar whirring sound and a cloud of freezing cold air enveloped her.

No! How can this be happening? The vortex doesn't take me from this timeline. I need to be here to fix this nightmare.

But then she was gone.

Willow Manor, Tudor Heritage Centre, York - Present day

There was a good turnout for the grand opening, with healthy press coverage which generated interest in the Cavendish stately home and the family's link to the Tudor court and Henry VIII. The centre was bustling, and visitors milled about admiring the exhibits, which had been meticulously curated by Kate and George.

'The place looks terrific,' said Cara to George as she took a sip of the pink prosecco the server handed to her as she arrived.

'Doesn't it just? What do you make of the ceiling?' he asked.

'I didn't even realise there were Tudor beams in the barn,' she said. 'How wonderfully authentic it all looks.'

'The builders really outdid themselves with the exposed beams,' said George with a satisfied smile.

The barn had been transformed into a light and impressive space, with its old Tudor features brought back to life. Kate had decorated the place tastefully, with a sprinkling of locally sourced antiques, wall tapestries, and artful lighting to draw the eye to the exhibits.

They moved around the centre, catching up with old friends and acquaintances and welcoming unfamiliar faces. A line had formed by the priest hole exhibit and visitors were being funnelled through to the library to see it for themselves after reading about the Jesuit priest who had been saved from certain execution by the now legendary Cavendish tutor.

'Do you know the name of the tutor who saved the priest?' enquired a reporter, eager to get an inside scoop for his article.

'I'm afraid we haven't been able to find out,' said George, shaking his head.

The reporter looked disappointed and trailed out of the centre after the others on the quest to see the priest hole.

'We don't want anyone digging about and noticing how many of the same names we had in those days,' said Cara, quietly. 'Your name will come as no great surprise with so many of your lineage named George, but the fact that your Tudor ancestor also married a woman named Cara is quite odd. Add to that, another Edward Makepeace, and we may arouse suspicion. You know what reporters are like.'

'True,' said George. 'And historians,' he smiled. 'I hadn't given it much thought, but you're right. Although, I shouldn't think it'll be a problem. When I researched the priest, I couldn't find anything beyond what we read in the family history book. Besides, are people likely to jump to the conclusion we're time travellers, just like that?'

Cara saw a beaming face heading towards them.

'Lord and Lady Cavendish,' Sylvia said in a low, warm voice as she approached them with outstretched arms. 'How wonderful to see you back at your family estate where you belong.'

They hugged and Sylvia toasted them with her glass of prosecco, her dangling earrings twinkling in the light as she talked. 'May you have many happy years together in your beautiful home.'

Cara jumped as a hand touched her shoulder. 'Eddie! There you are. I would have come to get you from the station.'

'I wouldn't miss this for the world,' he said. 'Or even for those pesky students of mine. The train from London got in a bit late, so I grabbed a taxi. How's it going?'

Cara filled him in on the reporter asking for his name, and then led him with exaggerated ceremony towards the elevated exhibit which explained about the tutor and the priest.

'How marvellous,' he said, the pride evident on his face, and his cheeks pink. 'Even though I don't remember how we rescued him, I am proud we accomplished something so significant.'

Cara whispered, 'It was you Eddie, you saved him.'

'To friends old and new,' he said, raising his glass, and Cara, George and Sylvia all chinked their prosecco.

Kate appeared at Cara's shoulder. 'There you are...'

'You remember Eddie and Sylvia—you met at the wedding?'

'Of course,' she said, her animated features aglow.

They chatted for a while and then it was time for George and Cara to say a few words to commemorate the opening. Reporters snapped and flashed their cameras, and the audience clapped enthusiastically when the couple officially declared the centre open. The occasion was recorded for posterity and would appear in *The York Press.*

Cara wondered whether a future version of herself would look back at the article, trying to piece together what had happened in this life.

'I'm glad that's over,' said Cara. 'It's been such a long time coming. I was a bundle of nerves, but now we can relax and enjoy it.'

'We pulled it off,' said George. 'We've been working towards this day for so long, I confess; I can hardly believe it's done.'

Cara reached for his hand and assured him he'd done an amazing job and the fruits of his labour would pay off for them long term, not just at the opening. 'This is where the fun begins. We have brought our own heritage centre to life and have the perfect base to live and work, not to mention a way to fund the estate.'

Later that evening, after the last of their visitors left the grounds, George handed Cara and Kate a pre-dinner drink, and Kate said, 'You know how I was telling you earlier about my strange dream?'

Cara tensed and prepared to handle more of Kate's probing questions. She tried to stay calm and took a swig of wine to bolster her courage and buy herself a moment as she sat down on the sofa. George poured himself a glass and settled into a nearby armchair.

'Well, I entered the priest hole again early this morning on my own,' she continued.

'Oh?' said George. 'You kept that quiet.'

'I wanted to experience it as a visitor would—entering for the first time. But I had that deja-vu feeling again, like I've been there before.'

'Goodness,' said Cara. 'Maybe Sylvia's psychic powers are rubbing off on you.'

'Well, you have been there before,' said George, to distract his sister even though he knew she wouldn't be put off so easily.

'You can both make fun of me, but I had this really clear vision of myself in another time—the one I told you about in the dream where you were my governess. And my name was Olivia… I don't know how exactly, but that priest hole is connected somehow.'

George and Cara exchanged a look.

'What is it? What do you two know that I don't? I've had a feeling you're keeping something from me, ever since I arrived,' she said.

CHAPTER 27

Willow Manor, York - Present day

Cara and George enjoyed a precious couple of hours alone when Kate had gone into the city. She insisted on making an appointment with Sylvia to see what she could discover about her mysterious dream.

'Sylvia promised not to reveal anything about us, but I imagine it'll be tricky,' said Cara.

'Do you think psychics have a confidentiality agreement like lawyers?' said George.

Cara laughed. 'I have no idea if they have an unwritten code, but we can trust Sylvia not to reveal our secret intentionally. My concern is more about her revealing something unintentionally when she's in one of her trances. You know how dogged Kate can be with her questioning!'

'I do indeed!' Now it was George's turn to laugh at the vision of his sister interrogating Sylvia. 'Do you think Kate could really be connected to Olivia?'

'Well, they say that souls reincarnate with the same soul groups, so I don't see why not. Let's hope that's what it is because the other possibility would be much more difficult to handle.'

George narrowed his eyes, trying to think what the other possibility could be, and then looked at Cara questioningly. 'Which is?'

'Well, she might be a time traveller too—a sleeper traveller like Swifty, but the priest hole is updating her memory.'

'Oh, goodness. As if trying to keep our situation from Kate isn't difficult enough already...'

'We must keep the family history volume from her, or she might read about Olivia and realise her dream was accurate, and who knows where that will lead?' Cara said.

'Unless she read the volume already at some point and the memory was in her mind and simply resurfaced with all of our talk of the history of the house?'

'I believe we may have a sceptic on our hands,' Cara said, prodding him gently in the arm. 'You'd think after all we've experienced, that you'd be a bit more open to the mystical realms...'

Swifty was in the kitchen on a tea break, visiting his mother, Mrs Lightfoot, and they heard Cornelius barking as a newspaper thudded onto the hard tiles by the back door. George jumped up to retrieve the paper and was back in a flash, leafing through the pages.

'Here we are. Not an altogether terrible photo of us...,' he said.

'Let me see. You are always so photogenic, but I generally look dreadful in these pieces.' Cara peered at their picture in *The York Press*. 'Ew, just as I feared.'

'I don't know what you're talking about. You look gorgeous,' George said, and then read the article aloud. 'Willow Manor had been in the Cavendish family since the early Tudor period, until the family's fortunes declined, and the estate stood derelict for years before being converted into a charming hotel...'

'Well, at least we've made it into the paper, and it's a big article. That's good—should get us some more bookings. We've had some come in overnight, actually.'

As they walked around the gardens and down to the river later that morning, making the most of the idyllic late summer weather, Cara told George how the vortex had come for her in Georgiana, and she'd had no choice but to leave.

'I wondered what was going on, but didn't want to press you. Why do you think that happened suddenly?'

'I don't know. I've been meaning to call Eddie and see what he makes of it.'

'Let's do it now,' said George, pressing Eddie's name on his phone. They had the sunny blustery riverbank all to themselves so they could speak freely when Eddie picked up.

'That sounds like time pushing back. You've experienced it in the past in different forms. Remember?' said Eddie.

'I remember you explaining that when we try to overwrite a timeline, it can cause all sorts of problems.'

Cara held George's hand, and he squeezed hers.

'By time travelling on demand, you are now effectively hacking the system and have taken it to another level, so it doesn't surprise me that time would push back—hard.'

'Was it something particular that triggered it?' Eddie said.

Cara sighed. 'George is so pig-headed, and it upset me.'

'Not again. That could have done it,' Eddie replied. 'I can't be certain, as we don't have enough data yet, but I suspect that when our emotions are heightened, it can push the system to the limit, and then we're more likely to summon the vortex and travel again. We've seen that happen quite a bit in other timelines.'

'I don't know that there's any more I could do, anyway.

George has returned to court, and he's going to ask Charlotte to marry him regardless of his feelings for Caroline. In typical George fashion, he thinks it's selfish to prioritise his own needs, and doesn't realise that putting his reputation above his happiness is just his ego running the show.'

'I am here, you know,' said George, dryly.

'What a complete fool,' said Eddie. 'Has he learned nothing from Tudorville?'

Cara rolled her eyes. 'Apparently not, although in fairness he is the new and improved version of himself and is behaving in a not all together surprising way for his time. But I always get the sharp end of the stick. I must have done something incredibly bad in one of my past lives to deserve this karma!'

George kicked a stone from the edge of the riverbank, and it skimmed the water with lightning precision for several seconds before it disappeared.

'Well, it was a man's world back then, but for what it's worth, I am sorry for being so dense, my darling,' he said.

Cara replied, 'With me gone, I fear the original timeline will play out just as it was written in the family history book before the text disappeared and hid its secrets from us. If I don't get back there, I think we're all headed for disaster.'

Eddie advised her to wait a few days and give her memory a chance to update, and then they would decide whether she should attempt to travel on demand again.

'I see why you're worried, but we must not forget that there's always just as much chance of messing things up by going back at the wrong time,' he said.

Eddie excused himself and rushed off to take a class.

'I think Eddie's still haunted by the error we made in the time travel experiment when we almost lost you at the Tower, so he's a lot more cautious these days,' remarked Cara. 'But I'm worried that if we delay, we will miss our opportunity to reset the timeline, and you—I mean—he, will already be betrothed, and then it will be too late to change the course of our fate. George won't tarnish his reputation as it is, so imagine how much more difficult it will be to change his mind if he's already promised to Charlotte.

'I wish there was something I could do to help,' said George. 'I feel impotent when this kind of thing happens.'

She squeezed his hand. 'You're here with me now, so we have made progress, or we wouldn't be together in this timeline. Besides, it's not your fault. We just need to let it play out and see if there's an opportunity to tilt the odds in the direction that we want without causing damage in other areas.'

'What's Charlotte like, by the way?'

'Oh, she's lovely. If we weren't Twin Flames, she might even be a superb choice. That makes it all the harder in Georgiana. When I was there, I could feel Caroline's sense of inadequacy about her lower-class status weighing me down and pulling me away from you. I didn't have the strength to fight for us like I have done in the past because I felt like there was no chance of winning. We are unequal in a way we haven't been before, and it presents a whole new set of challenges.'

They trod carefully over the tufts of grass and dry mounds of mud which had hardened in the recent hot weather on the footpath. The water sparkled in the sunshine and the willow trees cast deep shadows across its peaceful surface.

'This is a magical place,' said Cara. 'We're lucky to have spent so many lifetimes together in such a beautiful part of the country. When it all gets a bit much, I remind myself how fortunate we are. I imagine few couples can say they've lived and loved each other for hundreds of years like us.'

'True. I wouldn't have it any other way, no matter how difficult you have been through the years…'

She raised an eyebrow, and he laughed as he pulled her close and they walked back to the house.

The one constant through the centuries was the invisible chord which bound them to each other and transcended logic, class and time.

Willow Manor, York - Georgiana

Olivia was in tears and the countess attempted to console her daughter, to no avail, as Caroline looked on helplessly, wringing her hands and feeling like her heart couldn't take any more pain.

'Is there not some other way, my dear? As you can see, you are very much appreciated here,' said the countess, passing Olivia a silk handkerchief to wipe her wet face.

'I shall be most sad to leave you and wish there was another way, but I'm afraid my dear aunt is alone and much in need of my assistance due to sudden illness.' Caroline bowed her head.

'I received her letter when I visited my father several days ago, and I must now go to her,' said Caroline. 'I have delayed more than I should already for I do not wish to leave you, but unfortunately leave you I must.'

The tears bubbled in Caroline's eyes, and she fought to compose herself.

Olivia was distressed and Caroline's heart twisted and turned as she saw how upset was the poor young girl by her unexpected announcement.

Caroline had lain awake for much of the night battling with her inner conflict of whether to remain at Willow Manor as she wished or to leave and go far away to put space between her and George; as her conscience informed her, she must. She had decided and told them after breakfast, and it was quite as terrible as she feared.

'George will be most displeased,' said Olivia, her chest heaving as she gathered her strength and appealed to Caroline. 'He values you greatly and I feel certain he would wish you to notify him before leaving.'

'It pains me to leave without more notice, but I am equally certain that Lord Cavendish will understand my situation and that I must go to my aunt. He is such a kind-hearted master,' she added.

'When will you go?' said Olivia, her voice shaky.

'As soon as I can arrange a coach,' she replied.

'Nonsense, you must have one of our lads accompany you as far as the horses will last and then help you find a coach to take you the rest of the way,' said the countess.

'You are too good to me,' said Caroline, her eyes filling again as she weakened but clung to her resolve.

The following morning the countess and Olivia walked her to the carriage to bid her farewell, and they talked until the horses grew restless and swished their shiny tails and stomped their hooves.

'We had best let you be on your way—you have miles ahead of you, my dear,' said the countess, her affection for Caroline reflected in her eyes so reminiscent of George's.

Caroline held herself together carefully because if she were to let herself go, she would fall apart and not have the strength to leave.

'Please do not cry,' she said to Olivia, after the countess said farewell and returned to the house.

Olivia clung to Caroline's hands.

'I will miss you, my dear Olivia. You have been like a sister to me, and I shall never forget the way you welcomed me into your family, and your generosity of spirit.'

'But you shall return, shall you not… once you have done your duty by your aunt?'

Caroline did not see how she could ever return to the home she adored, so she said, 'Fret not, my sweet Livvy. All shall be well, and soon enough Lord Cavendish shall return with his new wife on his arm, and you shall have a true sister; one who is worthy of your place in the world.'

'But I do not want another sister, Caroline. You are my true sister,' she sniffed.

As they embraced, tears slid from Olivia's eyes, and Caroline's tender heart ached as she pressed a pretty ornate brooch into her hand. 'I want you to have this small token to remember me by and whenever you are in need of comfort, you shall know you are in my heart simply by looking at it.'

Caroline had already breakfasted with the servants and Cook came running out from the kitchen, wiping her hands on her apron, flustered and pink cheeked. 'Oh, I am glad I caught you. I wanted to be here to wave you off, my lovely one. You shall be missed indeed.'

As the carriage, emblazoned with the Cavendish family crest, rolled down the willow tree-lined drive, Caroline waved to her small entourage and only when the horses turned out of the estate and onto the bumpy track, did she allow her tears to fall freely.

Caroline did not worry overly about Olivia—she would be well taken care of, but she would miss her dreadfully. And she dared not even think about how much she would miss George. She wiped her face with the handkerchief he had given to her, and then she twirled it in her hands, running her fingers over the monogrammed letters: GC.

The vivid dreams had left her of late and the enchanting window which had given her a glimpse into another life and seemed so real, had closed. Caroline doubted the veracity of the dreams as each day the memories retreated further from her consciousness and their connection to reality weakened.

She wiped her eyes, tucked the handkerchief into her cloak pocket, and straightened her hunched shoulders. The time for crying was no more. Now, she must gather her wits to face the unknown path that lay ahead, for there was no sick elderly aunt in London anxiously waiting to welcome her beloved niece.

Caroline was alone and must begin a new life in London.

CHAPTER 28

East London - Georgiana

George alighted from the coach, which his man arranged, and alerted no one at the palace. They left by the back entrance, hoping not to attract attention.

He wrinkled his nose.

Whatever was that dreadful stench?

He didn't need idle chatter at court concerning his whereabouts—there were enough rumours flying around after Charlotte left court suddenly and was said to have returned to her family home in Derbyshire. Queen Caroline had requested George's presence and wished to know why the match wouldn't go ahead.

'I can't think of a finer couple, and it shocked me when Charlotte begged my permission to leave. I heard about your impending betrothal, so I must say I am sorely disappointed...'

George furnished the queen with as little detail as possible, only saying that they had not been as well suited as they both initially thought, and it had been a mutual decision not to make it a formal arrangement. They would, of course, remain friends, he had assured the queen with his most charming smile, which melted the frostiest of hearts.

'Well, it is surely a blow for poor dear Charlotte to lose the prospect of such an eligible husband, and I must say I feel for the girl.'

The queen had a soft spot for George, so she was soon distracted from the subject of his betrothal and allowed him to amuse her with his witty observations on the latest goings-on in London. He breathed a sigh of relief when he was excused once Robert Walpole arrived for his regular audience with the queen.

George bade the coachman to wait in the narrow side street and surveyed the tiny, shabby terraced house with the peeling paintwork, before walking purposely to the door and raising his hand to knock. No one answered at first, but finally he heard movement from within and the sound of shuffling feet. 'Hello,' said the small hunched over woman peering through the crack in the door. 'What can I do for you?'

'I'm here to see Mistress Caroline Radcliff,' he said, but immediately knew from the blank expression on the old woman's face she had no clue to whom he was referring.

He pressed, 'Are you by any chance Mistress Radcliff's aunt?'

'Never 'eard of 'er, Sir,' she said.

George pulled the letter out of his pocket and squinted in the harsh daylight as he checked the address in his mother's letter. 'Is this 8 Parson's Walk?'

The woman nodded. 'It is indeed, and I've lived here most of my life. Ain't no Mistress Radcliff here, I can assure you.'

The bells of the nearby church pealed out joyfully to

proclaim the morning service, and George looked around the filthy street, feeling anything but joyous. Perhaps he should be relieved Caroline wasn't here, after all. He couldn't abide the thought of her living in such squalid surroundings. Although her father's cottage in Willow Wick was no grand house, it was charming in its own quaint way and in a beautiful rural spot with clean air and situated only minutes from the river.

Here in the streets of London, beggars sprawled in front of the tavern, the cobbles were stained with piss and the stench was putrid. Not for the first time, he thanked God for his good fortune that he wasn't born to the lower classes.

George left the palace discreetly at all times of the day and night to make discreet enquiries about Caroline's whereabouts. He soon concluded she must have given a false address so he wouldn't be able to find her, and his heart was full of remorse at how he had deserted her when she was in such a state of despair. Churning the situation over and over in his mind, he asked himself what else he could have done. What should he have done? He had fully intended to follow through with his plan to ask Charlotte for her hand in marriage to fulfil his duties. He had believed it to be the right thing to do. But each time the moment presented itself when they were alone and he might formally ask her, he heard a fierce internal whisper telling him not to do it, and then Caroline's face loomed before him. Eventually, Charlotte grew frustrated at his failure to declare his intentions and she confronted him.

Meanwhile, the dreams returned, and Caroline was in his mind constantly and consumed his every thought. He grew ever more conflicted, and the pain and exhaustion showed on his handsome face. It was not the face of a besotted suitor about to be united with his love.

Charlotte had not taken the rejection well and left in a fury, storming out of the room and later he heard she had left the palace.

He regretted hurting her, but his heart felt lighter, and he was relieved to be free to return to Caroline. They could obviously not officially be together, but he must be near her —that much had become clear to him when they were apart. He made plans to return to Willow Manor and his spirits were noticeably lifted at the thought of being in her company again soon.

Then he was felled by the casual reference in one of his mother's letters, where she informed him that Caroline had left unexpectedly to tend her sick aunt. When he enquired about more details, his mother confirmed the governess did not intend to resume her post at Willow Manor, and they were all very sorry to lose her.

His heart raged with sorrow, and he had never known a feeling of such emptiness each morning as he awoke. He could not foresee a life without her and resolved to risk searching for her, so he may bring her back to Willow Manor. At least she would be safe, and he could take care of her in the only way society permitted, without bringing disgrace upon all of their heads.

He had even considered setting her up in a house in London where they might be together, and she could be his mistress, but he had soon banished the notion as grossly unfair to her. The thought of his family, as well as her father learning of their disreputable arrangement, sent chills of horror through him.

George had trouble admitting, even to himself; he was ashamed of his dire failing in being in love with a woman of such inferior social status.

Why had this happened to him? His path was so clearly

laid out for him by his father, the earl, for as long as he could recall, and George was disappointed at his own lack of willingness to follow through on securing his noble bloodline. He was certain he would love no one but Caroline in this all-consuming manner, but marry her he could not, so he found himself in a painful bind with no way out. He was only grateful his father was not around to witness his fall from grace.

Cara awoke to shrieks from the hallway and the sound of women arguing. She pulled the cover over her head, seeking the bliss of sleep, but it was no good—the peaceful interlude was shattered, and reality blasted into her mind. Cara had entered the priest hole and time travelled to Georgiana again. She must put things right with George. Her dreams warned her that if the Twin Flames were left to their own devices, they would spiral into disaster. She had been given the opportunity to reset the timeline, and that was what she intended to do.

She arrived to find Caroline wandering the streets of London en route to a cheap boarding house, which was all she could afford with the meagre savings she hurriedly crammed into her stays.

More shrieks from the hallway prompted her to rise reluctantly from the narrow bed with the lumpy mattress, which was a world away from the luxurious four-poster bed in her peaceful green chamber at Willow Manor.

Caroline had planned to seek a new governess position and had the foresight to request a letter of recommendation from the countess. She suspected George would follow her even if he were betrothed to Charlotte.

A quiet voice whispered to her it was not over between them, no matter how far she ran.

She went down to a meagre breakfast and shivered in her gown, wishing she had worn her cloak. There was no roaring fire lit by the servants to warm her tired body and weary soul, and she worried how she would find a new position with no friends in the city. She was only offered the position at Willow Manor because of her father's connection to the countess.

Before leaving, Caroline visited her father stealthily, taking a longer route to Willow Wick to avoid any chance of bumping into Ralph. Her father tried to discourage her from leaving, and she told him she couldn't explain now, but he must trust her and if anyone from the big house came calling, she begged he confirm her story of a sick aunt.

It was a paper-thin fabrication, and George would see through it if he went in search of her, for she had merely made up an address when the countess pressed for one.

Caroline's memories flooded into Cara's consciousness, and she knew what had happened, but not how to fix it. She longed to return to Willow Manor, but couldn't go back after making such a dramatic exit and deceiving the countess and Olivia.

Or could she?

Willow Manor, York - Present day

George returned from the Tudor Heritage Centre to find Cara preoccupied in the library, gazing out of the window with a heavy tome perched on her lap. 'I know that look. What's going on in that busy head of yours?'

She stretched and returned his kiss. 'I can't hide anything from you, can I?'

'I can read you like a book, but the question is, what did you find in that one?'

'It's the Georgiana volume. I was hoping some of the gaps might have been filled in again, but the pages are still blank, so it looks as though nothing is resolved and the timeline is still in flux.'

'Do you know what's going on with Caroline?'

'Last thing I recall is she left Willow Manor and is staying in some dreadful boarding house in a dismal area of London.'

'Why on earth did she leave York? I thought she was Olivia's governess.'

'To cut a long story short, she left after George went to court. She thinks he will return betrothed and obviously can't face it, so she made up some lame tale about a sick aunt and fled to London with nowhere to go and only a few shillings to her name.'

George raised one eyebrow and sat down next to Cara.

'Forgive me for saying, but isn't that just like you, my darling… to be so headstrong and impatient? To leave instead of waiting for me to come to my senses! Cara, Caroline—whatever your name is and whatever the century, you really are one and the same.'

'Oh, don't,' said Cara. 'I was too late to stop her—she had gone before I got back. I should have listened to my gut instead of delaying and listening to Eddie.'

'I suppose that's a lesson we both seem to have to keep learning,' he said, raising her hand to his lips and tenderly planting a kiss on her palm. 'Never mind, I'm sure it will work out. You'll find a way to sort it. You always do.'

'I'm not so sure. This travelling on demand malarkey is unfamiliar territory for me.'

George shifted the Georgiana volume onto his knees and flicked over the pages of fine parchment. 'This book is a marvellous thing of beauty,' he said, admiring the eighteenth-century artwork and reading some of the passages.

Cara smiled. 'It's good to see you back in your element with rare manuscripts.'

'Hold on, look! The text is rewriting itself,' George said.

They watched as a spidery line of rich dark letters formed on the page and then the writing ceased with a flourish.

'If I hadn't seen that with my own eyes, I wouldn't believe it!' George said. 'It sent tingles down my spine.'

Cara leaned over his shoulder. 'On October 17th of our lord's year 1729, Lord George Cavendish fought a duel to the death with his arch enemy, Ralph Knight.'

The following section was still blank.

'That definitely wasn't there before! The timeline is resetting as we speak. And that's a recent development—whatever has changed is because of my time traveling on demand and acting differently to how Caroline did the first time around. A quantum time loop must have triggered an alternate history,' she said.

'Are you thinking what I'm thinking?' George asked.

'If I don't find a way to stop this duel, you might die sooner than you were supposed to, and all our future timelines will be reset because you'll be reincarnated at different times.'

'I don't like the sound of that,' said George.

'Me neither. I've witnessed something similar to the text rewriting like that at the National Archives when Ralph Knight was following me through time, remember?'

George nodded. 'Yes, I do. That blasted karmic warrior is determined to finish me off, isn't he?'

Cara wrapped her arms around George and said, 'Please don't be blasé about it—he is a formidable opponent, and he will do his best to destroy us. Even our current timeline could disappear if he has his way.'

'How soon is October 17th in 1729?'

'I know it's October, so we don't have long, but I don't know the exact date. It's not as though you see the date very much in those days. Hopefully, I'll remember reading this so I can try to stop it, even though it means pushing back on time.'

'I wonder where the duel will take place?' George said.

'It will be somewhere near Willow Manor—probably in Willow Wick. Ralph has been itching for a fight ever since eighteenth-century George rode in as my saviour.'

'He's got it coming to him. I only hope my duelling skills are all they need to be, and I'll show him what for,' said George, unconsciously slipping into the role.

'Well, not if you're drunk, you won't,' said Cara. 'According to what I read before; you were in a terrible state the night of the card game.'

'Before the text disappeared, it said there was a card game, but now I'm wondering whether it's reset to a duel,' said Cara.

'What can we do?' he asked.

'There's nothing to do but wait,' said Cara, taking a sip of water. 'I just hope I get an update soon and Caroline is aware of the urgent need to get back to York rather than wandering around London seeking a new governess post.'

'Is there anything I can do?'

'I think you've done enough!' she said, wrinkling her nose at him.

'Oh, don't be like that, darling. You know I never screw it up intentionally…'

'Of course, but if Caroline doesn't get back in time to stop the duel, you could die by Ralph's sword and who knows what the repercussions will be for us all?'

George sighed and ran his fingers through his hair. 'I don't want to make things worse, but honestly, I'm terrified.

Every morning, the first thing I do is check you are next to me. We could be snatched from each other at any moment and find ourselves in a different life, married to someone else.'

'I know,' said Cara, reaching for his hand. 'Try not to think about it. Let's hope this will all be over soon.'

CHAPTER 29

Willow Manor, York - Georgiana

George was not his usual self—he was in a dark place, and everyone knew it. There were whispers throughout the estate, as no one would risk being overheard talking about the master of the great house.

But as gossip has a way of doing, it soon made its way to Willow Wick and it wasn't long before Ralph Knight heard George was in a bad way. Depending on where you heard it and who you heard it from, some said his lady love had jilted him at court, while others said he'd taken a fancy to the governess, and she had rejected him and broken his heart.

Only tiny fragments of these whispers reached the ears of the countess and Olivia, but they spoke of him in worried snatches of conversation.

'Mother, what do you think ails George? He isn't himself since his return—he said it's over between him and Charlotte, and I fear he has taken it badly, has he not?'

The countess paused in her needlework, which was a pastime she had reluctantly resumed since Caroline vacated her role and Olivia had no one with whom to pass the long October days. The weather took a sharp winter turn and Willow Manor lost its summer sheen and was shrouded in gloom, as though reflecting the state of its devastated master.

'I must confess I know not what troubles George. He said he had made the decision not to go ahead with the betrothal, so I do not understand why he is in such low spirits,' said the countess. 'We must do our utmost to rally round and cheer him for I have never seen the dear boy in such a sorry state.'

'He drinks at all hours of the day, and has taken to gambling in the village, you know,' whispered Olivia, feeling traitorous. The need to tell her mother what was on her mind outweighed her fierce loyalty to her beloved brother. 'Just yesterday, I mentioned I was missing Caroline, seeking to divert his mind from thoughts of Charlotte, but he fair snapped my head off,' continued Olivia, close to tears at the memory of George's scolding.

THE WHISPERS REACHED Ralph as he worked on the farm early one morning, when his brother came to break the news.

'Word has it that Caroline—the governess—has left the manor and gone to London.'

Ralph replayed the conversation in his mind all day, and his anger smouldered at the memory of the smug look on his brother's face when he mocked him by referring to Caroline as the governess. He could not bear to be ridiculed and had given his brother a short, sharp punch in the stomach.

He was in a black mood and thunderous that Caroline had escaped his grasp without having the decency to tell him she was leaving. Ralph still saw her as his fiancé, no matter how many times she told him they would not be man and wife.

He blamed George for the rift that had arisen between him and his childhood sweetheart, and for her leaving. He was determined to get her back, and his mind turned over possible courses of action continuously. Caroline and George dominated his thoughts, and a desire for vengeance on them both consumed him. Something deep within told him that George's sour mood was nothing to do with some fancy courtier, but was because of Caroline. The noble earl was in love with her. Ralph had seen it on his face when he had come to her defence, and he was damned if he would allow her to get away with spurning him, and George to get away with stealing his woman from under his nose. The fires of injustice blazed within him and plagued him day and night.

And then one day, an opportunity presented itself.

Early one morning when he and his brother were cleaning out the horses, he heard about an upcoming card game.

'The earl has been leaving heaps of silver around the village, playing cards like a fool possessed,' said his brother as he scattered the dirty hay loose from the prongs of the sharp fork. 'You are lucky at cards. I was of a mind that you might want to take him on and win some coin... we need a new roof on the outhouse.'

Ralph raised his head and stared at his brother; his blue eyes gleaming. 'Luck has nothing to do with it,' he said, arrogant as ever.

They chatted a while longer and his brother told him all he knew as Ralph questioned him. 'The next game is set for tonight at The Lion's Heart.'

'Is that so?' said Ralph, already envisioning himself stripping George of his wealth and showing him up to be the drunken fop he was. He would rip out his heart at The Lion's Heart—how fitting.

The earl had ruined his life, and he meant to make him pay. This would be the perfect way, and a plan formed in his mind.

George sat at the corner table in the tavern, waiting for the other players. He continued his dissolute habit of playing cards deep into the night and drinking until he could barely stand. Even by court standards, his behaviour was reckless, so he had decided to return home to nurse his heartache away from the scrutiny of the strait-laced king and queen. It wouldn't do for them to see him spiral downwards, and he couldn't seem to get a grip on himself no matter how he tried.

Each day stretched before him, and he felt Caroline's loss so keenly he struggled to breathe. It was as though there was a hole where his heart used to be, and he had lost all enthusiasm for living.

Knowing she was safe at Willow Manor had made their parting bearable, but when he learned she had left and subsequently disappeared in London and he could not track her down, he blamed himself and a gloomy cloud darkened his every thought and movement. Life didn't seem worth living any longer, and if he didn't have a glimmer of hope that she might return soon, he would leave England and take a trip to the continent to escape his sorrows. Everything about Willow Manor reminded him of her, and even in sleep he knew no peace, for his dreams were filled with her sweet face.

He questioned the meaning of it all. What was the point of having a grand estate and title, and all the riches bestowed on him by his heritage, if he were to spend his days pining for his true love whom he could never have?

He did his best to pretend all was well, but there was no joy in his heart, and it was plain for all to see.

He warmed his cold hands by the blazing, popping fire and clicked the heels of his boots on the hard floor, impatient for the game to begin. Playing cards was the only pastime which held his attention long enough for him to not dwell on thoughts of Caroline, which gave respite to his aching soul. Drinking only deepened his melancholy, but he sought oblivion and consumed copious amounts of whisky.

He heard the harsh winds beating against the tavern walls, and cold air whistled into the room as the door banged and George turned to see who would play across from him this evening.

'Good evening, my lord. Is lord the right term or should I call you earl?' Ralph mock bowed and spat on the floor near to George's boots, before removing his heavy cloak and sneering. 'I hope you are ready to be beaten today.'

George, who was already in his cups, rose to the bait, just as Ralph intended.

'I know where Caroline is, by the way,' Ralph taunted. 'She said she had to get away from you and your kind, and now she is safe in London.'

George stared at him, thinking about how he would love to flatten his nose into his smug face.

'What are you talking about?' he said, trying to compose himself in his whisky soaked state. He must not let this devil get the better of him or reveal anything to him about Caroline. He didn't know why it was so imperative, only that it was. He must protect her from this blackguard at all costs, and God help her if Ralph tracked her down when she was alone without his or her father's protection. George had no doubt he would force her to marry him or turn her into his whore.

'You can pretend you don't know what I'm talking about. The word is you are pining for your fine lady from court, but I know better. You've fallen for my Caroline, haven't you?' Ralph hissed as he spoke and lay a pack of playing cards on the table. 'It is a shame because she will never be yours. The lass is too good for the likes of you.'

A muscle twitched in George's face, and he held his fists close to his thighs below the table.

'Are we to play cards, or did you come here only to insult me?' asked George, his usually velvet-edged voice, steely and cold.

'We have waited long enough. No one seems to be willing to brave the foul weather this evening so let the games begin,' said Ralph. 'I shall relieve you of your silver and whatever else you wish to bring to the table, soon enough, and we can be on our way.'

George regretted drinking so much and could see his opponent had a vindictive clarity about him and if he wasn't careful, he was liable to lose the contents of his purse. But he must play... he wouldn't bow down to this low-born fool.

Ralph downed the topped-up glass of whisky served by the eager-to-please wench.

'So be it. What will we play for?' George replied.

Caroline and Cara's consciousness were as one and she knew she was time travelling and that George was in terrible danger.

She passed another miserable night at the boarding house and cursed her impetuosity. She should have stayed at Willow Manor—at least she was safe and would know what was going on with George. When she finally drifted off to sleep despite the drunken shouts from the street below her window, it wasn't long before she awoke in a panic; trembling, her damp shift stuck to her body from night sweats. Vivid images from her dreams flashed through her mind—she saw herself sitting with George in the present day as the family history book updated, and then she saw George in this timeline, playing cards with Ralph in Willow Wick.

Am I Caroline or Cara?

She shook her head, overwhelmed by the two conflicting realities competing for her attention. She made up her mind, and rose quickly from the narrow, bug infested mattress and dressed hurriedly, pulling her gown over her damp shift to make herself look presentable. Looking in the glass, she saw her cheeks were red and feverish, and she appeared as flustered as she felt.

I must get to Willow Wick. There is no time to waste.

She was certain the timeline was now resetting, but she didn't know what would occur, other than what she and George had learned from the legend and from the Georgiana volume. There would be a fire—unless she could stop it, and the Cavendish family would somehow lose ownership of the estate. She must prevent it, or they would lose everything, and when she returned to present day, what would she find?

The thought of what awaited her sent a chill down her spine, and she shivered. What if George wasn't there when she got back? Would they lose their future together after all they had been through to make things, right? Would Willow Manor still be theirs or would the timeline reset again, so it had never come back into their family? Everything depended on what happened next, and she left the boarding house, determined to reach York as soon as possible.

She decided the sensible course of action was not to return to the house, but to go to the village. If necessary, she would stay at her father's cottage and keep her presence a secret.

Progress to York was slow. She boarded a coach to leave the city and get onto the Great North Road, but then she was deposited outside an inn where she must either borrow a horse or secure a place on another coach.

Memories of past journeys on the familiar road accosted her mind, and she remembered their dear friend, Madame Alicia, who would be long dead, but perhaps the inn would still be there. She trudged for several miles, holding the skirts of her gown so they wouldn't trail in the mud as she headed toward where she thought the building had stood in 1536.

Already weary, her belly aching for sustenance, she pushed herself to place one foot stolidly in front of the other until she spotted a building that resembled the establishment Madame Alicia was so proud of in the Tudorville days.

She paused to catch her breath as a fierce stitch gripped her side—then walked slowly towards the front of the building but as she approached, it became clear the place was nothing more than an old, ruined shack; a shell of its former glory. Sadness consumed her whole being as she remembered Madame Alicia, and the kindness she had shown them when they had been fleeing for their lives during their time at Henry VIII's court.

The memories of all she had lost—dear friends and familiar places—shook her, and she moved to the side of the road towards a clearing where she would be out of sight. Tears streamed down her face and for a time, she could not think clearly.

At this moment, her memory of multiple lives seemed more a curse than a rare gift. While people who lived ordinary lives must inevitably endure the loss of their loved ones, she was reminded over and over of the friends who were no more, and of those who were still with her but whom could be wiped from the timeline at any moment with a careless reset. More images flashed through her mind as Caroline's memory updated, and she saw Madame Alicia dressed in all her finery, followed by Anne Boleyn's sombre, dark eyes as the sword was about to wipe her elegant head from her neck. And then, hardest of all, she saw the sweet, innocent faces of their children, Thomas and May.

Will I ever see them again or am I destined to move in and out of timelines only when tragedy occurs?

The pain of her past lives rose to the surface like a festering wound and spurred her on back to George. She must find him and stop Willow Manor from ending up like this old, abandoned place. She must find him before Ralph, their old enemy, destroyed their union, as he had sworn to do in 1536.

She raised her tired limbs from the grassy mound where she had rested a while, and with resolute steps, resumed her journey on the muddy road in search of a coach to take her to Willow Wick. She must reach George before it was too late, whether they were to be together in this life or not.

CHAPTER 30

Willow Manor, York - Present day

THEY FINISHED BREAKFAST, and George read the paper and Cara flicked through the Georgiana volume, hoping for inspiration, when Kate burst into the room.

'I had another one of those crazy dreams,' she said.

Cara pulled out a chair for her sister-in-law and Kate sat down and pushed a stray lock of hair away from her eyes.

'What was it about?' Cara asked, as George's eyes moved from the article to his sister's face.

'What put you in such a spin?' he said.

Kate poured herself a glass of orange juice and looked from George to Cara. 'I'm afraid you'll think me quite mad, but the dream seemed so real—like a window into another life.'

'That ship sailed long ago,' George said, a teasing smile crossing his lips.

Cara rolled her eyes. 'Don't mind your brother, Kate. Go on, what happened in the dream?'

'Well, I was in this very house, but it all looked different—like we were in the Georgian era again. I was wearing this old-fashioned floating gown, and my name was Olivia… the same as last time.'

'I see,' said Cara. 'And did anything happen, or was it more than just the feeling of being in another time?'

'No, if only! I woke up in a terrible panic because Willow Manor was on fire. You know how it is in dreams when you see something, but you can't do anything to stop it? It was like that, and a terrifying sense of doom haunted me.'

Kate leant back against her chair and took a deep breath. 'Even thinking about it makes me tremble.'

Cara patted Kate's arm. 'I know dreams can seem so real, but it was just a dream. The memory will soon pass.'

'I hope you're right, but honestly, I don't know what to make of it all. The strangest things have been happening ever since I arrived. There was that weird deja-vu in the priest hole and repeated instances of feeling like I've been here before. Could Olivia really be our ancestor and I'm actually remembering a past life?' She lowered her voice, stunned by her own question.

'It is bizarre, that's for certain. What did Sylvia have to say about it?' asked Cara.

Kate shook her head. 'She said it is possible that I'm experiencing karmic memories. I came out of there more confused than I went in, to be honest.'

'Would you like some breakfast?' George asked, reaching out to pat his sister's arm in a comforting gesture.

'No, thank you, I don't think I can eat.' Kate turned to Cara. 'Does it say anything in that Georgian family book about a daughter named Olivia and a governess called Caroline?'

'I don't think so,' replied Cara carefully. 'Although swathes of the text are illegible.'

'May I have a look?' Kate asked, nodding towards the book, which now lay closed in front of Cara on the table.

Cara pushed it slowly towards her. 'Of course. I couldn't get much from it with so much of the text faded. George said the quality of the ink hasn't stood the test of time.'

Kate pored over the book and Cara did her best to stay calm and act normal, but her heart beat riotously, and she exchanged an anxious look with George as they waited to see what Kate would find.

'So, you found this book when you moved in?' Kate asked, after what seemed an age.

Cara nodded. 'Yes, I dug it out of one of those big old storage cupboards in the kitchen. Who knows why it wasn't in the library? It was fortunate I stumbled across it.'

'This is amazing,' she said, engrossed in the old book, as she turned the delicate pages, taking care not to rip them. She raised her eyes to meet Cara's. 'Even though I've known about our family history since I was a kid, it barely seems possible that our roots go back so far in this same house.'

Cara watched Kate's gleaming eyes and knew with a sinking feeling that she wouldn't be easily distracted from trying to uncover more of the secrets of the past. She didn't want to lie to Kate—it was true she had read nothing specifically about Olivia or Caroline—yet… She felt deceitful not telling her what she knew, but if she did, she would sound like a lunatic.

Well, it's like this Kate... George and I are time travellers through the centuries, and it looks as though you may be a reincarnation of Olivia, George's sister, and yes, I was your governess in Georgian times. Um. Maybe not.

Cara sought George's eyes again and gave a slight shrug of her shoulders. What could they do other than hope she didn't find any tangible proof? They could hide things from her, but they couldn't stop her from dreaming and the dreams were becoming more insistent.

Kate left for her shift at the centre, and Cara breathed a sigh of relief.

'What should we do?' she said.

'Absolutely nothing. We'll just have to let it unfold and see what she figures out.'

'Are you sure we shouldn't tell her?'

He shook his head. 'We would do her no favours by bringing her deeper into this—let's leave it and see what happens, if anything.'

Cara nodded, then pointed to where the new text now marked the faded pages.

George laid his newspaper down on the table and shifted his full attention to the book. 'Here,' she prompted, again.

'It's amazing,' he said.

Cara stared out of the window, lost in thoughts of Georgiana. She was experiencing sporadic memory updates, but she didn't understand what was going on, other than she had been on her way back to York to stop the house burning down.

'What did you make of Kate's dream? She saw the fire!'

'Do we know what happened to Olivia?'

Cara shook her head. 'We don't know much at all. There are so many missing pieces to the story. I don't even know if George and Caroline got together in the end, but I don't suppose they would have been able to marry without bringing disgrace on the family. Imagine the noble George Cavendish falling in love with a penniless governess—just an educated servant, really.'

George peered at her over his spectacles, which rested on the bridge of his nose. 'I know it's difficult, but it might be best to do nothing… at least for now.'

'But I'm worried about Olivia and the countess. Not to mention the rest of the household. What if someone gets seriously hurt? Every time we tinker with history by going back to relive it, we risk making things worse.'

George reached for her hand.

'Kate's dream was either a karmic memory update or she had a premonition of what is about to happen,' said Cara. 'We just have to hope Caroline gets back in time to stop George setting fire to the house.'

George looked startled. 'What? No matter how much whisky the eighteenth-century version of me drank, I find it hard to believe I would actually destroy my own house.'

'Me too, but that was what they told you in Victoriana, remember? The legend is that the earl was heartbroken and tried to burn the house down after losing the estate in a card game.'

'Let's hope you get there in time to stop the game, so you can save him from his drunken idiocy!'

Cara rose from her seat. 'I can't wait around like this doing nothing. I'm going to call Sylvia and see if she can fit me in today.'

George studied his wife's face. 'What are you hoping to find out?'

'Sylvia has a way of seeing things and I think the more we understand about what's going on, the better.'

'Would you like some company, darling? I worry about you when you're like this.'

She leant over and kissed him. 'No, I'm okay. Nothing to worry about. You stay here and keep an eye on Kate. Who knows what she'll remember next? You're in charge of keeping her off the scent, at least until this thing plays out. You're right—if we were to tell her what's going on now, we'd only scare and possibly even endanger her.'

'Okay,' he said. 'No problem.'

Cara blew him another kiss and slipped out the door.

That afternoon she settled into a chair opposite Sylvia and told her the latest about the book updates and asked for guidance.

'My intuition tells me this is not a day for Tarot, but we must seek assistance from the ascended masters.' Sylvia shuffled the oracle cards and signalled for Cara to tell her when to stop as she placed them on the table, one by one.

'Now,' said Cara, her heart drumming so loudly she heard it ringing in her ears. Her eyes moved to study the card Sylvia flipped over.

'Ah, the ascended master, Saint Germain, is with us. Let me see what he may tell us about the book,' said Sylvia as she rested her hand on the card, closed her eyes, and began to sway gently from side to side.

The room grew warm, and Cara studied Sylvia's face and waited as the psychic sank deeper into one of her trances.

Patience, Cara, patience.

Willow Wick, York - Georgiana

A small crowd gathered around a table at The Lion's Heart and the group of villagers stood transfixed as the stakes grew ever higher in the game of whist.

George revealed some lucky hands and his confidence was growing even as his lucidity diminished. The serving girl topped up George's glass whenever Ralph nodded discreetly in her direction.

George's luck had turned sour, and his judgement grew more and more questionable when he was down to his last heap of silver coins stacked on the table between him and his opponent. George's words slurred as he upped his bets and his pockets were all but empty.

'Shall we call it a night, your lordship? I fear we have had enough,' whispered George's servant, Taylor, discreetly in his ear.

He then moved to cover George's glass with a firm hand when the girl made to top it up once more. He shook his head and signalled for her to retreat.

'No, leave me be,' said George. 'I have more in me yet and I feel certain my luck will soon turn again.'

At the end of the round, Ralph neatly swept the pile of coins off the table into his hand and added them to the heavy weight in his pocket. 'What shall we play for next? The great earl surely won't allow a lowly farmer such as I to defeat him so brutally,' Ralph taunted. The smile on his handsome face was bitter, and his blue eyes held menacing shadows in their icy depths.

George straightened and looked at his enemy, curiously lucid for one so drunk. 'You are right, Master Knight. Play on, we shall. Such a one as you, shall not beat me, and believe me when I say it has nothing to do with your birth and everything to do with your lack of honour.'

'If you insist on insulting me in that manner, earl or no, I shall demand satisfaction and we shall decide who is the more honourable of us by the blade of our swords,' said Ralph, his voice low and hostile.

The crowd whispered, and the air was charged as they looked at the two men: one bent on beating the other at any price, and one bent on finishing the other off, at the cost of the destruction of all he held sacred.

One of the local tenants, who knew and admired George, rallied his courage and spoke. 'My lord, shall we not see you home?' He then turned to Ralph, and said, 'This is below even you, Knight. The earl has clearly had too much whisky to play another round or to give you satisfaction in a duel. Let us reconvene tomorrow and play fair.'

The crowd booed, and Ralph snarled, 'Be away with you man if you haven't the stomach to witness his defeat.'

George's groom leant over to talk in his ear again, but George swatted him away like a tiresome fly, not recognising his folly in his paralytic state. All he knew was that he must beat this devil who continually goaded him and who threatened Caroline.

'So, what shall it be?' said Ralph, sensing his opponent had sunk to his most vulnerable and determined to press the advantage.

George considered for a moment, trying to decide what he would gamble to show his confidence and finish Ralph once and for all. The idea that flashed into his mind shocked him, but he sipped the dregs of his whisky, steadied himself, and met Ralph's glare head on. 'I add Willow Manor to the pot.'

Ralph's icy blue eyes gleamed.

'Hold on, and what will Ralph put into the pot for he has nothing of an equivalent value? How is that fair?' George's groom, Taylor, interjected as he tried to pull George aside to talk some sense into him.

Ralph's voice rang out, 'I will add my farm to the pot. It isn't the same monetary value, I grant you, but it is all I own, and so in that sense it is an equivalent bet.'

There were murmurings as various parties in the crowd discussed the terms of the pot and whether it was fair.

'Are you the sole owner of the farm?' George asked.

Ralph nodded. 'I am the eldest son and my father passed away last year; God rest his soul.'

Ralph's brother protested, but was quickly silenced with a firm hand.

'Then I accept your terms,' said George. 'Let us play on. I propose two-handed whist.'

Ralph nodded.

A hushed silence fell over the room and all eyes moved to the deck of woven silk cards, shuffled by the nominated dealer who dealt thirteen cards to each player.

Ralph was only too pleased George had picked a game that required a sharp memory and strategic thinking, while his opponent was in such a sorry state.

After some time, they reached the second stage of the game, where the object was to win as many tricks as possible. George won his second trick in a row and drew the top flipped up card. Ralph's face was dark as he concentrated on his hand. They continued as George won several more, and then Ralph won three tricks in a row and George looked on, his expression strained.

It was a close round, but on the deciding point, Ralph produced a king and waved it jubilantly in George's face.

Ralph laid the last card down on the table, triumphant. 'I declare myself the new owner of Willow Manner estate.'

George gasped and shook his head.

'I think not, my good Sir, you are mistaken, for if ever there was a cheating hand, that was one. I saw you switch that card from the other pile, which is against the rules. Let us end this nonsense forthwith.'

Ralph stood and upended the table with his large, calloused hands. The cards scattered to the floor, and he moved towards George, violent rage clearly etched into his features, his mouth set in a grim line.

Taylor, who was also a big burly man, captured Ralph's arms to prevent him from approaching George, who had lost his balance on the other side of the fallen table.

'I would rather burn Willow Manor down with my own

hands than see it in your thieving ones,' swore George as he rose and steadied himself.

'I demand satisfaction in a duel,' hissed Ralph. 'Your master repeatedly insults my honour and is a poor loser. If he won't admit defeat, I will give him a chance to settle this once and for all.'

'If you touch a hair on my lord's head, I shall run a sword through you myself,' said Taylor.

'What are your terms?' George said, straight-backed and alert, as the reality of what he had done dawned on him. Images of his mother and Olivia filled his head, and then he saw Caroline's face as clearly as though she were in front of him.

'Step down,' said George to Taylor. 'A duel between us is long overdue. This blackguard has insulted not only me but also those whom I hold dear. He and his brothers have a record of poaching from my lands, and I shall gladly accept his challenge to defend my honour against his obvious lack of such a quality.'

One villager whispered to another, 'This isn't about Willow Manor, it is about the governess. They have both lost their minds over the Radcliff girl.'

'You are presumptuous indeed, Master Knight, to be so emboldened as to challenge a member of the nobility to a duel, but in this instance, I shall overlook it, for your sins abound and there is plenty to fight for. Let us formalise the details so we may abide by the duelling code and the outcome shall be final and rests only in the hands of God,' said George.

An eerie silence filled the tavern as George's eyes clashed with Ralph's, both men knowing there was no backing down now without losing face.

George had nothing to lose, for he had already lost his most cherished possession.

'You demanded satisfaction, so it is you who must challenge me formally,' said George, his voice quiet but firm.

Ralph said, 'Very well. We must keep it between us, or we will both be for the courts—even you are not above the law, Lord Cavendish.'

'It is not I who needs to be,' replied George.

'I challenge you to a duel at dawn in the clearing in the woods by the river—our meeting point shall be the old shack beneath the willow tree,' said Ralph.

George nodded solemnly and accepted, his voice clear and calm. 'I will see you at dawn. Mind to appoint a second. Mine will be Taylor.' He looked over at his groom, who nodded his acceptance.

The seconds will discuss the details so the duel will be fair and final.

'Are you proposing a duel to the death?' Ralph asked, a flicker of fear in his blue eyes.

'That is exactly what I propose. Sharpen your rapier, Knight, and bring your man with you at dawn. I am weary of your insults; we shall end this once and for all. May the best man win.'

George exited the tavern amidst a hubbub of noise, with Taylor close on his heels. The two men rode away to prepare for the dawn showdown. George sobered up abruptly as the chilly morning air roused his senses.

He could not lose the duel, or not only would he die, but his family would be cast out of their ancestral home, and he would go down in the family history books as the Cavendish black sheep who ruined them all.

CHAPTER 31

Sylvia's office, York - Present day

Sylvia fell into a deep trance and Cara watched in awe as the ecstatic expressions played over her face. Cara crossed and uncrossed her legs as she waited for the psychic to return to her usual level of consciousness and reveal what she had seen.

Sylvia's eyes flickered open, and she beamed at Cara. 'Was I gone long?'

'A while, yes. You looked so peaceful.'

Sylvia nodded. 'The divine love source was strong and stable. I connected with Saint Germain.'

Cara stared at Sylvia, speechless, and then swallowed. 'What did he say?'

'The book is linked to the Akashic Records. Does that mean anything to you?'

'No,' said Cara. 'What on earth are they?'

Sylvia patiently explained that the Akashic Records are

the accounts of all soul activity; past, present, and future.

Cara still looked blank, and Sylvia took a sip of water and tried to explain further. 'They comprise a body of knowledge that is believed to contain a record of everything a soul has ever thought, said or done—for all time. They are typically accessible only to spiritual masters, hence my reaching out to the ascended masters.'

'I see,' said Cara, looking intrigued. 'But what does that have to do with the book?'

'The book is your conduit to the Akashic Records which are being updated and it appears the book deletes and records events as the timeline resets.'

'I don't fully understand. How does that help us?'

Sylvia shook her head, a puzzled expression in her gold-flecked eyes. 'I'm not exactly sure,' she said, swinging her tortoiseshell glasses by one arm as she contemplated what she had witnessed in her divine trance. 'It's extraordinary. Mind you, it always is when you walk in here!'

Cara smiled politely, not wanting to dampen Sylvia's enthusiasm, but her heart sank. She didn't feel up to going deeper into the realms of yet more universal mysteries.

The familiar thought crossed her mind: *Why can't we just live a normal life?*

'I know what you're thinking,' said Sylvia with a knowing smile.

'You do?'

Sylvia nodded. 'You're wishing this wasn't happening to you again and you could just be normal.'

Cara sighed. 'How the heck did you know that? Can you see into my mind?'

'Aside from your face being an open book?' Sylvia asked.

Cara smiled ruefully.

'When I enter a deep trance, the effects take a while to wear off and my consciousness remains heightened for some time. I can sense your thoughts to a higher degree than normal. I am a psychic, remember…'

'Incredible,' said Cara, 'You never fail to astound me.'

'And you me,' replied Sylvia. 'Here's the thing. You are not normal. Twin Flames aren't destined to be normal—we have access to supernatural powers that others think only occur in movies.'

'Okay, so will the book tell me what to do?'

'If only it were that simple, but no… If I've understood correctly, the book will update as a direct reaction to your actions. It's like a sort of soul ledger,' said Sylvia.

Cara sighed again. She was tired and frustrated and had been hoping for more concrete guidance—something specific she could do to avert the disaster she feared was about to repeat itself two hundred years ago, only it could potentially be even worse thanks to her messing with the timeline. 'I must stop George from burning the house down in Georgiana.'

'If that was definitely going to happen, the text wouldn't have disappeared. From what you've said, the timeline is resetting, and you are free to create an alternative history for you and George in 1729.'

'How many shots do we have?' Cara asked.

'I don't know, but tread lightly. Only make the changes you feel clearly guided to make. The book could just seal again if other factors are at play, and then you will have to live with the past, present and future according to the latest version of the records.'

'That sounds terrifyingly fatalistic,' said Cara.

'It's daunting but look at it as an opportunity to redeem some of the lost one hundred and eleven years when you and George were separated because of past foolish decisions. Now you have a clean slate to do it all again, and it might come out much better this time around.'

They ended the session and Cara drove home on autopilot, the latest revelations running through her hectic mind like a ticker tape. The weight of their past, present, and future lay heavily on her consciousness as she considered the responsibility of directly affecting the mysterious Akashic Records.

Does it really mean I'm being guided to redeem our missing timeline and make it right for our past selves between 1729 and 1840?

When she arrived back at Willow Manor, she went immediately to review the book. She could swear it twinkled at her as it lay where she had left it on the table, tempting her to engage with it again. She turned the pages to the blank sections.

Her blood raced as she realised there had been a new entry after she left—the ink was fresh on the page as if it was recently written by hand:

"Lord George Cavendish lost the card game to Master Ralph Knight, and with it, the Willow Manor estate. The earl accused his opponent of cheating and Ralph Knight demanded satisfaction in the form of a duel. The earl accepted the challenge."

Cara closed the book with a thud and headed towards the door to look for George. But then she heard the buzz of the vortex and the chill of the freezing air enveloped her. She felt herself slipping away.

And then she was gone.

Willow Wick, York - Georgiana

The tall willow trees lined the outskirts of the clearing, like soldiers on guard to witness the duel.

George and Ralph stood at opposite ends of the small group of spectators. They swished their blades, practiced lunges, and readied themselves for the fight that would decide their destiny. They had a brief conversation with their seconds and then the opponents moved close enough to reach out and touch each other with their swords.

Ralph's second, his brother, stood nearby looking pale and anxious. Taylor stood near his master, and an ominous silence filled the clearing in the woods. The only sound was the gentle ripple of the waters flowing in the cold river.

'According to the rules of the duelling code I am beholden to enquire whether you wish to apologise, and I offer you the opportunity to call off the duel…,' said Ralph, after one of the small crowd of onlookers instructed him on the necessary protocol.

George didn't falter and immediately replied, 'I think not, Master Knight. It is you who cheated, not I. Let us proceed—unless of course you would apologise and are willing before these witnesses to forsake your ridiculous claim to my estate.'

Ralph's face darkened, and he swished his rapier sword through the air from side to side. 'No, Sir. You accepted my challenge and therefore we shall duel to decide the outcome. I have only one question.'

'Let us hear it, Master Knight.'

'We both know what we are about to do is illegal in the eyes of the court,' said Ralph.

The tension in the crowd was palpable and the cooing of a wood pigeon echoed through the clearing.

George inclined his head in agreement. 'Yes, and we must agree on the terms so there is no doubt as to the winner.'

'Are you still for duelling to the death, then?' Ralph asked.

A dense silence fell as the crowd of hardened gamblers and weary revellers from all layers of village society watched, mesmerised, as the duellists prepared for the fatal fight.

'Yes, to the death, or until one of us begs for mercy. And if I prevail, your claim to Willow Manor and my supposed gambling debt are wiped clean. Do I have your word before these many witnesses?' George's voice grew louder as he outlined the terms of the duel.

Ralph nodded and said, 'Yes, I accept your terms.'

George withdrew a leather glove from the pocket of his long coat and threw it onto the ground, which was a sign for the duel to begin.

The duellists took tentative steps, circling each other in the centre of the clearing. Their seconds stood by and watched as George and Ralph locked swords.

CAROLINE STOPPED ONLY to rest her aching limbs briefly and exchange horses at an inn before continuing her journey to York. An inner force propelled her onwards and battled her foggy mental fatigue and bodily exhaustion, and she sensed that hers and the fate of the man she loved hung in the balance, and depended on what she did next.

Her dreams had been a confusing mixture of past, present, and future and all she knew for certain was that she must get to Willow Wick to stop something dreadful happening, but she knew not what.

She had flashes of clarity when she was aware she was Cara, but then Caroline's consciousness took over and she lost the connection and was just a governess trying to find the man she loved. She had ridden through the night as fast as she could. Her pace was slow as the horse had been hesitant to move fast through the dark, and the chestnut mare jumped at the shadows and at every noise of the awakening countryside.

She steadied the mare as best she could, and they pressed on until they arrived at the outskirts of Willow Wick. The rising light told her dawn was already upon them, and she was freezing from the shower of icy rain which sprayed down on her head, causing her to shudder beneath the folds of the thick, velvet lined cloak which was a gift from dear Olivia.

As she entered the village, intending to knock on her father's door, her eyelids grew heavy from lack of sleep, and she longed to close her eyes and forget the sense of foreboding which nudged at her senses. But before she could give way to her desire for slumber, the smell of burning assailed her nostrils and throat until she coughed and spluttered. The night air was heavy with the acrid smell of smoke, and she wondered what the cause of it at this early hour could be. Even the most dedicated of servants would only just be thinking about preparing the fires in the hearths of the big house.

Cara's memory kicked in and the reality of what was about to happen flooded her mind.

There was a fire at Willow Manor! That was part of the legend of the house and why it had fallen into ruin all those years ago.

She spurred her horse on in what she gauged was the direction of the house and it wasn't long before she saw orange flames leaping and licking in the distance, like a mirage of doom. Caroline pushed the tired mare on and rallied her to go faster, and they cantered towards the flames. All she could think of was who was at home. She feared the members of the household would all still be asleep and trapped in the burning house.

Would George die in the fire in this alternative timeline? What have we done?

Willow Manor, York - Present day

As Cara slept, she saw Ralph enter Willow Manor stealthily through the unlocked servants' door. He picked up the night candle from the kitchen table and carried it to light his way as he walked through the dark, silent corridors of the great house. He looked around him as his boots trod silently on the cold wooden floors, and Cara could feel the vengeance and envy in his heart. His sole purpose was to enact his plan to destroy Caroline and George's future.

They would pay for what they had done to him.

In her dream, she was unable to move—frozen to the spot as she watched him tilt the candle flame towards the wooden furniture and wait until it caught fire, before he turned his attention to the next surface. She tried to cry out and appeal to him, but the words made no sound and he carried on, methodically setting the house alight.

Only after he lit several pieces of furniture and saw the flames begin to take hold and lick the wood, did he retreat from the room and hurry back through the wing and towards the servants' unlocked door. Cara was transfixed and powerless to stop him as he quietly let himself out and the flames spread across the room as everyone slept. She was an observer from three hundred years into the future. There was nothing she could do…

'The house is on fire!' Cara shouted, and she shot up in bed.

George fumbled to turn on the light. 'You're having a

nightmare. It's okay, darling. It's just a dream.' He wrapped his arm around her.

She jerked away from him. 'No! You don't understand. Willow Manor is on fire. We have to stop it, or Ralph will burn it to the ground.'

'Ralph?'

Slowly, Cara emerged from her sleepy haze and slumped back down onto the bed. 'Oh, my God. It was as if I was there. I saw him set fire to the furniture in one of the drawing rooms. It wasn't George who did it, after all! But I think it was a premonition.'

'At the risk of stating the obvious, you're talking about something that happened almost three hundred years ago, so how on earth can it be a premonition?' said George. 'It's too late to do anything about it now, anyway,' he said, rubbing his red eyes. 'Isn't it?'

'Maybe, but what if it was a warning that George dies in the fire? He didn't light it, but that doesn't mean he can't die in it!' Cara said.

'You mean if the timeline has reset and created an alternative future?'

'I need to see if the book has updated,' said Cara, as she jumped out of bed, galvanised into action, and haunted by the dream.

She sought the comfort of George's warm hand as he followed her downstairs.

Was their wonderful present-day life together about to come to an end?

CHAPTER 32

Willow Wick, York - Georgiana

THE FINE WHITE linen sleeves of George's shirt billowed in the early morning breeze as the blade of his sword sliced through the air, narrowly missing Ralph's shoulder as he side-stepped.

The two men were poised to strike. Neither had fought a deadly duel before and the nervousness showed in their tentative actions. Their boots were covered in mud and the soft ground from weeks of rainfall impeded their progress as they circled each other.

Ralph made a bold swipe at George. He missed sinking the blade into his opponent's side by a hair's breadth, but it slit the lace on his shirt instead, which dangled like an unravelled bandage.

George glanced down for a second and cursed; shocked how close he had come to being stabbed.

They resumed their circling once again in the silent

woods, like tigers waiting to pounce, each awaiting the right second to strike the killer blow. The onlookers stood like statues; transfixed, not wanting to distract the men whose life depended on the outcome of this duel to the death.

George raised his sword and aimed at Ralph's torso, who then countered the attack, and they struggled, equally matched in strength as their swords locked. George withdrew his blade and twisted away, and those in the crowd who favoured him, breathed a sigh of relief, but as he prepared to make his next move, the tip of Ralph's sword slit the soft flesh of his cheek and drew blood.

George gasped but extracted himself and put some distance between him and Ralph while he regained his composure.

Taylor approached the duelling pair and looked at George, whose face dripped blood, which splashed onto his now muddy shirt. 'I must ask, my lord, will you not consider calling this off?' He looked from George to Ralph, but soon saw by the murderous expressions on both of their faces that there was little hope of reconciliation.

George dismissed him with a shake of his head. 'Let us resume, if you are agreed, Knight?'

Ralph nodded without hesitating. 'I will only call it off if you apologise for the slurs on my honour. Otherwise let us duel to the death.'

'No chance, for every word was true,' said George, as he swiped at Ralph with his sword with renewed vigour, even as the blood dripped on his shirt and splashed onto his boots. He realised he must end this soon, for his face was bleeding heavily, his head throbbed, and his right hand was covered in blood, which made it difficult to grip the sword.

George had some friendly fencing experience and decided to trust his gut as he channelled his anger into combat. The long slender blade hit its intended destination, and the crowd saw it flash and heard it slither through the air as it cut into Ralph and he screamed out and bent over, clutching his stomach, his face drained of colour.

The cut on George's face stung, and the rage in his heart fuelled his fury. Ralph fell to his knees and then twisted onto his back and George pressed the tip of the narrow blade of the sword firmly against him so he wouldn't be able to escape even if he had the strength. Blood dripped from Ralph's wound, and he cried out again and begged for mercy.

Ralph's brother held up his hand to George, signalling for a truce, and he bent down to examine the wound and exchange words with the injured party. After a minute, he looked up at George and Taylor, and said, 'It is bad. I fear he may not live if we don't stem the flow of bleeding and tend to the injury. For the love of God, will you call it off, now?'

George indicated to Ralph's brother to move aside, and he loomed over Ralph, who lay shaking and ashen on the ground. George prodded his sword into the hem of his opponent's buckram waistcoat so it wouldn't cut into his flesh, but so he couldn't move without the risk of the blade slicing into him again.

'Although we agreed on a fight to the death, I have no taste for killing, unless it is your wish to continue the duel,' said George, his tone cold. 'Do you wish to surrender?'

Ralph nodded.

'Speak up, man. Which is it to be? Surrender or continue to the death?'

'Surrender,' whispered Ralph, his voice only just audible to the stunned crowd.

'As you wish,' said George. 'If I am to show mercy and release you, you must swear before all these witnesses that you withdraw any and all claims to Willow Manor and my estate.'

Ralph's brother bowed his head over Ralph, and they

exchanged a few words. 'He withdraws all claims to your estate,' he confirmed.

'As I thought. We must hear it from his lips, though,' said George.

Ralph took a shaky breath and shifted slightly under the tip of the sword. 'Move your blade, Sir, I surrender and withdraw my claims.'

George nodded, satisfied, and wiped his blood splattered cheek with his left hand, still gripping the sword firmly in position. 'One more thing,' he said.

'Speak up, then. I see a pint of my blood is not enough to quench your devilish thirst,' wheezed Ralph.

'I will accept an apology and we will end it there.'

'But it was I who demanded satisfaction—you insulted *my* honour,' said Ralph.

'That may be so, but it is you now calling for surrender with a blade near your throat. I advise you to choose your actions with caution, or this could be over swiftly.'

George pushed the blade harder against his waistcoat, a steely resolve in his dark eyes.

Ralph slumped further into the ground. 'So be it. I apologise,' he mumbled.

'Speak up so we can hear you, Knight, and be a good fellow and be clear about what you are apologising for,' said George, his tone clipped.

'I apologise for insulting you.'

George looked down at Ralph for a few seconds, then stepped aside and passed his blood-soaked sword to Taylor.

The crowd slowly dispersed, and George and Taylor retrieved their horses.

'Are you all right?' asked Taylor.

'I'll survive. Let us rouse them at the tavern and see if we may get some water for me to clean up. I can't return home in this state.'

Ralph stumbled to his feet and quickly bound the wound with his brother's assistance, and then fled the woods in the opposite direction, his hand pressed to his stomach.

CAROLINE WAS conscious she was Cara as she rode along the footpath, luminescent slivers crossed the sombre grey morning sky, and she started, for the hairs on the back of her neck rose. She sensed a presence and heard the slight rustle of someone passing nearby.

'Hello? Who goes there?' Her heart thumped, and she feared she may slip from the saddle as her limbs froze, such was her terror at the unseen force.

Her call was met only with silence, but then Ralph's dirt-smeared face loomed before her.

'Ralph! What are you doing sneaking around at this hour?'

'Say nothing of seeing me.' His voice was full of menace, and he gripped her wrist until she cried out. 'Remember, I know where you and your precious earl are,' he growled.

'And I know what you did. How could you set the house on fire with innocent people inside?'

'If I can't have you, he's not having you or Willow Manor.' He met her eyes briefly and then slipped into the trees without another word.

After a few seconds of hesitation, she forced herself to ride on towards the burning flames. There was no time to waste. She must get to the house and warn the others.

It seemed like hours but was only a few minutes before she entered the grounds and approached the house. The mare neighed in fright as they neared the orange flames, and she dismounted and tethered the horse to the fence near the stables, at what she gauged was a safe distance from the fire.

Willow Manor lay in quiet morning stillness amidst the glow, and it seemed no one was alerted to the fire yet.

She shouted, drawing on all the power in her lungs, 'Fire, fire! Wake up, the house is on fire!'

The flames didn't appear to have reached the central portion of the building, but it wouldn't be long, so she dashed inside the servants' entrance which she prayed would be unlocked as usual, and called as loud as she could, running from room to room, through the maze of dark corridors.

Not surprisingly, the servants stirred first, and Cook came running into the kitchen. 'What is it, lass? Fire—what's this about a fire?'

Soon people were milling around, and the servants sprang into action, filling pails with water from the well and quickly dampening the flames on the burning wing of the house.

Caroline called out, 'Where are the countess, the earl and Olivia? Has anyone seen them?'

There was no response, so she didn't hesitate. She raced to the family's rooms, which were adjacent to the burning wing, and as she neared, the smell of burning intensified, and choked her. She shouted again and was rewarded with noises of movement and to her great relief she saw the figures of the countess and Olivia in their night shifts, stumbling towards her. She urged them to leave the house in haste.

The smoke was thick, and she spluttered. 'We must get out of here. But where is George—where is the earl?'

Olivia began to cry, and Caroline looked at the thick smoke and flames, trying to figure out the best route to reach him.

'George may not have heard your cries,' said Olivia. 'We must wake him,' she screamed.

Terror struck at Caroline's heart as the smoke thickened

on the stairs that led to George's rooms. She held her nose and tried not to breathe and allow the putrid air into her lungs as she ran towards his room, and her eyes stung with the effort.

'Lord Cavendish… George,' she cried. 'Wake up. You must get out of here—there's a dreadful fire!'

She moved further into the centre of the chamber towards where he would be sleeping. Shards of pale light illuminated the opulent room, and she realised the curtains weren't drawn, and as she stumbled about touching the bed to wake him, her hands were met with cold sheets and an empty bed.

She heard Cook's voice. 'Come out, lass, before it's too late. You rushed off before I could tell you the master didn't come home last night—the countess is with Olivia, and she said she didn't hear him return. It's not uncommon for him to stay out all night when he's gaming in the village. Lord knows where he sleeps but he doesn't come home until the following day.'

Caroline turned and fled the smoky room, following the sound of Cook's voice, who waited for her outside in the corridor.

'Let us get out of the house,' Cook said, capturing her hand and pulling her along and down the stairs, towards the back door.

Caroline gasped and gulped for breath as the cold, smoky air hit her face and flooded her mouth. The smoke and lack of oxygen made her dizzy, and she stumbled and landed heavily on a mound of grass just beyond the door. Her final thought was of George, and she thanked God he was alive before she blacked out.

. . .

George raced into the grounds after spotting the fire on his way back from the tavern. Taylor followed close behind him, ever the loyal companion.

'What the devil is going on?' George asked, as he jumped off his horse and dropped to his knees beside Caroline. He leaned over her, oblivious to the others. 'Caroline, Caroline, you must wake up,' he said. He had cleaned himself up a bit, but his shirt was still coated in blood and the cut on his face was raw and angry looking.

'What on God's earth happened to you? You look like you've been in a war,' said Olivia.

'Never mind me. How did this fire start?'

'I don't know. Caroline rescued us! Will she be all right? ' Olivia said, anxiously peering over his shoulder.

'She has to be, or I will never forgive myself,' he said, and his voice echoed with anguish. 'It's all my fault.'

'Of course, it isn't your fault,' said the countess as she appeared at his side, her tone hushed so the servants wouldn't hear. 'You weren't even at home when the fire started.'

George hung his head. 'Oh, if only that were so, Mother. But it's all my fault. I ran away because I couldn't face the truth, and she left because of my callous, unfeeling behaviour.'

The countess stared at her only son; confusion apparent in her eyes.

'Why are you covered in blood? You look dreadful. I fear you must be in shock, my dearest boy. Go and rest, the worst of the fire is over, and we will see to Caroline.'

George shook her hand off him and moved closer to Caroline, who still lay there, unresponsive. 'I'm afraid it's been quite a morning, and I am responsible for the fire,' George said, his voice empty and flat.

'But whatever can you mean? You've been drinking and are not thinking straight,' said the countess.

'I have indeed been drinking, and I lost our estate to a depraved individual in a reckless card game, and I fought a duel to defend my honour.'

Caroline spluttered and coughed, and her eyes opened. 'You are safe,' she whispered, her eyes seeking George's.

'Thanks to your bravery, everyone is safe,' said George. He reached for her hand and brought it to his cold lips and kissed it.

'We can never thank you enough. We might all have been burned alive, but for your return. Thank God you are okay,' said Olivia, sobbing with relief.

'How did you learn of the fire, dearest Caroline?' George asked, continuing to clasp her hand, despite his mother's stunned expression.

'I had a dream,' she replied, still disorientated, too weary and shocked to guard her tongue. Cara's memories flashed in and out of her mind. 'I knew you were in danger, and that I must come. Once I arrived in the village, I smelt the smoke and raced over here. Ralph started the fire—I met him in the woods, and he ran away after warning me not to say I saw him there. Thank the lord, I made it in time,' she said. A faint smile passed over her pale lips as she looked into George's loving eyes, before she slipped out of consciousness again.

'Where is the doctor? Is he coming all the way from London?' George snapped. 'Taylor, have you any word?'

'It would appear we have certain matters to discuss in private,' said the countess, as she appraised her son, and interrupted his torrent of questions.

'All in good time, Mother.'

Taylor approached and told George the latest on the state of the fire and assured him the doctor was on his way.

'We have had the good fortune to narrowly escape a

disaster to end all disasters, thanks to Caroline.' Tears trickled down George's face onto his muddy, blood-stained shirt. Emotion overcame him and he was exhausted from the duel but could not rest with Caroline in this state.

He turned to the countess. 'We are safe—our only concern now must be Caroline, for without her we would all surely be in mortal peril.'

'I fear Caroline isn't the only one who needs the attention of the good doctor. Your cheek bleeds, George,' said Olivia, both disturbed and fascinated by the morning's intrigue in equal measures.

The doctor arrived shortly after, and as he pushed Caroline's cloak aside to examine her more closely, a gold monogrammed handkerchief fluttered from one of the pockets and landed on the ground at the feet of the countess.

She stopped to pick it up. 'This is yours,' she said dryly, one eyebrow raised as she passed it to George, and looked into his eyes.

He averted his gaze and spoke to the doctor.

'She will live,' the doctor pronounced, a few minutes later. 'She's a lucky young woman, given the extent of the smoke she must have inhaled.'

'Are you certain she will make a full recovery?' asked George, who paced about as near to her as the doctor would allow.

'Yes, I am confident she will recover, but she will need a period of convalescence. She is weak and doesn't look like she's had a good meal in days, perhaps even weeks, so as soon as she comes around and is rested, see that she eats to regain her strength.'

The doctor then examined George's cheek. He assured him it was nothing to be overly concerned about, but may leave a small scar.

'I heard about the duel,' he said, his tone disapproving. 'Dare I ask what became of the other party?'

'I have a feeling we won't be seeing him for a while,' said George, as the doctor bid them farewell and promised to return to check on Caroline the following day.

Taylor assisted George to move Caroline, who had now regained consciousness, to the other side of the house, well away from the smoky wing. She fell into a deep sleep and didn't wake for hours as George hovered nearby.

When she opened her eyes, George was still beside her bed, despite his mother's protestations.

He held her hand and kissed it once more. 'Thank God you are alive. I cannot stand being parted from you—I would rather die, and I confess I almost did this morning. I have been a fool of the worst kind. Can you ever forgive my stubbornness, my love?'

Caroline squeezed his hand and tried to reply, but no words came out, only a croak.

'Don't speak for your throat is sore. Nod if you can forgive me,' he said, as he kissed the palm of her hand, and the tears welled in his eyes again.

Caroline nodded. The light of hope leapt into her heart as she realised he had come back to her.

All is not lost.

Her eyes closed, and she fell into a deep slumber, oblivious to the scandal which swept through the estate and the quiet village of Willow Wick.

CHAPTER 33

Willow Manor, York - Georgiana

DURING THE AFTERNOON following the fire, there was a knock at the door and the maid ushered in a short, officious looking man. He requested to speak with George, who had refused to leave Caroline's side, even to rest from the morning's ordeal.

'George, the parish constable is here,' said the countess, entering Caroline's chamber. 'I tried to dismiss him, but he insisted on speaking with you—he says it's urgent. I presume you are aware duelling is against the law,' she said, lowering her voice. 'Please weigh your words carefully, or he may report you along with the other fellow. Who was he, again?'

'Knight, Ralph Knight. It's that scoundrel they should be after. It was him who tried to burn the house down.'

The countess looked startled. 'I thought Caroline meant it was some kind of accident—I couldn't make out what she said and didn't realise someone intended to harm us.'

George shook his head. 'I am certain it wasn't an accident, but proving it is another matter entirely.' He ran his hand through his tousled hair. 'I spoke in anger, Mother, when I lost the card game. I wasn't thinking straight, and it was all my fault in that sense.'

'Goodness, this is becoming more complicated by the hour. Well, I suggest you explain all that to the constable, so he leaves us in peace.' She touched George's arm. 'I will stay here and watch over Caroline, while you are gone.'

'Thank you, Mother. I am deeply sorry for bringing shame upon you and the family name,' he said, and then quietly left the darkened room where Caroline still slept.

THE CONSTABLE ROSE from his seat when George entered the drawing room.

'Good afternoon, Constable, and to what do I owe the pleasure?'

'Good afternoon, Lord Cavendish, I'm afraid I am here on some rather unpleasant business,' he said, frowning as he spoke, not able to meet George's eyes.

George waited for him to continue. He thought it wise to discover what the constable knew before he revealed anything about the duel or the fire.

'I have been informed you fought a duel with the eldest of the Knight brothers.' The constable coughed and looked uncomfortable, clearly out of his depth. 'And people are saying you were responsible for the fire this morning.'

George took a deep breath, straightened to his full height, and towered over the small man. 'There must be some mistake. Why on earth would I damage my own property?' He skirted smoothly around the subject of the duel.

'I cannot imagine; if you hadn't been so fortunate, the fire could have killed all of your household and destroyed this illustrious estate. This is a serious matter, but I suppose if you wish to set fire to your own house, there is little I can do about it.' The constable shook his head. 'Thank goodness no one died.'

'Indeed. We are blessed. However, we are the innocent victims of this incident, and I'm surprised you come here to accuse me. It is quite preposterous… I didn't set fire to Willow Manor, but I know who did,' said George.

The constable twisted the brim of his hat in his hands. 'We have a witness who heard you say you meant to burn it down after Ralph Knight won it in a card game,' said the constable. 'I must confess, I thought it a most unlikely wager.'

'I concede I acted like a fool last night, but it is not me who set the house on fire. It was Knight—I am certain of it, and I intended to pay you a visit to ask your assistance in apprehending that villain and bringing him to justice. He deserves the noose for his evil deed.'

'I see,' said the constable. 'In that case, I must apologise for the misunderstanding. I was reluctant to come—I knew your father, and he was a fine man, but as you may appreciate, I am bound to abide by my duties in keeping law and order, no matter how unappealing.'

George nodded. 'I appreciate your diligence, Constable.'

The constable coughed again, and studied his shoes, before he raised his eyes to George, and said, 'I'm afraid we still have the matter of the duel to address.'

'Ah yes. Things grew heated, and I acted in haste, which I now regret, but if you are looking to apprehend criminals, then once again, I must point you toward Ralph Knight. He and his brothers have regularly poached from this estate. It was he who challenged me to the duel, and when he lost, he acted in cowardly vengeance by setting the house alight. I should think he would be accused of attempted murder.'

The constable considered for a moment, and then said,

'Well, when you put it like that, it gives me an altogether different view of events. And those Knight brothers are a bad lot.'

'What do you propose, Constable?' George said, using all of his charm to appease the man, who took his duties seriously.

'I think in the circumstances, I will make enquiries about Ralph Knight's whereabouts, and if necessary, enlist the help of my volunteers to track him down. Of course, it is no simple thing to find someone who doesn't wish to be found.'

'I understand,' said George, visibly relieved the constable had backed down in his accusations against him.

'I have but one more question before I take my leave,' said the constable.

George indicated for him to speak, with a nod of the head.

'Are there any witnesses to swear Ralph Knight was responsible for the fire? You were witnessed threatening to burn the house down, so to bring a case against the Knight fellow, I fear we would need more than your word alone, which would be questionable given the circumstances.'

'There is someone, but she was injured and isn't in a state to be questioned right now. Knight admitted he started the fire and threatened her before fleeing.'

The constable took Caroline's name and said he would return to speak with her after he had made his initial enquiries.

'I shall see what I can do, but in such a case, I have to say, it's unlikely we will find him, unless he's hiding in the village or hereabouts.'

'I trust you will do all you can, and I cannot ask more of you,' said George.

'Good day, my lord. Once again, I apologise for speaking

out of turn, and wish you and Mistress Caroline a speedy recovery.'

They shook hands and George rang the bell for the maid to see him out.

'One more thing,' George said.

'Yes?'

'May I count on you to forget the matter of the duel and not bring it to the attention of the court?'

The constable inclined his head. 'What duel?' A smile crossed his narrow lips. 'As I said, your father was a fine man and I have no argument with the Cavendish family—you have done nothing but good for the village.'

After the constable left, George sank into the chair, exhausted. The wound on his face throbbed and his head pounded, and the lack of sleep was catching up with him.

George guessed Knight would be miles away by now. He wouldn't risk being accused of instigating a duel, and attempting to burn Willow Manor to the ground with the entire household asleep inside. No, he would be long gone. George consoled himself that something good had come out of his reckless behaviour.

And Caroline is home.

Willow Manor, York - Georgiana (One month later)

Caroline and Olivia finished morning lessons in the library. Caroline was no longer Olivia's governess or lady's companion in an official capacity, but they naturally resumed studying together because they enjoyed each other's company.

'I am thrilled at the prospect of having you as my real sister. I loved you from the beginning and I just knew there was something special about you—it was as though you belonged here all along,' said Olivia.

'Dear Livvy, I could not wish for a more sweet-natured and wonderful sister. I too am overjoyed.' Caroline clasped the girl's hand and thanked God for the happy turn of events.

She would never have believed things could work out so perfectly, and that soon she would be Lady Caroline Cavendish, and a countess.

Caroline and George were to be married in a modest ceremony in the pretty little church in Willow Wick, where Caroline had attended services with her parents when her mother was alive.

After the initial shock, even the countess had resigned herself to George's intentions, on the one condition that he and Caroline took an extended trip to the continent after the wedding to allow the scandal of their marriage to die down. 'I can't abide gossips. I shall have my dear sister come to keep me company while you are away and soon enough there'll be something new for them to tittle-tattle about,' said the countess.

The newly betrothed happily agreed to the terms and were busy preparing for the wedding and the trip.

Caroline snapped back to the present and noticed Olivia examining the tall shelves.

'Are you searching for something in particular?' she called from her position on the window seat.

'Yes, now you are my sister; there's something I want to show you, but I can't quite recall exactly where it is.'

'I'm intrigued,' said Caroline, and then switched her gaze back to the window and watched the workers as they continued their restoration of the wing of the house that had been so nearly destroyed in the fire.

'Here it is,' called Olivia, running her hand over the frame of one section of the heavy oak bookshelves. 'Come over here and I'll show you what I mean.'

Caroline crossed the room to stand beside Olivia. As she stood there, a memory flashed into her mind. It was rare for Caroline to experience one of the vivid visions she experienced so often before the fire—they had faded into her consciousness, almost as though they never happened. The strange period when she was aware of living two lives simultaneously had passed as quickly as it had come, and she hadn't mentioned it to George, even after they were betrothed. It had not seemed like the right thing to do, and so she had kept her own counsel.

Don't go in there.

Caroline started as she heard the familiar voice in her head.

'What is it?' asked Caroline, as she watched Olivia's face grow pink with excitement and fumble about trying to locate what she was looking for.

'There's a priest hole hidden behind the shelves,' burst out Olivia.

'Gracious,' said Caroline, her heart racing as the memories of the wormhole flooded back and spun around her mind.

That's why I'm being warned.

Caroline took a step backwards. She instinctively knew she shouldn't risk getting too near the wormhole.

'Our ancestors saved a Jesuit priest from persecution during the reformation. I entered the hole alone when I was a little girl, and my father was so angry, you wouldn't believe! I remember crying for days because he wouldn't let me go back in there and he ordered it be sealed over permanently,' she whispered. 'It is best Mother doesn't hear us talk of it. I had a weird experience in there, you see, although I remember little of it.'

'How fascinating. What do you remember?'

'Only that for days after it happened, I kept talking of someone called Kate, and I believed I was her in a future life!'

'Goodness, that must have been disturbing for you and your parents,' said Caroline. She had seen George's sister, Kate, in her dreams. How bizarre that Olivia should have experienced something similar.

Did Olivia experience the same kind of visions of the future as she did?

'I think they thought I had gone mad and were worried they would put me in the asylum if anyone heard my claims, so they acted in haste. No one has entered the priest hole since,' said Olivia, raising her finger to her lips. 'Let it be our little secret now we are true sisters—even George must not know of it.'

Caroline patted Olivia's shoulder. 'Do not fear. Your secret is safe with me.'

'Let us talk of happier things... Have our gowns arrived for the wedding yet? I am quite beside myself with excitement—I can barely believe the day will be upon us soon...'

'No, our gowns haven't arrived back from the seamstress yet, but I expect them any day. Did George mention we are to visit the church and meet with the new vicar this week?' asked Caroline.

'I was sad to see Father Cuthbert leave, but they say his replacement is a young, forward-thinking man,' remarked Olivia.

'That is good news indeed, given our circumstances,' said Caroline. 'There are quite enough people who disapprove of our union.'

'Well, that is only because they do not know you. Anyone who met you would see immediately that you are exactly where you belong,' said Olivia. 'You belong in this family. It feels like you've always been with us...'

'Whatever have I done to deserve a dear sister like you, Livvy?' said Caroline. 'Come along, enough reading for one day. Let us go and find George. Perhaps we may take a ride to Willow Wick this afternoon and enjoy some fresh air.'

And just like that, the wormhole was forgotten.

CHAPTER 34

Willow Wick Church, York - Georgiana

Caroline entered the church on her father's arm, who was dressed in his Sunday best. George had offered to send his tailor to measure him up, but Master Radcliff politely declined, saying he couldn't abide the fuss and would dress well enough for the occasion. He promised Caroline that he would not let her down, and as they walked down the aisle to the sharp notes of the organ music, it was clear he was a father who glowed with pride. He was still a good-looking man and cut a fine figure in his colourful knee-length coat, breeches, and dark leather shoes.

Caroline's gown was made of cream coloured silk, and as she walked, she wondered whether she was having another strange dream and this fairy tale wedding was just a figment of her imagination. Perhaps she was dreaming about Cara and George's wedding in the future?

But no, Caroline knew it was real when she turned her

head slightly to the side and caught sight of Olivia, carrying the delicate train of her gown with great care. She wore the pale blue bridesmaid gown, which was sewn especially for the wedding and complemented her blonde hair and luminous fair skin.

As Caroline neared the altar, she shook inwardly, but then George's dark eyes locked onto hers and immediately reassured her. His presence was enough to calm and remind her they were doing the right thing, even if the wedding felt like a fairy tale.

Her father stepped aside and symbolically gave her away, and as Caroline joined George in front of the vicar, her heart palpitated so violently, she feared it must resound throughout the church like the organ music, all the way up to the high vaulted ceiling.

Because of their unorthodox circumstances, they had agreed there would be but a few family members and close friends at the ceremony, which Caroline was infinitely grateful for because her new social status overwhelmed her. When they married, she would hold the official title of Countess, for George was the 4th Earl of Gloucester, and she couldn't quite believe it.

She still reeled from the shock that George's mother had accepted their marriage and given her formal approval. Caroline knew the match couldn't have been what the countess had imagined for her beloved son, but the lady of the manor continued to be as kind and gracious to Caroline as she had since she first assumed her governess role. George's revelations of their love and their desire to marry had taken the countess by surprise, but she had taken it in her elegant stride. Caroline thought her mother-in-law was the epitome of nobility and deserved her title. She hoped that she, too, would learn to be worthy of her fortunate position over time.

The organ music stopped abruptly, but Caroline's heart continued to thump, and her bouquet of lilies shook in her hands as she passed the vibrant flowers to Olivia and tried to compose herself. The church fell silent as the new vicar appraised the couple before him, and he readied himself to perform his first wedding ceremony in Willow Wick.

'We are gathered here today...' The vicar recited the familiar marriage ceremony words.

George looked at Caroline and squeezed her hand, and she leant against his shoulder slightly to bolster her courage —she was weak with nervous anticipation and, as ever, he sensed her tumultuous emotions.

'Wilt thou have this woman to thy wife and love her and keep her in sickness and in health, and in all other degrees be to her as a husband should be to his wife, and all others forsake for her, and hold only her to thy life's end?' said the vicar, looking at George.

George nodded and said in a resolute voice, 'Yes, yes I do.'

'Wilt thou have this man to thy husband, and be buxom to him, serve him and keep him in sickness and in health?' The vicar turned to Caroline and asked her to pledge herself to George.

Then it was time for the ring. George's best friend, Anthony, withdrew a large shimmering diamond set in an elegant gold band from the pocket of his coat and passed it to George, who turned to Caroline and slipped it onto her wedding finger, saying, 'With this ring I thee wed.'

'I now pronounce you man and wife,' said the good-natured vicar, with a sparkle in his eye.

'You may kiss the bride.'

The newly weds turned to each other and kissed to the cheers of the small crowd.

The countess's sister had arrived in time for the wedding, for she had recently been widowed and would stay at Willow

Manor for the duration and keep her sister company while George and Caroline took their extended honeymoon on the continent.

At that intimate moment, the countess's eyes briefly met Caroline's father's, and they smiled at the irony of the situation, both at peace with how life had kept them apart but allowed their children to traverse the class barrier in this bold new century.

The newly weds prepared to leave the church and approached the vicar.

'Thank you for officiating over such a beautiful ceremony, Father Edward,' said George. 'And once again, welcome to Willow Wick. May you have many happy years, blessed with many more auspicious occasions such as this.'

Caroline thanked Father Edward, and then George helped her into the Cavendish carriage, which was gaily adorned with flowers from the manor gardens. They settled into their seats, waving at a few smiling villagers who had gathered to wish them well. She turned to her husband and said, 'When we went to see Father Edward before the wedding, I had such a strong feeling that I already knew him. I meant to tell you, but it slipped my mind. Has he perhaps lived in these parts before, do you know?'

'I don't believe so. Mother said he travelled extensively and served in the holy land for years prior to accepting this post,' said George. 'I understand he is now ready to settle down after somewhat of an adventurous time of it.'

'Goodness, that sounds fascinating,' said Caroline. She had a feeling that she would remember how she knew the vicar. There was something strangely familiar about him, but the more she tried to pin it down, the more elusive it became. She resolved to stop trying to clutch at the whisper of a memory and trust it would come back to her when it was ready.

All in good time, whispered a voice in her mind.

Father Edward promised he would follow on and attend the reception at Willow Manor.

THE GUESTS STOOD after the meal and toasted the couple, and George's best man said a few words and wished them many years of wedded bliss. The afternoon whirled by, and it was soon time for them to change and collect their luggage, ready to depart for their long journey.

Olivia hugged them both and her eyes shone with unshed tears.

'We'll be home before you know it, dear Livvy—there's no need for tears,' said George.

'If I weren't going to court next week, I would be completely bereft and sobbing,' she said.

George had finally relented and given permission for Olivia to attend court after a touch of persuasion from Caroline. He realised he couldn't live his sister's life for her and must let her fly the nest.

'I shall miss you both so much,' Olivia said. 'Whatever will I do without you?' she added, shaking her head.

'We shall write to you at Kensington Palace, and you shall be occupied with your wonderful new life at court. I imagine you will barely find time to reply!' Caroline said.

As they were about to leave, Caroline threw her wedding bouquet in the air and Olivia smoothly caught it without missing a step.

'I don't intend to marry within the year but thank you, my beloved sister,' she beamed at Caroline, and they embraced and kissed each other's cheeks once more.

The horses neighed and swished their tails as the couple settled into their seats, and Caroline and George turned to wave as the carriage lurched away from the house and headed down the long willow tree-lined drive, ready to carry them to new adventures.

The countess dabbed her eyes with her handkerchief and prayed the swirl of rumours would settle down by the time the happy couple returned.

Willow Manor, York - Present day

Cara and George waved off the small team of caterers after they cleared away their equipment. Several enquiries had trickled in about holding Tudor themed parties at the centre, and they had decided to give it a go and see how they got on.

'What's the verdict?' asked George.

'I think it was rather fun, and the guests seemed to enjoy it,' replied Cara. 'It's another string to our bow, although it might be too much to juggle if we go ahead with opening the hotel. We'd need more staff for the events besides the caterers.'

'True. But it could be an excellent source of income as long as the figures stack up, and it would help get the word out about the centre.'

'Fancy a cup of tea before we lock up for the day? My feet ache after all that running around.'

George pulled out a chair and gallantly indicated for Cara to sit. 'Take a load off, and I'll bring us something to nibble and make the tea.'

They sat in quiet companionship, munching the tasty sandwiches left over from the event, and sipping tea to the gentle strum of the rain on the diamond shaped Tudor-style windowpanes.

George wiped his hands on a napkin, pushed his plate

away, and turned to Cara. 'Did you tell Eddie he was the vicar who married us in Georgiana?'

Cara laughed. 'No, but I will. I haven't had the chance to speak to him yet. We've been playing phone tag. I told Sylvia that the family history book updated with our marriage.'

'Oh—and what did she make of it all?'

'She said she knew it would all work out.'

'Do you know what else happened in the new version of the timeline?'

'Only that you—well—the earl, was lucky not to be arrested for illegal duelling—fortunately there wasn't a professional police force in those days, and the parish constable believed him and trusted Caroline's account of meeting Ralph in the woods after he started the fire.'

'Thank God for that. I must have been an absolute clown,' said George, raising his hands in a helpless gesture. 'I couldn't have screwed it up more if I'd tried.'

Cara leant over to kiss him. 'Sylvia noticed that the wedding was on the eleventh day of the eleventh month. I didn't click initially, but it's the Twin Flame classic 11/11 symbol. Isn't that amazing? It's as if it was supposed to happen that way, but we'd gone off course all those years ago.'

Cara awoke at first light one morning with images of George and Caroline's wedding spilling into her mind.

She had jumped out of bed and rushed down to check the Georgiana history volume for updates, switching on the lamp in the snug and retrieving the old buckram bound book from where she'd left it on the table. She could barely breathe, such was her fear of the words that awaited her in the mysterious text.

And it was written, as if it had always been there:

"Lord George Cavendish, the 4th Earl of Gloucester, married Mistress Caroline Radcliff on 11 November 1729 at Willow Wick church in York."

George captured Cara's hand. 'All's well that ends well, my love, as a famous poet once said. It looks like we've made peace with each other in another timeline. How many is that now?'

'Four—we've achieved union in four timelines: Tudorville, Georgiana, Victoriana and here, of course.'

'Wonderful. Maybe we've paid our karmic debts and the powers that be will allow us to get on with our life with no more timeline emergencies…'

'Talking of karma—what do you think happened to Ralph Knight?' Cara said.

'I think it's fair to assume that the karmic warrior will continue to burn in hell after his evil shenanigans in the alternative timeline. He had a chance to redeem himself, but he didn't. Hopefully, we won't bump into him for at least another few thousand years…'

Cara shivered and slipped her jacket on. 'And while we're wrapping up the loose ends, do you think we should tell Kate about her link to Olivia?'

George shook his head. 'Not if we can help it. It will only complicate all our lives unnecessarily. Let's leave the past in the past.'

'I like that,' said Cara. 'Leave the past in the past… I only hope we can.'

There was a shuffle outside the door and Cara went to open it. 'Hello gorgeous boy,' she said, bending to stroke Cornelius's silky head.

Cornelius licked her hand and then ambled over to George, flopped at his feet, and closed his eyes with a contented sigh.

They were all home where they belonged.

THE COVENANT (TWIN FLAMES 4)

Willow Manor, York - Present day

Cara rose from her chair and crossed towards the rain-spattered window, seeking inspiration. 'There's something I didn't tell you.'

She turned to face George.

'Oh no, what?'

'This might not affect us at all,' she said.

'Go on…'

'There's been so much happening I had no chance to think about it, never mind tell you, but…'

'But?' George prompted.

'Okay, I'll just come out and say it.'

'I wish you would, darling! You're killing me with the suspense,' he exclaimed.

'Last time I saw Sylvia for a reading, she had this strange vision of us in another past life.'

'What did she see?'

'We were in Jerusalem at the time of the Jewish Second Temple before it was destroyed in the first century.'

George stared at Cara, not quite believing what he was hearing. 'So, hold on, are you saying we have been reincarnating together for two thousand years?'

'I don't know if it's true, but Sylvia's not been wrong yet…'

George shook his head. 'Just when I think our lives can't get any more complex, you throw something like that at me!'

'Look on the bright side. We averted disaster again—albeit narrowly. And even if it's true we had a past life in Jerusalem, it doesn't mean the vortex will transport us there.'

He looked thoughtful.

Cara walked towards him and wrapped her arms around his broad shoulders. 'I'm just so relieved we didn't lose each other in the Georgiana timeline reset.'

'Me too,' he said. 'But—you have to admit it would be mind blowing to be in the holy land at the time of the Roman Empire.'

Cara's forehead creased. 'Mind blowing? It sounds absolutely blood-curdling! I looked it up—it was all-out Jewish-Roman war. It would be our most dangerous timeline yet, so if you don't mind, I'd rather give it a miss.'

But she could see Sylvia's vision had captured George's imagination and he was far away.

After a few moments he raised his dark eyes to hers and said, 'I wonder whether we were Jews or Romans…'

Continue the adventure with *The Covenant* on Amazon.

EXCLUSIVE BONUS PROLOGUE

The Forgotten Meeting

Get the exclusive bonus prologue, *The Forgotten Meeting,* and read how it all began for Cara and George.

This is a new chapter I wrote especially for readers who want to know what happened even *before* book one.

www.Rachelhenke.com/subscribe

NOTE TO READERS

I hope you've enjoyed reading Cara and George's love story across the centuries.

If you enjoyed this book, I would appreciate a quick review on Amazon or Goodreads. Reviews make a HUGE difference to the success of the series and help new readers discover my books.

Thank you.

With much love and gratitude,

Rachel

www.RachelHenke.com

ALSO BY RACHEL HENKE

Book 1: Twin Flames

Book 2: The Uprising

Book 3: The Runner

Book 4: The Covenant

ABOUT THE AUTHOR

Rachel dreamt of writing novels since she was a little girl. Always an avid reader of historical romance and fascinated by the mystical and spiritual realms, she discovered Plato's Twin Flame phenomenon, and was inspired to write the first novel in the much-loved time travel romance series: Twin Flames.

Cara and George popped into her head and began telling their story of star-crossed soul mates in love for centuries.

Rachel is also the author of numerous bestselling non-fiction books, including Living Fearlessly. She lives in Surrey, UK, writing as many books as she can...

ACKNOWLEDGMENTS

I couldn't write these books without my brilliant editor, Russell Cooper. His insights make all the difference.

Special thanks to Greta Cooper, Anita Davis, Emily Mace, Clare Horrocks, Donna Preece, and Kim Kaase for the support, enthusiasm, and many hours of advance reading. You are the best.

Thank you to all my wonderful readers who take the time to review and recommend the series. I appreciate you!

Printed in Great Britain
by Amazon

84641415R00198